CHIMNEY BLUFFS

David B. Seaburn

Savant Books
Honolulu, HI, USA
2012

Published in the USA by Savant Books and Publications
2630 Kapiolani Blvd #1601
Honolulu, HI 96826
http://www.savantbooksandpublications.com

Printed in the USA

Edited by Katrina Robinson
Cover images by David B. Seaburn
Cover design by Daniel S. Janik

13-digit ISBN: 9780985250683
10-digit ISBN: 0985250682

Dedication

To my family.

Acknowledgements

I want to express my appreciation to Sarah Cypher for her invaluable help in the preparation of this book. Special thanks to my editor, Katrina Robinson, for her support and guidance during this project. Thanks also to Dan Janik.

PART 1

Chimney Bluffs

Chapter 1

Clarence Brisco, Clancy to his friends, peered through the driver's side window into the white VW van parked in the middle of the lot. He pulled on the door handle, but it was locked. *What the hell?* he thought, shaking his head with disapproval. There was a half-eaten banana on the dashboard and an open bag of peanuts on the passenger's seat, a few having fallen on the floor. There was a half-full bottle of water in the cup holder between the seats, cap off, and an unopened one on the passenger side floor. He walked to the back of the van and checked the license plate—New York. Clancy looked around the empty lot. The sign at the entrance was clear—Park Hours: 8 a.m.- Dark. He checked his watch. It was nearly 6 a.m. Clancy looked at the VW van again, its bumper rusted and its side panels scratched and dinged. He listened for the whir of his partner's truck, but all he could hear were mourning doves and a few woodpeckers. As usual, Bobby was late. The trail up to Chimney Bluffs was challenging during daylight for most hikers, but it would be nearly impossible to follow at night, especially in the rain. Last night's storm had left the trail muddy; droplets from the maple leaves left drizzled designs on Clancy's shoulders. He wondered if a bunch of college students had partied near the bluffs the night before, had gotten high on God knows what, and then had gotten themselves completely turned around and lost. "Damn fools," he said, right out loud, and then realized no one was there to hear him. He listened again for Bobby's truck. The main trail had to be checked before the park opened and families started pouring in. Clancy figured he'd better get going, even without Bobby.

The bluffs were so high and the erosion under them so deep that it wasn't uncommon for a few feet of trail to fall away in a massive jumble during the night, piling up on the beach below. It wasn't like the bluffs were a wall of granite. Chimney Bluffs was little more than glacial till, a mix of sand and silt and gravel pulverized and pasted together under the mountain of ice that had created Lake Ontario thousands of years ago. Wind and rain and time had carved the humped-backed drumlin into stunning, yet delicate, earthen pinnacles, razor-sharp at the top, scratching the air and drawing wonder-seeking visitors from miles around.

Whenever there was a nighttime collapse anywhere along the one-and-one-half-mile cliff-side trail, it was up to Clancy and Bobby to find it quickly, tamp down a trail detour for the hikers, line the new trail with decaying limbs and small boulders to keep visitors from wandering off the beaten path, and then hammer in a sign warning, "Unstable Bluff—Stay Back!"

As Clancy started up the trail, he turned and looked at the VW van sitting amidst the puddles. He shook his head again. The driver hadn't parked in one of the clearly marked spaces. Instead he had left the vehicle in the middle of the lot. Clancy couldn't wait to find the owner of the van that would create a nuisance for the park's more courteous visitors.

He took the Garner Point Trail through tall, wet grasses and up a slight incline until he reached Bluff Trail, famous not only for its panoramic view of the lake and the bluffs, but also for its eye-popping drop to the beach, sometimes causing the first-time visitor to wobble with vertigo. Clancy stopped at the top of the trail, where he gazed up the north shoreline as it wound its way toward the smoke stacks in Oswego, some thirty miles away. The morning breeze was cool, and sunlight insinuated itself through the tall oaks that lined the bluff, their young leaves a glistening green. Clancy looked out across Lake Ontario to the northwest, hoping for a glimpse of Toronto, but a fleet of last night's storm clouds lay on the horizon, blocking his view. A flock of Canada geese rose from the pond behind him, so near that he could hear the persistent whoosh of their beating wings as they organized themselves into a V, their desperate honking echoing across the water below; they were on a morning practice run before making their final flight across the lake to their summer home. Clancy smiled and squinted as a beam of light caught his eye. "My gosh," he said. Being a park ranger was a far cry from his years with Mott's before he was laid off. He had seen a lot of apples in his twenty years with the company, but little else. Every day on Chimney Bluffs, on the other hand, was a brand-new canvas.

Clancy headed up Bluff Trail and soon entered the woods, the temperature falling ten degrees. He pulled his collar up and zipped his jacket to the top. He stood for a long minute listening, hoping to hear the college students and planning what he'd say to them. "Damn fools." But there wasn't a hint of human noise in the air, just the cawing of restless crows and the occasional skittering of hungry chipmunks and squirrels. Above him, the canopy of slender maples leaned with the breeze, shedding the last drops of the nighttime storm. He continued down the trail, the floor of the woods wet, pools of water here and there. A small clearing of knee-high ferns surrounded him as he headed up the first slope. The trail made an abrupt left turn toward the cliffs, and by the time he reached the edge, he was already one hundred and fifty feet above the water. Dead trees lay across the path, while others tilted precariously over the edge. The cliffs sacrificed a dozen or more trees per year depending on how much rain, ice, and snow hit the shore.

For a while after leaving Mott, Clancy had made a modest living mowing lawns, cleaning gutters, and, in the winter, clearing driveways; his Dodge Ram had stayed healthy, and life was good enough. He had kept the house where he and Darlene had lived, even though it was a struggle to make the mortgage. Now in his early forties, Clancy wondered if his future would ever improve on his past.

Things had started moving in the right direction when he answered the state park service ad and was hired immediately at Chimney Bluffs State Park as a ranger, which sounded more impressive than it was. He traded in his dungarees for a navy blue shirt and trousers, a stitched name tag over his left breast. He and Bobby checked the trails each day, cleaned up any messes left by thoughtless campers, and answered endless questions from scores of visitors. Not much of a people person, Clancy preferred walking the trails where he could be alone but still do his job.

The phone on his belt vibrated. "Bobby," he said, shaking his head. "Where are you? I'm already on the trail."

"Sorry, man. The state boys out on 104 are checking inspection stickers, so I had to turn around and drive back to the cutoff."

Clancy listened but didn't speak.

"And, hey, Clance, it was lucky I came this way because the gas station just past Drumlin Road is about four cents cheaper than the one up on 104." Bobby laughed while recounting his good fortune.

Clancy finally replied. "Look, Bobby, when you get to the west lot, let me know if you see a white VW van still there."

"Okay, Clance. Anything wrong?" Bobby asked, but Clancy had already hung up.

Clancy shook his head. It was no surprise to him that Bobby had never gotten any further than his parents' basement and a drunken semester at Oswego State. Though he was in his early twenties, Bobby was still a kid in most ways. He'd spent much of his time smoking weed until his mother demanded he a job or else. "This is as close to being paid for doing nothing as you can get," he'd announced to Clancy their first day together as park rangers. For some reason, he thought of Clancy as a friend: "Me and you, Clance."

The bluffs were just ahead. Even after seeing them for six years, the sight of them made Clancy pause. Those tall gleaming spires looked like giant shark fins or switchblades, their tips long and sleek as if carved by a knowing hand. Clancy had never been much of a churchgoer, even though his mother had tried to make him into an altar boy at one point. "But, Mom, I thought we were Baptists," he'd shrewdly half-stated, half-asked, effectively nipping her dream of him taking up the cloth in the bud. He didn't see much evidence of God's hand in the world, which was always in some mess, what with terrorists and welfare cheats and crooked politicians, greedy bankers, and Wall Street scum. People were the problem as far as he could tell; they didn't appear to care at all about one another; everyone was out for himself, making excuses, never even taking responsibility for setting their alarms and getting to work on time. He thought about the VW van and how inconsiderate the occupants were. Leaving it right in the middle of the lot and wandering into the park when they weren't supposed to be there, just so they could have a good time.

Clancy took a few steps forward and stood right at the edge of the precipice. He gazed down at the moonscape that formed the base of the spires, its ruggedly sculpted surface angling quickly away to the water's edge. He took a deep breath. "How in the world did all this get here?" He looked at the pencil-thin horizon, the azure blue surf, a smattering of white caps, the sky awash with pale clouds dragging grey underbellies.

His phone buzzed again.

"Clance, it's me. The van's still here."

"See anyone around who might belong to it?"

"Nope."

"Okay. Meet me at the east lot. I'm near the bluffs."

"Hey man, I stopped at Tim Horton's and got you a large joe. Two sugars, just the way you like it."

"Thanks, but I'd prefer you just get yourself here on time," Clancy concluded and stuck the phone back on his belt.

Turning around and to head back, he noticed something near the base of a tree about ten yards away, something pale green but clearly not a plant, and definitely not an animal. Something different, something that stuck out amidst the fallen tree limbs and mud and knotted roots that surrounded it.

He walked towards it, knelt down to get a closer look, and then smiled. He picked up the light green teddy bear, not much longer than his hand, its button nose and eyes a little muddy from the fall.

"Someone sure cried themselves to sleep last night," he said, wiping it off on his sleeve. He looked at the bear, its fur thin and its joints limp. A smile crossed his face and then faded as his thoughts turned to Darlene.

The trail became steeper as Clancy headed towards his favorite spot. A green sign with a stick figure of a hiker was just ahead, a thick white line drawn through it. A slender finger of land jutted out beyond the trail. He stepped past the warning sign and walked slowly along the finger's spine like a tightrope walker on a high wire. He felt for firm footing on the grassy knuckle of the finger. Then he took three more steps forward onto its craggy tip. The west wind slammed him; his arms went out and he caught his balance, avoiding a fall to the rocks below. His brown hair swept back off his forehead; he squinted, watching a hawk glide by at eye level. He stretched his arms out, and his jacket filled with the chill morning breeze. Clancy faced west, looking at a line of jagged spires rising above the blue backdrop, Sodus Bay hidden beyond the next bend. In the distance, a speckled sail fluttered into view.

He took a deep breath and let it out slowly. Then another. And another. He felt clean and clear. For a moment, he was the only person in the world and nothing mattered at all: not his job, not Bobby, not

Darlene, not the past, not the future, not even himself. He held the bear in his right hand and gazed at the narrow beach some two hundred and fifty feet below.

Clancy had stood on this spot hundreds of times and had never noticed the two boulders below him at the water's edge. He settled his gaze, looking hard, examining them, wondering about the way they seemed to flutter in the wind, then realized they weren't boulders at all. They were two sacks lying still in the lapping waves. He took a final step forward and leaned out over the edge to get a better look. "My God," he said when he saw the bodies, one on its back, arms extended, clearly a man, the other curled in a ball. Both as still as the sacks by their sides.

Clancy gasped and his foot slipped. He righted himself and stepped back. He couldn't catch his breath, and the horizon started to waver. He sat down, head in hands, and then lay back on the grass, his stomach balling into a knot. He felt like throwing up, but kept breathing, until perspiration began to cool his body. He closed his eyes and there they were: two people dead on his beach, on his watch. "What the hell," was all he could venture.

He sat up just as the hawk soared by again, its indifferent eyes scanning the scene below. Clancy pulled the phone from his belt. "Bobby…yeah…you still in the lot? Listen, I'm out on the point, and there's something below me on the beach…no, just stay where you are; I'll be there in ten minutes…no, wait for me; we'll go together."

"Are you kidding me!" said Bobby as he caught up with Clancy and heard the news.

"No, I'm not," said Clancy, wiping his face with his hand.

"C'mon, let's go."

"What? Why don't we just call the cops? Do you really want to go out there?" Bobby's round face was flushed.

"Look, Bobby." Clancy took another deep breath. "Look, this is our park and this is our responsibility. Stay here if you want, but I'm going." And with that, Clancy headed down the beach. Bobby waited a minute. He didn't want to go. He didn't want to see. But he also didn't want to let Clancy down, so he followed.

"Whadaya think happened, man?"

"Don't know. If it was night, they could have missed the sign and just stepped out into nothing."

"Oh, my God, can you imagine it? Falling that far. I mean, they must have been freakin'."

"Not for very long." Clancy was thinking about the van and the half-eaten banana and the bag of peanuts and what must have been an overnighter; they must have figured it didn't matter where they parked, because they'd be gone in the morning before anyone was the wiser. College kids. He was glad someone else would have to call the parents.

Around the second bend, they could see the sacks soaking in the shallow water. Beyond them, the bodies.

"Look, man, I don't know..." said Bobby, shaking his head and sliding his hands deep into his pockets.

"Just stay here, then," said Clancy, a snap in his voice.

"Look, Clance, don't get upset," said Bobby, but Clancy had already walked away. "Okay, okay," called Bobby, already twenty yards or more behind Clancy.

Clancy was standing over the bodies when Bobby reached him. The man's face was cut from the fall and clotted with blood; his hand was curled and one leg was twisted across the other; he didn't move. The other body was a woman in a fetal position, her arms pulled tight to her chest and her knees up to her elbows, hair covering her face. There was a flashlight lying beside her. These weren't college kids out for a romp.

"Jesus," said Bobby.

"Call 911," said Clancy, and then he walked over to the sacks.

Clancy knelt down beside the first sack, which had a gash in its side. He pulled on the hole, and out fell a toy tractor. He reached in and pulled out a stuffed dog and then a plush cat and a green dinosaur and a handful of Hot Wheels cars and a Fisher Price farm set full of plastic animals and a farm family. Clancy stared at his find.

"What is all this?"

Then he went to the second sack, which was pulled tight at the neck and tied shut. He tried to pick it up, but it was heavy and awkward. He pulled out his pocket knife and slashed the neck of the sack. He reached in and his face turned white. He opened the sack further to take a look and then fell back, completely limp. He knelt in the water, unable to stand; he knelt there hoping that he was wrong, hoping that what he had touched was something else altogether. He looked at the sack again, afraid. He crawled on all fours, took the sack up in his hands and tore it wide open.

"Oh, my God!" There he was: blonde hair, a sleepy face, not much older than three or four, wearing a hooded sweatshirt, faded blue jeans and Nike sneakers. A little boy. And not a breath.

Chapter 2

Kate Duncan laid the banana on the dashboard and tossed the bag of peanuts on the floor. She flicked the switch on the flashlight to make sure it worked, then cradled it in her lap, her head bowed. Mitch opened the hatch and tossed one of the sacks in the back of the van. Several minutes passed before Kate felt a slight dip on the rear driver's side of the van as Mitch lay the second sack gently into place beside the first. It was quiet for a moment, and then Mitch slammed the hatch shut, startling Kate.

Mitch fumbled with the keys. Then he stopped. He tried again, this time succeeding at inserting a key in the ignition. "We should get going."

Kate turned her head from Mitch and looked through the windshield into the darkness.

"Yes, I guess we should."

Mitch reached for her arm, gently squeezing it. "Kate?"

"I know."

"This is the best way," said Mitch.

"Uh huh. It's just..." Kate's voice trailed off as she looked out the passenger side window.

"What?"

"It's just, there's nothing 'best' about it. If I'd have…"

"Kate, don't."

Mitch turned the key. The engine coughed and sputtered and then roared. He pressed the gas a couple of times until the engine purred. Mitch put it into reverse and backed slowly out of the driveway and onto the road. Kate took a long look at their darkened house. She couldn't remember if she'd locked the back door. She was about to say something but realized it didn't matter. She stared at the road as the striped lines rushed by.

Her mother's death was the only other loss she had ever experienced. She'd lived with her mother well into adulthood. It was her mother who woke her every day to go to work at the grocery store, whether Kate need waking or not: "Katie! Get up! You're gonna be late!"

One day, Kate, having slept through her own alarm, woke up to silence. "Mom?" she called out, then called a second and third time. She walked on tiptoes across the cold linoleum to the other end of the trailer. "Mom?"

When her mother didn't answer, Kate leaned over her mother's bed and nudged her gently on the shoulder. She hadn't move.

Kate had bought a black dress for the calling hours at Patterson's Funeral Parlor—first new dress in years. On the way to the checkout counter, she saw a butterfly broach and bought it on impulse. "Tacky," her mother would have said.

Folks from work came and some old high school classmates and some of her mom's friends, as well.

"God must have needed her," they said.

"Yes, I'm sure that's true," answered Kate.

"She was too good for this world," they said.

"Yes, I'm sure that's true," said Kate.

"Everything happens for a reason," they said.

"Yes, I'm sure that's true," said Kate.

Her mother would have laughed at this. "When you're gone, you're gone," she would have said bitterly.

When the last of the visitors had filed out of the parlor and into the parking lot, Kate stood over the casket looking at her mother's pasty face and wood-like hands, feeling nothing. She noticed a speck of dirt on her mother's powdered cheek. She reached down and flicked it away.

"Honey?" Mitch reached across the console and nudged Kate's arm.

"What?"

"Please eat something. You haven't eaten since, well, you haven't eaten much since…"

"Not hungry," said Kate.

"Here," he reached for the banana, peeled it, and gave her half. She took the banana, examined it, rolled down her window, and threw it out. Mitch looked at Kate and then tossed the rest of the banana onto the dashboard.

"I think this is the right thing to do. For Danny. For us. Everything is going to be okay. You just have to have faith," said Mitch. He blinked his brights at an oncoming truck, its headlights quickly turning on.

Kate looked at Mitch and took a deep breath. "I thought for sure it was just an ear infection, a little stiff neck." Mitch's back tightened. "That's all. I mean, how many earaches has he had in the last six months?" Mitch didn't answer. "No, really, how many? A lot, right? I mean, after all he'd been through, with the surgery and everything, what was an earache?" Mitch's foot pressed more firmly on the gas.

"I mean, it was so normal," said Kate. "It was such a nothing for him to get an earache; usually they said, 'Don't bother to bring him in, it's going around.'" She stopped talking for a moment. "Really, Mitch, how many times did Danny get an earache?"

"Lots of times," said Mitch in a controlled whisper.

"Lots of times," said Kate. "So why did this time have to be so different?"

Mitch shifted his weight and folded his hands tightly over the steering wheel, his knuckles white. "I don't know, Kate. It's one of those things we're not supposed to understand. At least not yet."

"Who says we're not supposed to understand it? Who makes up the rules?" She looked at Mitch, but he stared straight ahead. Mitch looked just like Danny. The crease between his eyes, his smallish ears, the pointed chin. *Is that what Danny would have looked like?* Kate wondered. She imagined being an old woman riding in the car with her son, that he was a grown man and he was taking her to see his family, her grandchildren. And that he was about to laugh and his eyes were about to narrow into a squint and his ears were about to turn red like they always had. She looked at him through the long lens of memory, of first steps, of school bus rides and football games, of learning to drive and finding a first love, of disappointment and joy, of all the things that are lined up along the road of life, all the things that are waiting there for you.

"Kate?" said Mitch. "We're going to make this be all right."

Kate's eyes refocused and she turned away, looking out the window again. "Why didn't I see it coming? It wasn't his fault, it was mine, so why should he…"

"Kate. Stop. We've been over this. Everything will be fine in the end. You'll see."

"I don't know…"

"I *do* know. Look, soon none of this will matter. We will all be together. Forever. I promise."

They drove through a fog as it folded in on top of them. Kate looked out the passenger window as the trees swept by in a milky blur. Mitch guided the van slowly into the Chimney Bluffs State Park parking lot and rolled to a stop. He turned off the headlights and took the keys out of the ignition.

"Are you okay now?" said Mitch. "I mean, I know…"

Kate's eyes filled with tears. They were sitting in an empty parking lot long before the first hint of dawn, their son and his toys in the back of the van and a plan in their minds that was unspeakable. Kate and Mitch got out of the van and walked to the back. Mitch raised the hatch and gently lifted his boy. He shuddered at Danny's stiffness. He steeled himself—all the more evidence that Danny, his loving, playful boy had departed—not died, but departed this body, this world, and was alive in a world where rigor held no sway. He cradled Danny and switched on the flashlight. Kate took the other sack in her arms. She had filled it with Danny's toys at Mitch's insistence.

"But why?" she had asked. "Because he'll need them," he had replied, as if the answer was obvious.

For a moment as Mitch looked at her, Kate feared that he saw in her face that she did not believe they were going anywhere together—that she did not believe that Danny needed anything anymore. But just as quickly, the look on Mitch's face had passed. Kate had chosen Danny's favorite toys: the Fisher Price farm with its happy farmer and wife, the smiling cow and horse and dog, the barn that opened on the side; his collection of Hot Wheels, many of which he had parked in the barn with the farm animals; a few stuffed animals. There was one more toy. It had grown up with him, which is how they thought of Little Green Bear, the name Danny had given it when he was finally old enough to name things. She had taken Little Green Bear from Danny's bed, kissed it, and put the bear in the sack.

There was only a single light in the far corner of the Chimney Bluffs parking lot, but it didn't matter. They had been there so often that they could have found their way blindfolded. Mitch closed the hatch, and for a long moment they stood together in the darkness, a sack flung over each of their backs. The sky was like pitch, and with no glaring lights to filter their view, they looked out across the lake at a three-quarter moon, Venus and Jupiter just off its shoulder, and surrounding them, more stars than Mitch and Kate had ever seen before, all arrayed in soft splashes against the night, a few standing out as if calling attention to their respective clusters. In the far eastern corner of the sky, sitting atop the horizon, flashes of lightning warned of a coming storm. There was no reason, though, to point out the moon that Danny had loved so much, its partially hidden face peeking, or to call out the names of the planets like they were old friends, or to whisper comforting words about the storm, so distant it could not bother them.

"We'd better go," said Mitch, and with that they stepped onto the trail and into the woods, Mitch leading the way, flashlight in hand. The moonlight faded in the advancing storm clouds, and the blackened trail quickly became a confusing maze studded with treacherous roots, low-hanging limbs, and unexpected tree stumps. Kate held onto Mitch's belt, and he pulled her along. They finally found the upward path that turned towards the high cliffs just as Kate slipped to the ground, exhausted, the sack of toys tumbling over beside her.

Mitch lay Danny down and knelt beside Kate, shining the flashlight in her face, catching the fear in her eyes. Mitch's jaw was set; he must stay strong and they must go forward.

"Can you walk?" he asked.

"Yes."

Mitch reached for her hand and helped her to her feet. He picked up the toys, put them back in the sack, and gave it to Kate. He gathered Danny into his arms. He took Kate by the wrist and started to walk up the incline to the bluff.

As they walked, Kate's resolve began to weaken. If she and Mitch died, there wouldn't be anyone to remember Danny; there wouldn't be anyone to remember his laugh or the way his eyes closed when he smiled; there wouldn't be anyone to remember his short life, his fleeting exuberance, his having been here in this world. There wouldn't be anyone to note the birthdays and anniversaries of so many things, to count the days that were and might have been, to keep the sadness.

There wouldn't be anyone to carry it all; there wouldn't be anyone to suffer for what had brought them to this unforgiving moment. Every fiber that had linked Danny to this life would be gone. Kate couldn't bear the thought of such an absolute ending.

Mitch breathed quickly and deeply as they reached the finger of the cliff where two hundred and fifty feet below, the lake grumbled as the storm approached. He sighed and adjusted Danny in his arms. Kate stood at his side, tears staining her face. The wind blew hard and the stars that were so brilliant had all but disappeared. They stood together. Mitch took Kate's hand and squeezed it. Mitch knew he was about to step off this world and into another, where every ache and pain of this life would be left behind and all that would remain was eternity.

"Kate, I love you."

"I love you, too," said Kate.

He took her hand and said, "It's time."

They inched forward, a stiff wind in their faces, waves clapping against the shore, a chasm of emptiness below. Kate looked at Mitch, but he didn't return her gaze. He smiled and squeezed her hand. He leaned into the wind.

"Mitch, wait, please," said Kate.

Chapter 3

"Jesus Christ almighty! What the hell?" said Bobby. The woman lay at his feet rolled in a ball, her eyes open. "Are you okay?" he asked. She lay like a shell thoughtlessly thrown on the shore. "Are you hurt?" He bent over but didn't touch her. He stood up and looked at Clancy sitting nearby, his face white as the sand. "Clancy?" said Bobby. He waded through the shallow water to Clancy's side. Clancy held the sack tight against his chest. Bobby leaned over to look, but when he saw the boy's face through a hole at the top of the sack, he gasped. He put his hand on Clancy's shoulder to steady himself.

"This isn't possible. It can't be happening."

Bobby backed away and then fell on the rocks. He struggled to get up, leaned over, and vomited. He stood and looked north at the undulating shoreline. He leaned over and got sick again. Then once more.

Bobby wanted to walk, but his legs convinced him not to. He leaned against the rocks again and then slid down to the sand. Before him were two sacks, one dead man, a half-dead woman, and his only real friend. He pulled his legs up to his chest and wrapped his arms around them.

Clancy couldn't move. He couldn't speak. He sat at the water's edge, his legs stretched out before him, a lifeless sack beside him. He pressed it to his side, as if the contact might make a difference, as if by linking himself to the sack, he might jump-start its contents back to life. And when it made no difference, he held it tighter.

If he could not stop them from coming to his park in the pre-dawn of the day, if he could not stop them from going to the edge of the bluffs, if he could not stop them from jumping, if he could not stop them from dying, then the least he could do was stay with this boy, hold him tight and not let go. If he let go, who knew what might happen. No, he would hold the sack, forever if necessary.

There were five at the base of Chimney Bluffs now, five on the shore where the waves came haltingly, five in the silent aftermath, five waiting, the sun crawling into place, the spires leaning, the gulls circling, complaining. When the EMTs finally arrived, Clancy was still sitting at the water's edge, fist clenching the sack.

"Sir?"

Clancy looked up.

"Sir, you can let go now. We can take it from here." Clancy held tight. He looked at the sack. He still couldn't believe it didn't move, that the little boy lay perfectly still, unaffected by the water and the cold morning air. He could have taken him up in his arms, but it wouldn't have warmed him. There was nothing Clancy could do. His white knuckles were wrapped tightly around the neck of the sack.

"Really, sir," the EMT said. "We'll be careful." Clancy looked up at the EMT, his young face, his coffee-breath, his pierced ears.

"Sir," said the EMT, this time more firmly, insistently. Clancy let go of the sack. "Thank you, sir," said the EMT with a nodding smile. He waved off the stretcher and picked the little boy up in his arms. His tiny hands were stiff, his fingers fanned out, eyes closed in permanent sleep, his hair drying now, responding to the breeze.

"Make sure he's okay," said Clancy, so quietly that no one heard him.

Bobby leaned against the spire, watching the woman at the water's edge. He could see her shivering. He walked unsteadily to her side again. Her matted hair concealed her face, her eyes the only things visible. He knelt beside her as the EMTs approached. "Ma'am?" said Bobby. This time he placed his hand on her shoulder. "Are you okay?" She didn't answer. She didn't blink. She didn't see.

"We'll take over," said the EMTs, politely but firmly.

Clancy looked at the dead man, his eyes wide open in shock, as if he knew he had made a mistake as soon as he had committed to thin air. Clancy studied his face, the crisscrossing cuts, his missing cheeks, his split lips, his gouged teeth, his shattered nose; the man's hands were closed, thumbs over index fingers, knuckles battered, and wrists broken.

Clancy wanted to care, but he didn't. His fists were clenched. He left the man in the water and walked over to the woman, still in a fetal position, shivering, her lips blue with cold.

"Clancy, I can't believe she's still..." Clancy stepped in front of Bobby and the EMT. He leaned over the woman. "Do you know what you have done?" he said, his face contorted. She didn't respond.

Clancy knelt at her side and leaned down so that his face was in her view.

21

"Hey, wait a minute," said the EMT. "Get back, please."

"Don't pretend you can't hear me; I know you can."

"Sir!"

"Clancy?" said Bobby, standing up and stepping back again.

"Why did you do this? That's what I want to know. What were you thinking?" Clancy's jaw was set, his eyes like a shark's. "Look at me, dammit." Her eyes were fixed. Clancy got closer. "You killed that little boy. You did." Her whole body shook, but her eyes never moved.

"Jesus, mister, get the hell back!" yelled the EMT.

"Let me tell you something," said Clancy, "you're going to pay for this. You are going to burn in hell." The EMT pushed Clancy away. Clancy glared at her, but she didn't twitch or blink or sigh. The EMTs carried one body away on a stretcher, face covered. A cop helped the woman up and wrapped a blanket around her as she sat leaning against the silt tower.

"Ma'am? Can you tell us what happened?" asked the other officer.

"She's in shock," said the EMT. "Not going to get anything out of her now. We've got to get her to a hospital." The EMTs helped the woman onto a stretcher, and they slowly labored down the beach.

Another officer searched through the sack of toys, itemizing the contents. He sat each toy gently on the sand—a tractor, a barn, cows and horses, a pig, a happy farmer and his smiling wife. He placed a stuffed basset hound, brown and white, floppy ears and big eyes, beside the other toys. It fell over on its side. Clancy sat the dog back up on its haunches, but it fell over again. He picked it up and leaned it against the barn so it wouldn't fall.

"Thanks," said the officer.

"That's okay," said Clancy. "Goddammit. Have you ever seen anything like this?"

"Can't say that I have. Been doing this for eighteen years and, no, I can't say I've ever seen anything like this." The officer paused, looked up at Clancy, grim-faced, then continued writing on his pad.

"What in the hell were they thinking?"

"Don't know." The officer sighed, clicked his pen, flipped his pad closed, and returned the pen to his pocket.

"My God, that little boy," said Clancy. There was a cluster of grey clouds sitting on the horizon, watching.

"Lot of crazies in the world, I guess."

"Crazy?" Clancy's eyes narrowed, his cheeks knotted. "They knew what they were doing. They understood. This was no accident. This was no God-made-me-do-it bullshit. The only ones responsible for this are them. As far as I'm concerned, that's not crazy—that's evil. No other explanation. Didn't give a damn about anything, not even their little boy."

The police officer looked at Clancy. He was about to say something but thought better of it.

"Life doesn't mean a thing to people anymore," said Clancy.

"Yeah," was all the officer said.

"Some people never even get the chance to have..." Clancy fiddled with the wedding band that he carried in his pocket. He looked at the officer, who had turned his back to speak to another cop. When the officer was done, Clancy was still at his side.

"I'm sorry, you were saying?"

"Nothing," said Clancy. The other officer put the toys back in the sack, threw the sack over his shoulder, and headed down the beach.

"Do you mind if I ask you some questions?" said the officer, removing the pen from his pocket again. Clancy recounted everything that had happened since he had arrived in the parking lot that morning.

"One last thing," said the cop. "Aside from the van, did you find anything else? Anything that might help us understand this mess? Anything at all?"

Clancy reached for the stuffed bear in his jacket pocket and then thought better of it.

"No, nothing," said Clancy.

Chapter 4

Clancy threw his truck keys on the table and stood in the middle of the kitchen with his arms out straight, looking at his hands. They were trembling. He shook them hard and held them out again, but there was no difference. He took the wedding ring out of his pocket and laid it on the spoon rest beside the sink. Then he took the bear out of his jacket and held it. He put it to his nose, trying to smell its owner but sensing only the dampness and the dirt of the bluffs. His eyes welled with tears. He laid the bear on the counter, turned the cold water on, and soaked his face, letting the beads drip wherever they wanted. Clancy took a glass from the dish drainer and filled it. He took a drink, put the glass down, and looked out the window at the garage. He picked up the glass again and took another drink. As he lowered the glass, it shattered in his fist; the blood ran down his arm in tiny rivulets into the sink. He watched it for a moment, feeling white-hot, his lips curling in disgust. Clancy reached for a dish towel and wrapped his hand. He turned from the kitchen sink as the phone rang.

"Hey, man, it's me," said Bobby. There was a long silence. "Clancy? Are you there?"

"Yeah. I'm here."

"How you doin'? I mean, are you okay, 'causeI sure ain't. I mean, to tell you the truth, it sure did a number on me. I can hardly think straight."

Clancy smelled Buffalo wings and heard Elvis on the jukebox when he pulled into John Dan's parking lot. Bobby was standing alone near the front door, his shoulders hunched in the cool evening air. When Bobby saw Clancy, he waved like they were meeting at a baseball game or something. *Jesus*, thought Clancy.

"Thanks for coming, buddy," said Bobby. "I mean it. Thanks. I just couldn't sit still. I was jumping out of my skin. Hey, what the hell happened to your hand?"

"Nothing. It's nothing." Clancy flexed his gauze-wrapped hand slowly. They walked into the restaurant and Clancy nodded at a handful of regulars along the bar, each with a Genny beer in his fist. He walked to the bar and ordered.

"Hey, John, a Blue Moon and a…" He looked at Bobby with a question mark on his face.

"Molson," said Bobby.

"Blue Moon and Molson coming up," said John. John stared at Clancy's hand. Clancy just shook his head. John pulled the tap handle slowly and watched the brew fill the glass, a snowcap foaming on top. He tilted the glass back level, dropped in an orange slice, and slid it to Clancy. "On the house, gentlemen," was all he said. Clancy took a long draw, wiped his mouth, and put his glass back on the bar.

"Hey, Bobby," said John, and slid one his way.

"Thanks, John; I never needed a beer more than I need it tonight."

"So I hear," said John.

"I mean to tell you," said Bobby. "It just messed me up awful."

"I'm sure," said John.

"I thought I'd never stop puking," said Bobby, looking at his glass. He glanced at Clancy, hoping he would say something.

Clancy just looked at his beer, turning the glass slowly.

"I mean, that kid couldn't have been any older than three, maybe four, I'm telling you. Right, Clancy?"

"Uh huh," said Clancy as he lifted the glass to his mouth.

"Clancy'll tell you," said Bobby. "He was just a little kid. Just a little kid all curled up in that damn sack. I mean, what was that about? How could they, I don't know, just how could they? I mean, what in the world were they trying to do? And the kid's toys were in the other bag. I'm telling you, it was just crazy. No other word for it." He looked at Clancy again.

"Another beer, John," said Clancy.

"Sure, Clance."

"Clancy'll tell you. It was something out of a damn movie." Bobby took a long draw and set his bottle back on the bar. "I was thinking, what if that little boy had a brother or something, and the brother was left all alone with no one? You know, like maybe they shared the same bedroom or something."

John replaced Clancy's beer with another, and Clancy ran his forefinger across the top, smoothing out the foam.

"I don't think there were any other kids," said John. "Just the one."

"Well, I guess that's one good thing. It would be awful to be left behind," said Bobby.

"Small consolation if you take a little time to think hard about it, Bobby," said Clancy.

Bobby shifted in his seat and fell silent for a moment. "Yeah, I guess you're right on that," he said. Clancy didn't look at Bobby, and Bobby didn't know what else to say. "Better hit the head. You never buy the beer, you just rent it. Set me up another one, John," said Bobby. "I'll be back in a minute." He headed off to the men's room.

"Still just a kid, isn't he?" said John.

"Barely," said Clancy, finishing off his beer. John slid a basket of peanuts and pretzels his way.

"So, was it as bad as everyone is saying?"

"Yes," said Clancy, "and worse."

John ran his towel across the oaken surface and leaned on the bar.

"Killed a little kid," said Clancy. "He never did anything to anybody. You know, you have to get a license to drive a damn car, but anyone can have a kid." Clancy stuck his hand is his jacket pocket and held the bear tight.

Bobby crossed the bar and slid back onto his stool. Clancy stiffened.

"Hey, John, don't forget me down here," said Bobby. John nodded at him and slid a bottle of Molson in the man's direction. "I mean it, serious now; can you believe that two people would jump off a cliff with their son? And one of them lived. I sure wouldn't want to live with that on my mind for the rest of my life."

Bobby took some peanuts and then slid the basket back to Clancy, who didn't touch it.

"I mean, living after a kid gets killed, you just don't get over it; I know what it did to my father when…"

"Maybe the woman will die, too," said Clancy.

"Hmm, yeah, maybe that would be best." Bobby waited again, but Clancy didn't speak.

"Anyone else ever survived a jump off the bluffs, Clancy?" asked John.

"Not that I know of," said Clancy. "This was my first, though I've heard there've been ten before. Maybe more; I don't know for sure."

Bobby took another handful of peanuts and let his back slump into a curve.

"God," said John. "You know, when I'm up on that trail looking out over the lake so far below, I have to tell you, it's like a magnet. Don't get me wrong, I ain't never wanted to kill myself, but there's been times that I had to force myself back from the edge. It just sucks at you. All that wind and sky."

Clancy understood the lure, too. After Darlene had left, he had often gone to the cliffs on his days off, not because he wanted to kill himself, but because he wanted to clear his head. But sometimes he felt such an empty, peaceful feeling standing at the edge—looking out over the lake, birds flying below, wind calling him—that jumping seemed natural.

John walked away to tend another customer. Bobby stood up and arched his back. He leaned against the bar and tipped his glass back until there wasn't any more.

"Yeah, you're right, Clance; they must have been crazy. No one in their right mind would kill their own kid." He sat down again. "It's like I was saying, when my brother…"

29

"Another, Clancy?" called John from the other end of the bar.

"Sure," he said.

"So…" said Bobby.

"Some more peanuts, too, John," said Clancy. He turned to Bobby, his eyes narrow, his lips pursed. "What is it?"

"Nothing," said Bobby, shaking his head. He leaned across the bar, catching John's attention.

"Another one here, too," was all he said.

Chapter 5

The EMTs lay the stretcher carefully on the pavement as two more approached with a gurney.

"Okay, one, two, three," said the two young men as they hoisted Kate Duncan onto the gurney and strapped her into place.

"Careful, careful, she doesn't need another fall."

"Are you okay, ma'am?"

"No point in asking. She hasn't said a word yet."

"Don't worry, ma'am; we'll take good care of you. We'll get you to the hospital as quick as we can." He hesitated over her, waiting for her to nod or smile or even blink. "Okay, let's go."

They rolled her across the pavement to the waiting ambulance. Kate turned her head in time to see the VW van in the middle of the lot, looking like a beat-up old dog. She opened her mouth, feeling she should say something as she passed. But she couldn't. She closed her eyes. Once in the ambulance, one of the EMTs unzipped Kate's jacket and opened her blouse. The stethoscope felt cold. The other EMT strapped a cuff around Kate's arm and started pumping. Both listened closely for the beating of her heart and the pulsing of her blood. "Elevated," was all they said with a shrug. "Maybe a little hypothermic, but okay." There was a long silence.

"Does anything seem odd?" whispered one to the other.

"Yes."

He went forward to speak to the driver and then returned to Kate's side. The driver called the hospital.

"On our way with a female, late thirties; possible fall from Chimney Bluffs." The driver waited and then spoke again. "No, nothing that we can find."

"Okay, guys, we're heading out." The EMTs grabbed seats and the ambulance turned onto the road, no lights flashing, no sirens blaring.

The emergency room was bustling. Kate's stomach turned as she looked at the pale green walls with directional striping, so familiar from their trips to the hospital with Danny. The EMTs helped her off the gurney and onto a bed.

"I hope that everything turns out...I hope that you'll be okay," said the youngest, his eyes sad, his mouth thin. Kate looked at him.

"Wow, she actually looked at you," said the young man's partner.

"Shut up, man; she can hear you."

"I don't give a shit if she hears me," came the reply.

Kate turned her face to the curtain. On the other side, a woman moaned and a man tried to calm her.

"Honey, honey, it's gonna be all right. Hey, can anybody do something here?"

Soft-soled shoes squeaked across the linoleum. Someone barked orders. The woman fell silent. They rushed her in a blur down the hall.

The atmosphere of urgency pressed Kate's temples like a vise.

Danny had been so little when they had come to the hospital for the surgery. After being admitted, they were ushered to the phlebotomist's, where a nurse tried in vain to prick Danny's finger while Kate cradled him in her lap.

"The nice lady's not going to hurt you," she had said, knowing it was untrue.

"Mama!" cried Danny, clutching his mother. The nurse, sliding her rolly-chair closer, looked on, unmoved.

"We've got to do this. They need a sample before he goes in for surgery," said the nurse.

She tried and failed three more times. Danny thrashed and swung his arms, hitting the nurse on the bridge of her nose. She picked up her glasses from the floor and rolled backwards in her chair, glaring at Kate.

"Can you do this?" she asked Kate. Mitch looked on, red-faced and silent. Kate gave Danny Little Green Bear.

"Here you go, honey; he'll help you feel good." Danny grabbed his bear and buried his face against his mommy's shoulder. He was still weeping, but tired, his strength gone.

"Can we try again? I have other patients," said the nurse in a huff.

With that, Mitch yanked Danny from his mother's arms and held him tight, one arm across his chest and the other hand clenching Danny's hand. Danny was white with fear. "There, take what you want!" he said, his voice shrill with anger. Danny lay petrified as the nurse pricked his finger time and again. Kate began to cry and when it was over, she took Danny in her arms and rocked him back and forth while pacing the room. She wouldn't look at Mitch.

"What?" said Mitch, sullen and edgy.

The nurse slid a shoebox across the table. "He can pick a sticker."

At the time, Kate couldn't have imagined a worse moment, a moment of greater helplessness. Yet now she yearned for that moment. She yearned to hear Danny's cry. She yearned for the tempest of his surgery. She yearned for the good news that had followed. Instead, she had nothing, and no amount of yearning could change that.

When she looked up again, a white coat and two blue hats were standing over her.

"Mrs. Duncan? Is that your name?" asked the doctor. Kate studied the face staring at her: the smooth skin, the wide and steady eyes, the black goatee with a crumb nestled in it.

"We found some identification in the van," said the first police officer. She was short, coming only to the shoulder of her partner, a barrel-chested man with tiny eyes and a wide jaw who seemed annoyed that she had spoken first.

"Mrs. Duncan, I am Dr. Herald," said the physician, leaning in ahead of the police officers. "The police would like to ask you some questions. If you don't want to answer them now, I can ask them to come back. You've been through an ordeal, I know…"

"I'm Officer Crukshank," said the diminutive woman, whose hair stuck out at right angles from under her cap.

"I know this is very difficult," continued Dr. Herald. "I wanted you to know that we have not found anything physically wrong with you, but we would like to keep you in the hospital for observation."

"What exactly happened last night, Mrs. Duncan?" asked the barrel-chested cop. When she didn't answer, he went on. "Your son and husband are dead. We want to understand the sequence of events."

Kate watched his mouth opening and closing, sometimes grimacing as he spoke; he stopped from time to time, waiting for something that never came, and then he went on. He shifted his weight from one foot to the other as his face turned red; he put his hands on his hips, then folded his arms over his chest, then waved his arms while his mouth picked up speed and his eyes bulged further out of their sockets. The lady cop was stiff. She stepped back from her partner and put her hand on his shoulder, but he shrugged her hand away. The doctor's forehead was creased, and his mouth lay open but didn't move. He reached for the red-faced, barrel-chested officer, laying a hand on his wrist, but the officer glared at the doctor, who then removed his hand, straightened his posture, gathered himself with a deep breath, and spoke calmly to the cop.

"I suggest you leave," said the doctor. "I suggest you leave now."

The thunderous wall of dark blue receded, disappearing behind the pale green, striped curtain, leaving only the glare of an overhead lamp and the bleached silence of the physician's coat.

"Wait, Mitch, please!" said Kate.

The doctor turned his head, his face stark and expressionless with fear, much as Mitch's face had been.

"Wait, Mitch, please! I have something I want to..." she said. Mitch's hand had slipped from hers, and he had disappeared into the blackness without a sound, Danny in his arms.

"MITCH!" she screamed.

"Nurse!" called the doctor.

Kate had stepped closer to the edge. She had looked into the black hole where her family had disappeared. She had hoped that Mitch was right, that he was with Danny and that they were happy and that they would understand. She had hoped that they were in each other's arms, and together were at peace, that they were safe from all harm, from all suffering—that they were...home.

Standing alone on that cliff, she had begun to cry because, in truth, she didn't believe that this was the case. She didn't believe in a heaven above or a hell below. She didn't believe in an ever-after where all worldly wrongs are righted, where the suffering of this life is justified and explained and finally erased, where all the wounds are closed and the scars are healed and there is no pain anymore.

It took Kate an hour, flashlight in hand, toys on her back, to make it down the trail to the parking lot and then up the beach to where Mitch and Danny lay so still that she gasped when she came upon them. She knelt down beside Mitch. She covered her face in her hands, unable to look at his eyes. She threw her head back and tried to scream, but nothing came. Finally Kate reached for Mitch, brushing his hair back from his face with a trembling hand. She closed her eyes and leaned forward, kissing his bruised cheek. She looked at him, stunned that he didn't move. "I am so sorry," she said, lying on him and rocking back and forth.

Danny was several feet away. She kissed the top of his head. Kate opened her sack, searching for Little Green Bear to put by his side. It was then that she realized the bear was gone. She wept again and fell to the pebbled beach. "My poor boy."

In the East, the horizon had gone from black to purple. The storm swept across the water, rain like needles pelting her face, a pinpricking rain that made her skin feel as numb as her heart felt; it was a punishing rain, a rain that beat her, as it should, for Danny's sake. Kate had curled into a ball and lay shivering at the base of the bluff.

The nurse came quickly, hypodermic in hand. She swabbed Kate's skin and then thrust the needle into her arm. The numbness spread until there was nothing left but sleep.

Chimney Bluffs

Chapter 6

"Mrs. Duncan, did you hear me?" said the psychiatrist. "Do you have thoughts of hurting yourself?" The psychiatrist wore a white coat, a pin-striped tie on a blue collar, neatly pressed pants, the crease blade sharp. "Perhaps more to the point, do you want to kill yourself?"

Kate felt his words circling her like birds of prey.

"We don't want you to do anything that would jeopardize your recovery, your..." His voice faded. He sat up straight in his chair. He leaned forward for emphasis.

"Mrs. Duncan, please..."

Kate was hollowed out, empty. Everything had seeped out onto the beach and had been swept away.

"I can wait, if you need time," he said, crossing his arms.

There were sea gulls outside the doctor's window, gliding effortlessly on an invisible cushion. Such trust.

"I don't want to live, if that's what you mean," she said.

Kate was immediately transferred to the psychiatric wing. She wore a hospital gown but little else. They took her shoelaces, her sheets, strings of any kind; they removed all sharp objects; the windows didn't open, and outside the windows were bars. Throughout the first day and then the second and finally the third, she was repeatedly checked by staff to make sure she didn't do anything rash. Throughout, she steadfastly and calmly maintained her desire to die.

On the fourth day, she was visited by a social worker with a tight blond bun intended, it seemed, to make her look older than her twenty-odd years. She wore practical shoes and dark-rimmed glasses and a white coat several sizes too large with sleeves rolled up to her elbows. She sat in the straight-backed metal chair and smiled constantly. She wrote notes in her chart with religious fervor, head bent over and hand curled awkwardly like a middle school student trying to write an essay about what she had done on her summer vacation.

"You're not suicidal?" said the social worker.

"No."

"That's good."

"I just don't want to live."

"That's not so good," she said with a broad smile. "Help me understand this. You don't want to hurt yourself, but you also don't want to live."

Apparently this was a contradiction of some kind, although it made perfect sense to Kate. Kate didn't think it would be necessary to take action of any kind. She assumed that, much as night inevitably follows day, death could not be far behind her. She felt it close on her heels. When she had lain on the beach, she thought, *I will lie here until it comes.* It seemed so simple, so obvious at the time. She would join them—not in the afterlife, but in the not-being-here.

"Yes," said Kate.

The social worker explained that she didn't think that Kate was a "high-risk" patient and that she would recommend she be moved to a regular room on her unit. She also explained that she would be meeting with Kate daily while she was in the hospital.

"I look forward to getting to know you," she said, shaking Kate's hand as if they were meeting in a wedding reception receiving line.

The next day, Kate stood at the hospital window, looking out across the expansive parking lot at the grey, granite headstones that dotted the adjoining cemetery. She wore a pair of blue jeans cinched tight with a long belt and a Nike sweatshirt that was two sizes too large, the best she could do at the consignment shop on the first floor. She paced the floor in front of the young social worker, who sat patiently in an over-stuffed chair beside her desk, another chair opposite her. Kate reached the office door, turned, and walked back to the window. She took a deep breath and let it out, a suggestion from the social worker to help her relax. With each breath, though, the muscles in her neck tightened as if to hold her head squarely on her shoulders. She leaned against the window ledge and looked at the people below, coming and going from the hospital entrance, some in a hurry, others walking slowly, each with a story to tell, each with a loved one in distress. She felt she knew them intimately—too intimately, perhaps. She turned from the window and the social worker —Carrie-somebody—smiled.

"Why don't you take a seat?" she said.

Kate wrapped her arms around her shoulders. "No thank you, this is fine."

The social worker seemed a little disappointed. She adjusted her position on the chair and tried again. "Would you like a cup of coffee?"

Kate nodded. The social worker got up from her chair and walked to the coffeemaker, pulling an extra cup from the rack on the wall. It said, "A Smile on Every Mug."

"Cream and sugar?"

"No, thank you," said Kate.

Carrie-somebody handed her the coffee and gestured toward the chair. Kate declined and walked back to the window as the social worker returned to her seat. Kate leaned against the windowsill and took a sip of the coffee, which burned the tip of her tongue. "Sorry, I should have warned you; I guess I'm used to it super hot," said the social worker with an apologetic smile. Kate shifted her weight from one foot to the other. She looked at the diploma on the wall behind the desk—Carrie Evelyn Goodwill, awarded a master's degree in social work, Syracuse University.

"I know you aren't suicidal, but are you still having those thoughts?"

Carrie Goodwill had asked this question every day since Kate had been transferred to psychiatry three weeks earlier. Some people greeted each other with "Good morning," but here it was different. The answer to the question was always the same "Yes." But Kate learned to vary her response to satisfy her questioner. Sometimes she said, "A little," while other times she said, "Not as much" or "Less often." These seemed to be satisfactory answers even though they amounted to the same thing—she still had thoughts of dying every day.

"From time to time," was the phrase Kate chose for today.

"In time, I'm sure you won't have those thoughts at all," said Carrie Goodwill. She leaned over her chart and wrote. When she was finished, she clicked her pen and put it down on her desk. She looked at Kate and smiled. "So, Mrs. Duncan, how are you doing *overall*?"

Another favorite question. The EMTs had asked her this over and over again as they wheeled her to the ambulance and then again on the ride to the hospital; they had asked her again in the emergency room when they were puzzled by her lack of injuries, then on the medical floor where they observed her for several days until they concluded that she was no longer in shock—she was just not talking. And, of course, once she got to psychiatry, it was always the second question they asked, just after the one about suicide. The only person who hadn't asked her that question was the man who had stood over her on the beach, the man who had found her. "Okay," she said, an answer that usually held the questioners at bay for a while.

"Good. I'm glad to hear it, though I doubt you're really doing okay." Carrie Goodwill paused, letting her response sink in, as if to say, "I'm on to you."

The social worker always smiled. Even when Kate saw her in the hall and no one was around, she was smiling. Kate wondered how this could be. How could someone be living in the same world as Kate and always smile? "I mean, you've lost so much; I can't imagine," she said, still smiling, her eyebrows meeting in sympathy. Kate sipped her coffee and looked out the window again. An ambulance was pulling into the emergency entrance, a car behind it. She watched as family members piled out of the car and ran into the hospital.

"Mrs. Duncan, you haven't said much about Mr. Duncan. Can you tell me a little about him? His name was Mitch, right?"

"Yes, it was. Mitch." said Kate, watching Carrie Goodwill take another sip of coffee, place the cup on her desk, and smile invitingly. "What do you want to know?"

"Well, what was he like?"

"He was a good man," said Kate, shifting her weight and avoiding eye contact.

"I'm sure he was," said Carrie Goodwill, pronouncing each word distinctly, as if she meant the opposite. "What else can you tell me?"

"I don't know," said Kate, looking into her lap, remembering.

Kate had lived in the Happy Valley Trailer Park with her mother all of her life. Her father—"He's the one who wanted a kid!" her mother reminded her—had left when Kate was an infant. After high school, Kate had stayed on at Wegman's Grocery Store, where she worked as a cashier and eventually as the front-end manager.

Kate's uneventful twenties were slipping steadily away, clearly proving her mother's dictum that "life ends up being one big nothing after another," when a young man with a cheerful voice and a confident smile came into the store one day. Every hair was in place, and his face had a fresh-scrubbed look about it, the face of someone you could trust. "Hi there," he said to the first person he saw. "Can I help you?" he said to a woman who struggled with her bags. "Excuse me," he said to another woman as he let her pass. Kate couldn't take her eyes off of him, not because he was particularly good-looking, because he wasn't, but because he shined—that's the only word she could think of. He shined like one of those neon arrows blinking outside an all-night diner—"Look at me! Look at me! Look at me!" He took a cart from the rack, and off he went down aisle one, whistling.

Soon enough, she looked up to greet the next customer and it was him. He was standing there, a big smile on his face like they were long-lost friends. "Hi," he said, "I'm Mitch Duncan. I'm new in town. Just opened the appliance store down on Fifth Street; maybe you've seen it." He paused as if she was supposed to answer, but she didn't know what to say.

"Paper or plastic?"

"Let's go with plastic. Save a few trees today, whadaya think?" His smile was broad and straight and unflinching.

Kate arranged the bags and gave him a half-smile without looking at him directly.

"And what is your name?"

"Kate. My name is Kate."

"Of course, how could I be so stupid? There it is right on your shirt." He laughed out loud. "Kate. I like that."

"Coupons?" was all she said.

"Excuse me?"

"Coupons, do you have any? This is a double value day. Each coupon is worth twice as much as usual."

"Really, I wish I'd known. That's a great deal, Kate." She liked the way he said her name, as if he'd known her for years. "Well, next time I'll remember my coupons."

She managed to look straight at him. "Okay."

"So long, Kate!" said Mitch.

She watched him push his cart towards the exit, wishing he'd turn around one last time. If he did, she'd smile and maybe even wave. She watched, but he was too busy greeting everyone along the way. In a moment he was gone.

"I'm going to make something of myself, God willing," he said to her on their first date, and she believed him. Something about Mitch touched Kate like nothing before. He looked at the world as if there were jewels to be found everywhere; you just had to look hard enough. When he talked to her, she believed everything he said. Soon enough, they were married, had a house, and not long thereafter, a child on the way.

Mitch made Kate see life's possibilities. "You've just got to believe, and everything will fall into place," he'd say with a broad, confident smile. When Danny was born, she knew Mitch was right; her life felt complete.

Kate looked at Carrie Goodwill, who sat patiently, smiling again as their eyes met.

"He was a good husband, and a good father," said Kate, as if to counter something that hadn't yet been said.

"I'm sure you feel he was," said Carrie Goodwill. She took a breath as if to continue, but then stopped. She took another drink of her coffee. "Would you like more coffee?"

"No, I'm fine," said Kate.

Carrie Goodwill leaned forward. Her face, softer; her voice, warm. "Your little boy, Danny; are you ready yet to talk about him?"

Kate's face flushed. She brought the cup to her lips again but didn't drink. She put the cup down on the windowsill and took another deep breath, and then another.

"I know it's hard, but it's important to talk…"

Kate closed her eyes, trying to see her son.

"Congratulations, Mommy and Daddy, you have a perfect little baby boy," Dr. Smythe had said. The doctor laid the baby on Kate's belly, and she cradled him in her arms, tears streaming down her cheeks. "Hello, there," she breathed. "Hello, Daniel Joseph Duncan. Welcome to the world." She looked up at Mitch, who was bent over beside her, his hand on his son's back, his face red with excitement.

Danny's bassinet was in their bedroom, and when he cried, they brought him into bed with them. Kate and Mitch lay beside him like protective walls of love. They rubbed his belly and tickled his toes. And with each passing day, they loved him more and more until it was difficult to remember their lives before Danny.

"…because talking can be healing and…" Carrie's voice continued in the background.

Danny smiled when they came in the room, and he yelled if they didn't look his way; he hid behind his daddy's hands when playing peek-a-boo and grabbed his mother's hands during tummy time. But all of this came more slowly for Danny. Whenever they went to the mall or to a restaurant and saw other couples and their babies, they always asked how old the babies were. It was clear to Kate that Danny wasn't progressing along the same timeline. Eating remained a problem. When she switched to bottle-feeding, he often chewed the nipple but wouldn't suck. Kate tried to spoon-feed him, but most of the squash and peas ended up on his chin or bib.

Mitch didn't seem to notice. "It's all in your mind." Things were always in Kate's mind. "God has blessed us. Why are you borrowing trouble? Really, he's fine. He'll get there. He's just going at his own pace. You worry too much."

Kate's worries deepened with each passing day.

"...more than anything, I'd like to see a smile on your face," concluded the social worker.

Kate opened her eyes.

Carrie Goodwill stood, walked over to the coffeemaker and pressed the button, filling her mug again. She leaned against the table. "I'm sure it's very hard to even think about your son right now, let alone talk to me about him."

Kate took another deep breath.

One evening after work, Mitch came home to find Kate sitting in the rocker crying, Danny in her arms.

"Honey, what is it?"

"I'm telling you, Mitch, something's wrong," said Kate.

"Kate, look, we've been over this; you heard what the doctor said; it just takes time. He'll catch up, you'll see."

"Mitch, why do you keep saying that? He's not catching up!"

"Stop it! Don't keep doing this! My God, every day you think of some new thing to worry about. Don't you understand that you're just making things worse? Stop comparing him to other babies. It's not fair."

"I'm not comparing him. I just know that things aren't..."

"Don't even think that! You're so damn negative. You've got to be more positive. You can't give in to that kind of thinking. It's not good for you, and it's not good for him."

Kate fell silent. Then she held Danny up to his father. "Take him, Mitch. Hold him. Look at him."

A tear trickled down her cheek.

"Mrs. Duncan, are you all right?" asked the social worker. "Did I say something to upset you?" She reached for the Kleenex box on the desk and gave it to Kate.

Kate took a tissue. "No, it's nothing…"

"Mrs. Duncan, please have a seat," she said, her hand on Kate's arm. Kate looked at the identification badge hanging around the social worker's neck. Her hair was shorter in the picture, but it was the same beaming smile looking back at her. Kate sat.

"How can I help you?" said Carrie Goodwill.

Kate looked at her, blank-faced. Kate rubbed her eyes and leaned back against the soft cushion. "I don't know," she said. "I don't know if there *is* any help."

"There's always help," said Carrie Goodwill. "Things can always get better."

Dr. Smythe had listened for the longest time to Danny's little chest. She pulled the stethoscope from her ears and draped it around her neck. She smiled at Danny and tickled his belly. She sighed and looked at Kate and Mitch. "Now, I don't want you to be alarmed, but I do hear something that I haven't heard before."

Despite her apprehensions, Kate had gone to Dr. Smythe with the same expectation as Mitch—that Danny was actually doing fine. Hearing this, she wondered if she had done something wrong, if she had missed something.

"Well, then, if there is something that needs to be fixed, and I'm still not convinced that's the case, but if there is, then I'm sure it will turn out fine. It's all just part of the plan," said Mitch with a broad, ill-fitting smile.

Mitch had always been a positive thinker, which was one of the things that attracted Kate to him. He had always looked on the bright side and had always flicked her doubts away like so much dust on his sleeve. Though he wasn't a churchgoer—"They're all hypocrites," he'd say—Mitch had inherited a deep belief in God from his mother. She had taught him that if you did well in this life, God would reward you when you went to "the other side." "Why else would you put up with all this crap?" his mother concluded.

"You know, Mrs. Duncan, I couldn't do this work if I didn't believe that things can get better, that life can change in positive ways, even when everything seems so awful." She reached out and put her hand on Kate's knee. "You have to keep hope alive," said Carrie Goodwill.

Kate glanced at the pictures and slogans on the wall and the coffee mug full of pens and pencils on Carrie Goodwill's desk. "I'm glad that it works so well for you," said Kate without expression.

Dr. Crandall, Danny's surgeon, had leaned forward on his elbows and had taken off his glasses, revealing greying, bushy eyebrows. "This open vessel between your son's lungs—a patent ductus arteriosus or PDA—this open vessel puts a strain on his heart that can lead to heart enlargement; it can elevate the blood pressure in his lungs; it can lead to infection. If it's not dealt with, it will likely have a deleterious effect on your son's overall health."

Mitch still insisted there was nothing to worry about. Kate, though, felt her insides seize up. She would have to take their infant boy to the hospital and entrust him to people she didn't know and hope that they cared about Danny at least half as much as she did. And they would put him to sleep—not the sleep of a baby swaddled in his crib, but an anesthetically induced sleep, necessary so that when they cut into his side he would neither feel nor remember the assault. And when he would awaken, he would be confused and afraid and in pain, and he would want to get away and they would have to comfort him and hold him in place so he wouldn't hurt himself; they would sleep with him in uncomfortable chairs and he would be startled awake by nurses checking his vital signs throughout the night and day. And all of this to make a little sound go away.

Neither Kate nor Mitch had been ready for what they had seen when they walked into the pediatric intensive care unit after Danny's surgery. He had lain behind a single curtain, a bright light over his tiny body, machines surrounding him on all sides, their rhythmic pinging sound like water on one's forehead, tubes in his nose and mouth, tape holding everything in place, his face barely visible, his body barely reaching the middle of the bed, where he lay amidst tubes and monitors, white sheets and pale green walls. They thought they had asked every question, but they had forgotten one: What will he look like?

There was a nurse in the room with Danny, looking like a professor standing over an elaborate science project. Danny's eyes were closed, yet he was struggling to turn over, reaching with his left hand, revealing a long jagged incision that snaked from behind his armpit to the middle of his chest. It was black with dried blood, visible through the clear tape that, for all they knew, was keeping his insides from spilling out on the linoleum floor. Kate lost her breath in the realization that, indeed, they had taken a knife and had cut her son open, had searched around his insides for the errant vessel, and then had stitched him up like a torn pillowcase.

When Dr. Crandall had spoken with them after the operation, Kate had been prepared for the dead weight of bad news but not the airiness of good. The surgery had been a complete success.

"Thank you," she whispered. "Thank you."

Mitch shook Dr. Crandall's hand for the longest time, not wanting to let go. "I knew it would be okay," he said. "I knew it all along. God bless you." At first, Danny was bent over to one side like a pretzel, the pain was so sharp, but with each passing day, his body loosened and unfolded and healed. In less than a week, he was home, looking good as new. Everything seemed to go back to normal.

When Mitch woke up each morning, he looked out across the day as if he were surveying calm seas and clear skies all the way to the horizon and beyond. When he considered their recent trials, he thought, *What an amazing world this is!*

When Kate woke up, she looked out across the day, worried that the blue skies and placid seas would surely give way to storm clouds just beyond the horizon. Though grateful for Danny's recovery, when she considered their recent trials, she thought, *What kind of world is this?* and worried that her mother had been right all along: that the world beyond their driveway was unpredictable at best, dangerous at worst.

As Mitch shed the last of his cares, Kate picked them all up like dirty laundry strewn across the bedroom floor. Danny would grow and thrive for the next eighteen months. And then Danny's earaches would begin.

"So, Mrs. Duncan, about Danny." Carrie Goodwill, her arms

crossed now, grinned hopefully at Kate. Kate stood and walked to the office window again. The family that had raced across the emergency parking lot below was gone. The sun was disappearing behind the hulking garage where she and Mitch had parked so often. To the north, clouds were mounting, as they often did over the lake in the late afternoon. Chimney Bluffs would be beautiful this time of day, softened by the fading light, the trees along its heights casting long shadows on the water below. Kate turned from the window.

"Do you have children?"

"Do I have children?" rephrased a surprised Carrie Goodwill.

"Yes, do you?"

"I'm not supposed to share personal information. We're here to talk about you. The fact that *you* had a little boy is the important thing. That's what we should be talking about."

Kate looked down at the floor in front of Carrie Goodwill's chair. "Do you have children?" she asked again, this time in a whisper.

"Like I said, I don't share…"

"I'll take that as a no," said Kate, looking up.

"Does it matter if I don't have children?" asked Carrie Goodwill, her smile vanishing briefly.

"Yes."

"There are many things that my patients have experienced that I haven't. I still think I can empathize with what you're going through."

Kate looked up from the floor into Carrie Goodwill's eyes. She could tell that the social worker was sincere, that she was saying what she truly believed, which saddened Kate all the more.

"It's just that if you've never had a child, someone to hold in your arms, someone who depends on you every minute of every day, then you can't possibly know the joy, and if you have never known the joy, then you can't possibly understand the sorrow," said Kate. She took a deep breath and looked Carrie Goodwill in the eyes. "And if you have never felt, as I do, that you may have cost your child his life, then you can't possibly know the pain, the regret, the guilt. And if you have never felt those, then you can't really help me at all."

Chapter 7

"Look, Clance, you may think you're all right, but you ain't all right, trust me," said Buddy Rollins, Clancy's boss, wiping coffee from his handlebar mustache, his belly hanging over his Harley-Davidson belt buckle. "Jesus, it's only been a few days! Nobody can go through what you just went through and then get right back on the horse. I know, I been there. Never seen a little kid, but I seen my share of jumpers. Their faces always look the same. Like they thought, 'Oh shit!' as soon as they became airborne."

Clancy protested, but Buddy wouldn't hear it. "That's that, so go home. See you Monday."

Clancy stood in the west parking lot of Chimney Bluffs, watching a dozen crows perched on a row of ash trees, arguing with each other. He leaned back against his truck, exhaling mist into the cool morning air. He pulled the tab back on the coffee lid and sipped the hot brown brew slowly, steadily. He looked around again, remembering the exact position of the white VW van in the middle of the lot. It had made him angry at the time, their thoughtlessness. My God, Clancy had broken up more than one fight over a stupid parking space.

Clancy took another sip of coffee. *You have a job where*

managing how people park is one of the most important things you do. It is always uppermost in your mind; it's always something that needs to be monitored. Jesus, he thought, *who cares?*

Clancy clicked the radio off and stared at the glove box. He leaned across the passenger's seat and turned the knob. He reached in, pulled the green bear out, and sat it on the dashboard in front of him. The bear slumped over slightly, its button eyes looking squarely at him.

"You know, there's only one thing that matters in this life," Clancy said to his limp companion. "And it's not whether you park your van in the right place or not; it's not trying to make it big, or having a lot of cash, or a fancy car, or a house that isn't falling apart. It's none of that. What matters is that you leave something behind: your name, your blood, something—something that lasts, something that's going to be here even when you're not. And you do everything you can to make sure nothing goes wrong with that one thing."

Clancy balanced the bear, its ragged arms outstretched, on the steering wheel. He held it to his nose. It smelled of old Cheerios and mashed peas. Clancy thought of Darlene. He sat the bear in the passenger's seat. He put the truck in gear and rolled toward the exit. He looked both ways on 104 and turned left, heading for Watertown.

Fifteen miles down the road, Clancy stopped at Sam Reynolds's BP station. Sam had an old Dodge up on the rack, but when he saw Clancy, he wiped his hands on an oily rag, smiled, and took his old friend's hand.

"I'll be damned, if it isn't Clancy Brisco," laughed Sam. "How are you doing?"

"Well, I'm doin', I guess," said Clancy. "How's your wife and son?"

"Noreen is doing just fine. Still working at Mott's," he said gently.

"Good for her. She was always a tough-assed foreman."

"I'll tell her you said so; she'll take it as a compliment."

"And your son…"

"Ricky."

"Yeah, how's he doing?"

"How's he doing! I'll tell you…" Clancy sighed after a few minutes, feeling edgy and disinterested in Ricky's accomplishments. Sometimes Sam's pride was overbearing; it sucked all the oxygen out of the garage. After ten minutes, Clancy found an opening.

"Yeah, well, that's pretty amazing," said Clancy. "Love to hear more, but I got to get going here in a minute. So, Sam, reason I stopped is, I got some tax notice thing in the mail from like years ago, and I got to do something about it; it involves Darlene."

"Oh my, what did she do now?" said Sam with a wink.

"Nothing like that, Sam, it's just that I've got to get her signature on a paper and I don't know where she lives anymore. I thought you could help me out."

Sam fidgeted with an empty coffee can full of cigarette butts, tossing it into a nearby barrel. "Well, I'm not sure…," he started to say, but the look in Clancy's eyes said, "Stop." Clancy and Sam had never discussed it, but both knew that Sam had been a frequent visitor to Darlene's apartment long after she and Clancy had broken up. Clancy heard he promised Darlene that he'd leave Noreen if she'd only be a little more available, which, as it turned out, meant jumping in the back of his truck cab every time he got the itch. Noreen wasn't nearly as accommodating or flexible.

He waved Clancy into his office and blocked the door shut with a brick. "It's been a long time, Clancy. I actually don't know; last time I, well, she wasn't living where she used to live the last time I was in Watertown. And she didn't exactly leave a trail for me to find her, so I gave up. I mean, I got a wife and son…"

"Know where she's working?" said Clancy.

"I never went to see her there, you know, 'cause it was delicate…"

"Sam, look, I don't care about all of that. Can you tell me where she's working?"

Sam shuffled a bit. "I'm pretty sure she's working at a place called the Double D. On Prince Street, if you know where that's at."

"Okay, Sam, thanks," said Clancy, turning to leave.

Sam took his arm. "Look, Clancy, we never had this conversation, do you hear me?"

"What conversation was that?" said Clancy.

After a droning hour on Route 104, Clancy turned into the parking lot of the Double D, where he could hear loud talk and louder music bursting through its seams. The sun was long gone; peepers called from the tall grass and bushes beyond the gravel lot. The long row of pickups across the front entrance looked like well-worn piano keys. A dozen Harleys roared into the lot, kickstands dropping, serpentine leather sliding through the front door. A few couples sat in cars, high-pitched laughter mixed with low guttural urging.

When Clancy had first started dating Darlene, the guys on the loading dock at Mott's had usually said something like, "My God, I wish I could have some of that." It was a well-earned response. When she walked into the break room, everyone looked and looked and looked some more. Not that she was a great beauty—more that she had a hypnotic sway. Her hips seemed to move independent of the rest of her body, to and fro, to and fro. And her breasts were full and firm, leading the charge. She had a few extra pounds, but they were distributed everywhere and didn't bunch anywhere. She had full lips and a tiny scar under her right eye from a childhood fall. And she was blond, not the lush blond of movie stars—more frizzy and thin—but its length more than made up for its lack of substance.

She understood her assets and wasn't afraid to use them. Clancy had heard the stories. How she'd gone down on her knees to get a job in the first place, and she wasn't down there to beg. How she'd hike her skirt or loosen a button on her blouse whenever the Big Bosses came through. How she'd made the dating rounds of the second shift, leaving men wobble-kneed and satisfied.

She was flirty with Clancy, but never more than that. He liked her smile and had to admit that he liked watching her walk away as much as anyone else. But he hesitated to ask her out. Something about all that body and all that boldness made him pause.

One day, she sashayed up to him on the dock and stood so close that you couldn't slide a piece of paper between them. "So, Clancy, I hear you're interested but don't know exactly what to do. So I'll do it for you. Let's go out Friday night. Pick me up at my apartment at eight. You choose the restaurant." She walked away, not even waiting for him to respond.

Clancy chose Denny's, but they never made it there. In fact, they never made it out of her bedroom. "My God, Clancy, you aren't so shy after all," she laughed.

Clancy smiled at the memory and got that old feeling just below his belt buckle. Darlene had that effect on men. Clancy looked at the little green bear lying on the seat beside him; the smile faded from his lips. He held it in his hand, then put it in the glove box and got out of the truck.

"Hey, man, got a light?" came a call from the truck parked beside him.

"No, I'm afraid not," said Clancy.

"No harm," came the reply. "I'll get it lit somehow," the stranger said, his female companion purring.

So this is the pot of gold at the end of Darlene's rainbow; this is what she left you for. The happiest moment of their marriage had been the first. They couldn't wait for a wedding, so they went to the justice of the peace and got married on a Wednesday afternoon before Clancy went to work. There was a look of complete surprise on both their faces when the judge said, "I now pronounce you man and wife." Clancy was thrilled—until he looked into his bride's eyes and she wasn't looking back. He decided she was overwhelmed by the suddenness of it all; he decided things were okay. The justice of the peace reminded them that they could kiss. When Clancy came home from his shift that night, Darlene was asleep.

It took six years before he accepted that things were not okay, never had been, and probably never would be. And it took four more before it all came to an end. She ran off to Watertown with Donnie Cardwell, an old classmate; they were going to make their fortune running a natural food store. A few months later, Clancy broke open a six-pack of Blue Moon to celebrate when Sam told him that Darlene and Donnie had broken up. Turned out that Donnie didn't know a damn thing about how to start a natural food store, which, between the two of them, made him the expert.

Clancy stepped through the swinging door of the Double D. They were three- and four-deep at the long mahogany bar, its foot rail covered with work boots, biker boots, and the occasional high heel. There was an American flag behind the bar, bottles in tiers in front of it, "In God We Trust" carved into a wood plank above it. Clancy breathed in the aroma of beer and stale cigarettes, sweat and sweet perfume.

There were two tenders at the bar: one a sexy young thing with her hair pulled up in a spray; the other, a well-worn middle-aged blonde with a ready smile and tired eyes. She wore a Rolling Stones t-shirt, the long red tongue disappearing below her belt buckle where her once widely dispersed weight had finally found a place to call home. She was moving as fast as she talked. Clancy sidled up to the other end of the bar, leaning in to get the young thing's attention.

"Hey, what can I get you?"

"Blue Moon," he said.

"With an orange slice?"

"Yes."

"Got it."

She chirped her way to the tap, passing in front of Darlene, exchanging a comment and a laugh. The men were all lined up for her attention. She would be taking home all the tips tonight. Darlene smiled, trying to look fresh, trying to draft in behind the young thing's appeal.

"Hey, honey!" called the guy two stools down from Clancy.

"Don't call me honey," said Darlene. "You still owe me from last time." She came down the bar, wiping rings as she went. "Hey, how are you doing? Haven't seen you in a while."

"Been on the road."

"On the road? For a month? Must have been a long road." Darlene laughed. "I missed seeing your ugly face around here."

"I'll bet you say that to all the guys."

"Hey, watch yourself, Stan; you know I only have eyes for you."

"I'll have a Sam Adams."

"Stan the Man. You can have whatever you want." Darlene's voice was gnawing. Clancy looked at her face. Her eyebrows were long gone, replaced by two penciled streaks of permanent surprise; her lipstick was a shade too red; her left eyebrow and right nostril were pierced; and her face was doughy. She looked like a Michelin version of herself.

Darlene didn't notice him. Clancy glanced at the mirror behind her. She was swollen and he was sagging. Time had not been kind.

"Here you go, Stan."

"Thanks, darling."

"And where is Stan off to tonight?" she asked.

"Well, Stan is off to his wife and kids tonight."

"Now that doesn't sound like any fun at all." She looked at him a long time as she backed down the bar to another customer.

"Jesus," said Stan, shaking his head disdainfully as he returned to his friends.

Clancy watched Darlene as she walked away. He drank his beer while she worked the other end of the bar. They were strangers, he thought. *What are you doing here?* He started to get up from his stool, but when the girl called, "Another?", Clancy shook his head and sat back down.

"Darlene, can you get this gentleman another Blue Moon with a wedge?"

"Sure, sweetie," said Darlene as she pulled on the tap and called to another guy down the bar. "Hey, Billy, what's goin' on?" She laughed when he waved and then turned to Clancy without looking. "Here you go."

"Thanks, Darlene."

Darlene blinked slowly and looked up. Her face went slack and age crept in at the corners of her mouth. She blinked again. "Well, I'll be. It's you, isn't it?"

Clancy smiled. "How have you been, Darlene?"

"Clarence Brisco, I presume. Come crawling back, have you?"

"I'm not the one that crawled away."

"Touché," she said. Darlene looked him up and down. "You've held together pretty well, Clancy."

"You, too." Their eyes met in the lie, and they both laughed.

"Well, at least we're here. A lot of people can't say that."

Clancy lifted his glass. "Here's to being here."

Darlene swiped the wispy bangs from her face and smacked her lips. She smiled, and for an instant Clancy could see the young woman he had married.

He asked about her work and she asked about his. Where they lived. How things had been. She'd heard about the jumpers and was sorry. He thanked her and was about to tell her what it was like but stopped. There was silence, and she waited on another customer. When she came back, she said, "You know, Donnie's long gone."

"Yes, I know."

"I guess that's that."

"Guess so." Clancy drank his beer. Darlene wiped the bar in front of him.

"Clancy, why'd you drive the whole way up here after all this time? I know it wasn't for the beer."

"True," said Clancy. He felt a slight tremor in his right hand and steadied it on his leg. "I need to talk to you about something."

"Shoot." Darlene put both hands on the bar and leaned forward, bracing herself.

"No, I mean in private. When are you off?"

"I'm closing tonight, so about two."

"Okay if I wait?"

"Suit yourself."

Clancy sat in his car, trying to gather his thoughts, and watched the comings and goings. He listened to the radio, and he sat in silence. He held the green bear and thought about heading home. Instead, he waited. He thought about Chimney Bluffs and the woman who had survived the jump. He thought about the toys in the sack. He waited. Around 2 a.m. the "Open" light went off and the "Closed" one went on. The last of the regulars swerved to their cars. The Harleys roared and the pickups spit gravel in their wake. Soon it was quiet. Clancy opened the truck door and crossed the lot.

When he entered the bar, Darlene was cleaning off some tables and resetting some chairs. There were two beers on a table nearest the bar. Clancy sat down and Darlene joined him, leveling her gaze into his tired eyes.

"So, what's this all about?"

Good question, thought Clancy.

Chimney Bluffs

Chapter 8

Clancy looked up from his beer as she looked down at hers. Darlene's hair framed her face, hiding the turtle-neck creases. She peeked at him through her hair. He had never noticed the green flecks in her eyes. How could he have missed them? She smiled and her eyes almost disappeared. Her smile, yellowed now, had always dominated her face, keeping every man focused, telling them what they wanted to hear; her smile struggled valiantly to lift her sagging cheeks.

"What *is* this all about?" said Clancy. He put the glass to his lips. "Well, it's been a long time, Darlene. Too long, maybe. I've been thinking about you. About us. I don't know. After all that stuff happened at the bluffs, I started thinking about things. Today I got in the truck and just followed my nose. I'm not sure what this is all about."

"Jesus, Clance, you're no better at talking now than you were back then," said Darlene. She took a deep breath and started over. "I was more than a little shocked when I saw your mug down at the end of the bar. But it's good to see you, no matter the reason." She leaned back and pulled a pack of cigarettes from her purse. "You mind?"

"No." He had often begged her to stop smoking. "So, how long you been working here?" Turns out that when Donnie left, Darlene was already involved with Douglas, one of the owners of the Double D. He promised her he'd leave his wife and they'd buy out his brother, Dickson, and they'd build a life together and they'd travel and his kids would learn to love her. Most of these promises were made while Darlene was flat on her back. But she believed the words he heaved so easily in the dark of night. In calmer moments, though, Douglas was more reticent. "You can't just rush into these things," he said. "There's lots of things I got to consider," he said. "I can't just break the family up," he said. "You've got to give me time," he said. But all his considerations didn't keep him off Darlene, and it didn't stop him from making promises when he wanted what he wanted. "I guess you never learn," said Darlene, shaking her head. It was Dickson who bought Douglas out after his wife discovered the affair. She threatened to divorce his ass if he didn't give up the business. They moved to Rochester, and Darlene only saw him a few times after that. No promises. Just grunts and groans. She had turned her attention to Dickson, who had all the same interests as his brother. But he didn't believe in making promises, and in time they got bored with each other as lovers and finally fell into a passable friendship. She had had high hopes, but standing behind the bar and taking a turn with a customer now and then was all she got.

"And what about you? Find the love of your life?" Darlene drew deep, leaned her head back, and blew a streak of smoke into the air. She picked tobacco off the tip of her tongue and looked back at Clancy while never breaking her smile.

"No, not really," said Clancy, turning the glass in his hands. Much as he had hated Darlene, he had never quite gotten over her. Something about her was magnetic, and no matter how far he pulled away, no matter how much he ignored her calls, he felt attached in ways he couldn't explain. Since they broke up, Clancy had dated a few times, usually when someone at work had fixed him up with a cousin or friend. He found he didn't want to get close to anyone again. It was too much work—talking about food and movies and reality TV, meeting their friends and their friends' friends, having to call them every day to talk about nothing. It was a painful way to occasionally have sex. After a year or so, he gave up on the whole enterprise. He discovered the adult ads on Craigslist. Here were women who didn't expect anything except money on the table. When the itch got too bad, Clancy would make a call. He'd walk away each time feeling a little extra spring in his step, knowing that the business transaction had left him free of everything he disliked about relationships with women. But eventually he tired of being called "hon" or "sweetie" or any name but his own, and the hotel rooms and the women started looking the same: threadbare. He didn't feel much of a spring anymore, just a sorry feeling, knowing that they were agreeing to take advantage of each other without a shred of care.

He smiled. "How could I ever replace the likes of you?"

Darlene threw her head back again and forced a howling laugh, guttural and angry. "I've heard that line before, Clarence Brisco; you better believe it," she said, this time her voice trailing off like a cicada's fading cry. A dog barked in the distance and silence fell over the table. Clancy reached for his beer.

"Jesus, Clancy, you are a mystery. Never could figure out what was going on in that head of yours."

"Ever think that maybe nothing was going on?"

Darlene chuckled at this. "I guess that's possible. But not likely. My bet is there's too much going on back there." She pointed at his head. "It's all packed in like a log jam in a muddy river. Needs to come out."

"You're giving me too much credit." Clancy shifted his feet on the floor and leaned forward in his chair. He took a breath. He had forgotten how much Darlene talked about how little he talked. It's no wonder she had chased after Donnie. He talked a mile a minute. Maybe that's all Darlene had wanted, just some sound coming back at her so the air wouldn't feel so empty.

Darlene dropped the butt on the floor and crushed it with her heel. She leaned her elbows on the tabletop and looked at him square. "I have a feeling that that log jam of yours is about to come undone. You didn't come the whole way to this little corner of hell just to have a beer with the woman who walked out of your life and left you high and dry." She wasn't smiling now. "What is it? Money? If it's money, you made a long trip for nothing, 'cause I don't have a red cent."

Clancy looked up from his beer. "Darlene?"

"Uh huh?"

"Did you ever wonder what it would have been like if we had had a kid?"

Darlene's foot stopped fidgeting. She sat straight up. "What?"

"I know it wasn't in the cards for us, but did you ever wonder?"

"I never thought you…"

"That's not what I'm asking. I'm asking what you think it would have been like. Would it have made a difference?" Clancy sat the beer on the table.

Darlene ran her hand through her hair, pulling it back from her face. "I can't believe you're asking me this. What difference does it make? The past is gone, Clancy. It's gone." Her jaw was square. She stood. "Look, it's late. I've still got to close up."

"I always wanted a kid," said Clancy. She looked at him. He spoke, as if to no one. "I don't know. I always wanted to be a father, a dad. I think I could have done it, you know?"

"Look, Clancy. Geez, I don't know where this is coming from."

"I think it would have made a difference. I think we might have made it." Clancy stood and walked behind the bar, poured his beer in the sink, and wiped his hands off on a towel. He stepped out from behind the bar. "Maybe I came to apologize."

"Apologize?" said Darlene. "Apologize for what?"

"For not being able to make it happen—for not being able to give us a kid." Darlene had always blamed him, made fun of him for "shooting blanks." Couldn't have been her, that's for sure. She'd gotten knocked up in high school, had gone the whole way to Syracuse for the abortion. No, it had to have been Clancy. He walked towards the door. "I shouldn't have come here." He turned to leave as Darlene stepped forward.

"Clancy, wait." She hesitated and then took a few more steps. Her eyes were tired. Her hands hung at her side, sausage fingers. "Clancy. It wasn't your fault."

Clancy was impatient with this. "Look, I know you're trying to be…"

"No, Clancy, listen to me."

Long past closing time, Clancy sat in his truck, headlights aimed at the entrance to the Double D as Darlene locked up. She turned and waved. He blinked his lights and watched as she got into her car and eased onto the road. Clancy put his truck in gear but then hesitated. He leaned back in the seat, his hands sliding off the wheel. He put the truck in park and turned off the engine. He repeated her words over and over, hoping they would sink in.

"Look, Clancy," Darlene had said, her voice softening. "Yes, I got pregnant when I was just a kid. My old man would have beat the ever-loving crap out of me if he'd ever found out, so I took care of it."

"This is old news, Darlene. I've heard this story a million…"

"Just wait. Listen for once. You never listened to me. Did you know that?" Darlene's voice sounded ragged.

Clancy looked at her. "Okay, I'm listening."

"I was just a damn kid, for chrissakes. I didn't know what to do. My friend Rhonda's brother's girlfriend lived in Syracuse and told Rhonda she could help me out. What did I know? I figured she knew a doctor, but she didn't. She knew a friend of a friend who knew someone who took care of pregnancies." Darlene's faced blanched. She shook her head and swiped her hair back off her face. "So, Rhonda took me, and I went into this woman's bedroom and she had this plastic tub of doctor's instruments and she told me to lie down."

Darlene breathed as if she had a fist in her stomach. Clancy had never seen this before, had never seen what was behind the smile and the make-up.

"Look, Dar, you don't have to…"

"Yes, I have to." She was quiet for a moment, pulling herself together, trying to find the words again. "So. She did it. It hurt like hell. I had to pretend I had the flu so my dad wouldn't get suspicious, but it was over and I just let it go, you know, like you let things go when you're a kid."

"You don't have to tell me all of this, Darlene. I know."

"You don't know anything." Darlene walked to a table, pulled a chair out, and sat. Clancy joined her reluctantly. "I thought that was it, you know. I thought I had dodged a bullet and didn't have to worry about anything. But I was wrong."

Darlene was right. He didn't know.

Darlene told Clancy that when she didn't stop bleeding, she had to go to a regular doctor. He was surprised by what he found. He was surprised at the devastation inside her. "I'm sorry," the doctor had said. She remembered those words more than any others. No one had ever said "I'm sorry" to her. "He was so gentle with me. I mean, he didn't really know me, but he was so gentle and kind." The doctor told Darlene that the bleeding would stop and she would get better, but the damage was permanent. She didn't know what that meant. "Permanent?" she had asked. He looked at her, hoping that she would understand by the look on his face. "Well," said the doctor, "I'm afraid that you won't be able to get pregnant again."

The dead weight of her words lay on the table in front of Clancy. More than listening to them, he looked at them, wondering if they could be rearranged or swept onto the floor.

"Clancy?" said Darlene. "Did you hear what I said?" She slid her hand across the table, reaching for his. She told him that she had always loved him and always would, that she was sorry for what she had done, for not telling him the truth. "Clancy, can you ever forgive me?"

Clancy waited for the anger, but it didn't come. He looked at Darlene's face, so full of brokenness and longing that all he could do was smile. All he said was, "It's okay," and even though the words sounded empty at the time, later he realized he meant them. Then he took her in his arms and held her as she cried. He couldn't remember ever feeling as close to her. Her honesty, her apology, so late in coming, didn't change the past, but for Clancy it made things a little better in the present; it pulled the shade over something that had been in the light for too long.

A police cruiser idled past the lot slow as could be, taking a long look at Clancy's truck. Clancy returned the gaze as a gust of wind blew hard against his face. He reached for the handle to roll up the window and then thought, *Let it blow*.

Chapter 9

In the eighteen months since the surgery, things had changed for Kate and Mitch. Kate finally went back to work after a couple of months watching over Danny, helping him get well and transition to pre-school. Mitch's appliance store was making money. Mitch had even added two more employees.

Mitch had also joined a Bible study group with some other business owners. Kate listened to his enthusiastic stories about how their lives and their businesses had been transformed by their faith in God.

"It is truly amazing; when I'm with these guys, I can feel God's presence," he had said more than once.

After everything that had happened with Danny, Mitch became even more religious. He read the Bible daily and prayed in the mornings on the way to work and in the evenings before he went to bed. Mitch, like his friends, believed there was a plan for everyone's life. If you lived a good life on earth, God would reward you with an even better one in heaven, where you would be surrounded by everyone you loved.

His friends tended to see proof of God's plan for their lives in business profits and losses, believing, though never admitting, that regular Bible study and prayer might help keep their bottom lines black. Buster Henderson always reminded them of Job and how he'd lost everything, but, because he'd kept the faith, God restored him tenfold. Mostly they ignored the part about Job losing everything and focused their prayers on the tenfold portion of the story.

Mitch gravitated to the belief that somehow faith and success in life went hand in hand. "Kate, I'm telling you, if you believe in God, it can only help; look what it did in Danny's case." Danny's success was evidence that they were blessed and that they would all do well.

"Should try it," he said to Kate from time to time, when he got his Bible out in the evening.

Kate would smile and say, "Maybe, sometime."

One day while watching Mitch and Danny wrestling on the living room floor, Kate noticed something. "Is he pulling on that ear again?"

"I don't know; don't think so," said Mitch.

Kate watched closely. "Yes, he is."

"Here we go again," said Mitch.

"Here we go again is right," said Kate.

They had been frequent visitors at their pediatrician's office once Danny had started pre-school. Sometimes Dr. Smythe laughed good-naturedly when she saw them: "So, let me guess, Danny. Mommy and Daddy noticed you tugging on those ears of yours, again. You don't want to look like an elephant, now do you?"

At first she prescribed antibiotics, mainly to help Kate feel less anxious, but eventually, she explained that antibiotics often weren't enough for most ear problems.

"Bring him in so we can make sure there's nothing else going on, but mostly he needs rest. Daycare centers and pre-schools are real Petri dishes, you know. In the end, his immune system will be better for it."

Usually this was enough for Kate and Mitch, although sometimes Kate worried that having so many infections wasn't good for Danny's heart. Dr. Smythe listened to her worries but was always quick to reassure her that there was no connection. And so went the choreography of their visits to Dr. Smythe.

"What do you think, Mitch, call Dr. Smythe?"

"I don't think it's necessary, but it's up to you."

Despite the success of Danny's surgery, Kate still watched his health like a hawk, although Dr. Smythe was no longer on speed dial.

Mitch and Danny continued to roll around the living room floor, playing a game of follow the leader. Danny was laughing and had stopped tugging at his ear. Kate reached for the phone to call the doctor's office, but then concluded it wasn't necessary. For once, she'd wait and see.

He didn't pull his ears at all the next day, although he seemed out of sorts, so Kate decided to give it yet another day. The following morning, Danny seemed listless, but once he ate breakfast, his energy level seemed to pick up.

He slept on the way to pre-school, which, again, was unusual, but, Kate reasoned, he had been up late the night before, wanting bedtime story after story. Kate reassured herself that, like the doctor had said, he just needed a little more rest. She watched him through the rearview mirror and smiled at his puffy, sleepy face. He held onto her a little longer than usual when she dropped him off, but he often did this when he was tired. She gave him a big hug and a kiss—"Have fun, Danny; I love you"—and then headed to work.

Kate was surprised when a few hours later she was paged and Miss Nancy from pre-school was on the phone.

"Sorry to bother you, Mrs. Duncan, but Danny just isn't feeling very well today. He's pulling on his ears again, and he's also crying off and on; I think he's got a headache. All he wants to do is lie on his cot with the window blinds pulled down. I've tried everything to cheer him up, but he's not a happy little guy today. Could you come get him? I think he needs his mommy."

Kate reached the parking lot, still talking to Miss Nancy. As she started the car, she called Mitch. When she got to the pre-school, Miss Nancy was waiting for her at the door.

"He's pretty sick. Our doctor is here."

Kate looked at Miss Nancy, her fresh-scrubbed, bright-eyed face blank as a slate. "Is he okay?" said Kate. When Miss Nancy directed her to the nurse's office without answering, Kate's stomach curled into a knot.

As she walked inside the nurse's office, the center's doctor met her.

"Poor Danny is not feeling well at all, Mrs. Duncan. He started vomiting a little while ago and he's spiked a fever. Hopefully just a virus, but I think you should take him to see your doctor today. Can you do that?" Kate looked at his calm face and thought, *Okay, makes sense.* But when she saw Danny lying on the cot, the window blinds pulled, she was shocked at how pale and lethargic he looked.

"Hi, honey. Mommy's here," she said. He was sweating and limp and didn't seem to care at all that she was there. When she carried Danny into the hall, he cried out and covered his eyes.

"There, there, honey, you're okay," said Kate. She hugged him as he buried his head in her shoulder.

"Here you go, Danny; here's Little Green Bear," said Miss Nancy, returning to her best pre-school voice. She patted him on the head. "Mrs. Duncan, I'm sure he'll be okay in a few days." She leaned in close to Danny's face. "Hope to see you soon, sweetie." Danny clutched his bear and turned away.

When Kate pulled in the driveway, she was relieved to see Mitch's van.

"How's he doing, honey?"

Kate was short of breath. "He's—he's—I don't know; on the way home, he kept trying to get out of the car seat and was crying, 'No, no, no!' like something was after him. Then he just stopped. I kept talking to him, asking him how he was doing, but he wouldn't answer. It was like I wasn't there." She leaned in to take him out of the car seat. "Look at him, he's burning up," she said. Danny's face was bright red; his legs were pulled up to his chest. "My God," said Kate. "He looks awful."

"He just needs some rest, that's all. Let's get some Motrin in him and put him to bed," said Mitch.

"Mitch, they said to take him to the doctor's today. We can't wait. We've got to get him there. I knew I should have called the other day."

"Look at him; he's exhausted. He needs to sleep and maybe then…"

Her jaw was set. She looked at Danny as she spoke. "Mitch. He's

79

got to be seen by a doctor. Now. Not later."

Dr. Smythe was already in the exam room when they arrived. Usually she greeted them with a broad smile and some chit-chat, but this time she wasn't smiling.

"Hi, folks. How's our Danny doing?"

"I don't know what's wrong. I thought it was just an earache. We thought we could just let it run its course, you know." She waited for Dr. Smythe to confirm that that was what they had always done, but she was looking intently at Danny. "But today they called me and said he was pretty sick."

"Yes, the center called." She still didn't make eye contact with Kate; instead, she studied Danny as if she were trying to solve a puzzle. Her face, usually calm and comforting, looked clouded and confused.

Kate looked at Mitch. Mitch raised his eyebrows.

"Look, Dr. Smythe, what's going on?" said Mitch. "I mean, Danny had an earache, and all of a sudden the school is calling us and then they're calling you and we're rushing around and we don't know what's happening!"

Dr. Smythe pulled up a chair and sat down. She crossed her legs and looked at her chart for a moment. "When the doctor called us, he was concerned about some of the things he was seeing. He said Danny was hypersensitive to light, that he didn't want to straighten his legs out at all, that he was much more comfortable with them pulled up to his chest, that he had spiked a fever and at times seemed confused and unresponsive when they tried to speak to him." Dr. Smythe paused, looking at Kate and then Mitch. She reached out to Danny, who was huddled in his mother's arms. "Earaches don't act like this, so we want to find out quickly if anything else is going on."

"Like what?" said Kate. "What else could it be? I mean, after everything he's been…" Kate's voice cracked.

"Look, Dr. Smythe, Danny's been blessed since the surgery. We thank God he's fine. So, what are you talking about? You're scaring my wife for no good reason, and I don't like it," said Mitch.

Dr. Smythe looked at Mitch and then at Kate. She opened her mouth and then closed it again. She took a deep breath. "I'm very sorry if I'm scaring you. That's not what I'm trying to do at all. But Danny's symptoms are concerning. It's too soon to say what it could be, but we need to find out if he's got a bacterial infection or what else it might be so we can start treating it immediately."

Mitch looked at Kate as she rocked Danny. He wished Danny would smile, just a little smile.

"What do you need to do?" asked Kate. She kissed Danny's forehead and reached for the sneaker on his left foot, shaking it gently. "Mommy loves you, honey."

Dr. Smythe explained that she wanted to admit Danny to the hospital, where they could run the necessary tests and she could consult with a pediatric infectious disease specialist. Kate stopped looking at Dr. Smythe. She could hear her voice, but Kate wasn't listening anymore. She felt Danny's warm body against her chest and noticed that there was perspiration in the crook of her arm. She kissed him and laid her head against his. She continued to rock. She could hear edginess in Mitch's voice, but she didn't know what he was saying, and she didn't care. She looked at Danny's sneaker. The treads were worn. He ran so much that he wore the treads down to almost nothing. For the first time, she would have to buy new shoes for him not because Danny had outgrown them but because he had outworn them. She smiled faintly. Such a big boy. Growing a little every day. She would take him to the store and let him pick out any pair of sneakers that he wanted. Even the ones that lit up when he walked. It didn't matter how expensive they were. She would buy them for him so he could run as far and as fast as he wanted, and when they were worn out, she'd buy him another pair and another and another. Then she heard something that brought her back.

"Meningitis?" said Mitch.

"That's what we need to rule out, yes."

Kate rocked Danny a little faster now; she reached for Little Green Bear, put it in his lap, and held her son closer.

Chapter 10

Mitch and Kate sat in the family waiting area on the first floor of the hospital.

"Don't worry, honey. Have faith. We've seen God's good work before; I'm sure things will be fine again. You'll see. This is just a 'rule out,' nothing more."

Kate took Mitch's hand and squeezed it. She didn't look into his eyes, though, because she knew he'd see her fear. She knew he'd see her fear and wouldn't know what to do. She'd have to convince him she wasn't afraid, just concerned. And she didn't think she could do that, so she held his hand and looked at the floor; the floor would not tell her it was wrong to be afraid.

The specialist did not introduce himself. He was in a hurry. "We have to do a lumbar puncture to withdraw some fluid from your son's spine. Once we look at it, we'll know better what we're dealing with." He smiled, turned, and was gone.

And so they sat together, other people around them waiting as well, all with their eyes cast down, leafing through magazines, sighing, looking at the clock, and avoiding conversation—each an island densely populated with private thoughts. Mitch realized that the doctor never said how long it would take. He went to the attendant, who was sitting at a small desk reading a book. She smiled and was polite but couldn't answer Mitch's question. He slumped back into the chair, Kate stiff as a board beside him.

Mitch reached for Kate's arm and squeezed it gently. Kate closed her eyes, imagining Danny running through the grass at Chimney Bluffs, laughing in the back yard, splashing in the bathtub, sitting on her lap while she read *Goodnight Moon.*

Why didn't you call Dr. Smythe sooner? she wondered.

She opened her eyes and looked at Mitch as he tore open two packets of Splenda and sprinkled them into his coffee. In recent weeks, he had told Kate more about his Bible study partners, how they talked a lot about "turning things over to God" and trusting that everything would be okay, no matter what happened. Floyd Markman, who owned the Dollar General, told them about his wife's cancer and how she wasn't supposed to live past six months. Mitch's eyebrows spiked as he shared the final detail: "That was six years ago."

"And that wasn't the most important thing," said Mitch. "Here's the thing. Floyd said they were ready no matter what happened. If Helen had died, they knew it would be okay; she would have gone to a better place and she would have been waiting for Floyd when his time came. That's what believing does for you." With this, Mitch had leaned back in his chair and shaken his head with approval.

All Kate had said in reply was, "That's something," although she could hear her mother's voice saying, "Those people are living in La-La Land."

Then Mitch had leaned forward, his eyes dark with concern.

"Don't you believe in God?"

Kate felt heat rising on the back of her neck. She looked away. "Not the way you do, I suppose. But, yes, I believe in something; I guess you could call it God."

"What about heaven and hell?" he asked. "You've got to believe in heaven or there's no point to being here at all."

Kate's shoulders tensed. They had been over this before, and she had always avoided a direct answer, deferring instead to his beliefs and her respect for them. She was afraid of how angry and disappointed Mitch would be if he knew her true beliefs.

She wished she could put Danny in God's hands; she wished she believed that everything would be okay if she did, but none of it made sense to her. Every time she got close to believing, she would see her mother sitting out on the driveway in her chaise lounge laughing at her. She knew in her heart that the only hands she could count on were her own. Of course she could depend on Mitch, and she loved Danny more than life itself, but when it came to answering big questions or making big decisions, she had only herself to turn to. Pray all you want, you're still the one getting up every day and trying to do the right thing.

She pondered Mitch's question. The answer was easy: She wished she believed in heaven and hell, but she didn't. She looked into Mitch's eager eyes.

"Doesn't everybody believe in heaven and hell?" she had said.

Mitch had smiled, measuring, no doubt, the eternal implications of her answer.

"Here he comes," said Mitch, watching Danny's surgeon, still in blue scrubs, stride down the hall.

He didn't wave. He didn't smile. But he made eye contact. Kate and Mitch felt a Christmas-morning adrenalin rush as he stepped off the linoleum floor and onto the carpeted waiting area. Mitch was eager to see what was under the tree; Kate was afraid all the needles had fallen.

"How did Danny do?" said Kate.

"Your son did very well. He came through the tests without any problem; he's resting comfortably and will be in his room shortly."

The doctor motioned to a small room adjoining the waiting area. Kate and Mitch took seats behind the round Formica-topped table. The doctor pulled up a chair, as well. He crossed his legs and then uncrossed them and leaned forward, his elbows on his knees. Finally he looked up. Kate caught his eye and she knew. She knew he was going to tell them something they didn't want to hear.

"I'm afraid it's bacterial meningitis," he said, his voice low but firm.

Kate gasped.

"What exactly does that mean?" said Mitch.

"Well, it means we've got to be as aggressive as possible fighting it. We've started him on several IV antibiotics. It's our best chance of knocking out the infection."

Kate looked at the doctor. She caught his eye again and could tell that he was going to try as hard as he could, but that it wouldn't matter. She looked away.

When Kate and Mitch reached Danny's room, he was resting on a cloud of white sheets, sleek plastic tubing dripping liquid into his veins, monitors scribbling and humming and beeping, his nurse leaning over him, adjusting his pillow. Kate resented the nurse, resented her trying to do what only a mother could do, resented her being in the room before her. She went to Danny's side, grabbing his limp hand.

"Hello, honey, Mommy's here."

She stared at Danny's face, studying his sunken cheeks and charcoal eyelids. She wanted him to open his eyes and smile at her. She wanted him to squeal and jump out of his bed, like he had pulled the funniest trick ever. She wanted to take him up in her arms and walk out of the room and down the corridor and out the front entrance into the parking lot and all the way home so he could sleep in his own bed in his own house surrounded by his own stuffed animals and toys and his own mommy and daddy. But it would not be. Not that day or the next or the next.

Kate rested that night and the following nights in a recliner beside Danny's bed while Mitch curled up on the love seat they had pulled in from the waiting room. They lay down out of habit but did not sleep. Instead, they held their eyes closed and listened to the sounds of their son's medical machinery battling the Lilliputian germs and bugs and bacteria that had overpowered his tiny body.

Danny didn't know that his mommy and daddy were there, although they pretended otherwise. They talked to him and told him what Big Bird and Elmo were doing on *Sesame Street*, and read to him and sang "Old McDonald Had a Farm." Sometimes the nurses joined in—at least the young blond one with the tattoo. She always joined in when it was her shift.

Mitch and Kate ate stale sandwiches wrapped in cellophane and drank weak coffee from Styrofoam cups and snacked on cheese crackers filled with peanut butter. Sometimes they didn't eat at all. Looking at Danny lying motionless, his legs reaching barely halfway down the sheets, made eating seem pointless. Buster and Floyd from the Bible study group met Mitch in the third-floor chapel and knelt with him at the altar and prayed that Danny would be spared and that Mitch and Kate would be strong because that's what Danny needed. And Floyd reminded Mitch about his wife and how Mitch had to turn it all over to God—then it would all work out for the best no matter what. Then Buster led them in the Lord's Prayer: "...for thine is the kingdom and the power and the glory forever. Amen," said Mitch.

Chapter 11

Bobby breathed a sigh of relief when he pulled into the parking lot and Clancy's truck was nowhere to be found. It marked the first time in months that he had arrived early. Not that getting to work first, or even on time, mattered that much, but this was Clancy's first official day back since Buddy had sent him packing ten days earlier. He'd never seen Clancy take anything so hard.

Clancy had seemed okay at first, just quiet, but next thing Bobby knew, Clancy was sitting in the water clutching that little boy's bag, just clutching it as tight as he could, his hands shaking like crazy, shaking like he was being electrocuted or something. That scared Bobby almost as much as seeing those dead people.

Bobby got out of his truck gingerly, balancing two cups of Tim Horton's coffee. He kicked the door shut and set the coffees on the hood. He turned and looked toward the road, knowing that Clancy would be pulling into the lot in no time. Sure enough, he was right. He waved, and Clancy raised four fingers off the steering wheel in return. Bobby stepped aside as Clancy pulled into the spot beside him.

"Here, I got something for you," said Bobby as Clancy got out of his truck. Bobby handed him the coffee, a smile on his face. "There you go, buddy."

Clancy took a sip. "Thanks."

"Wanted you to get off to a good start, Clancy." Bobby looked at him as if he expected something in return. After all, he'd been gone several days and hadn't answered any of Bobby's calls.

Clancy took another drink. "Just right," was all he said.

"Good to see you, Clance," said Bobby.

"You, too," said Clancy.

"I'm glad you're back," said Bobby.

Clancy smiled and raised his coffee. He drank a long gulp and then tipped the cup at Bobby. "How have you been doing since everything happened, Bobby?" said Clancy.

Bobby's face went blank. "What do you mean?"

"Well, you were there with me. But Buddy didn't send *you* home."

"Yeah, I guess so." Bobby put his coffee back on the hood. He looked down at the fender and scuffed it with his shoe. He looked back at Clancy. Usually by now, Clancy would have moved on to something else or he would have walked away, but this time he just stood there, waiting.

"I haven't slept much at all," he said. "And when I do sleep, all I can see is those two sacks; sometimes they're sitting right on my chest and I can't do anything about it. I want to get up and run, but I can't; I can't move, like I'm paralyzed. My mother got all nervous. I kept calling for my parents at night." He looked to see if Clancy was still listening. "They sort of thought I was going nuts, I guess," he said, a corner of his mouth trying to smile. "Made me go to the doctor. Gave me some medicine." He looked at Clancy, searching his face for any hint of derision, any waver in his eyes that might say, "Jesus!" But all he could see in Clancy's eyes was sadness, faraway and unreachable. "So, I guess that's how I'm doing, you know?"

"I didn't know. I thought you were okay," said Clancy.

"That's okay," said Bobby, smiling and putting his hand on Clancy's shoulder, then quickly removing it. It was quiet for a moment. Both men took refuge in their coffee. Bobby wanted to tell him the rest of the story, but he wasn't sure if he should. He wanted to tell Clancy that his mother had found him sitting in the corner of his bedroom crying and calling for his brother—"Mark! Mark!" That was the real reason she took him to the doctor.

"Guess they still don't know exactly what happened," said Bobby, deciding to take a safer route.

"I heard they thought the boy might have been dead before they jumped."

"I heard the same thing, too. I guess that's what the preliminary report said."

"Huh," grunted Clancy. "It sure didn't look like that on the beach. I would have bet..." Clancy's voice trailed off as he thought about the woman curled up in a ball, still as could be, eyes blank and cold. Clancy had damned her to hell. It had felt simple, clear and right. But since talking to Darlene, nothing seemed simple anymore. Turns out there's always a story behind the story, and maybe another story behind that. Life is just one damn puzzling thing. "What about the woman?"

"Still in the hospital. That's all I know," said Bobby.

The sun rose over the treetops and blinded Clancy for a moment.

He slipped on his sunglasses. "We better get going."

"Yeah, I guess so," said Bobby, not wanting the conversation to end. He felt some ice melting between him and Clancy, and he wanted to linger just a little longer so that it wouldn't freeze up again.

Bobby offered to check the trail to the bluffs, but Clancy wouldn't hear of it.

"You sure?" said Bobby. "Might want to take a day to ease back in. I know I couldn't go out there right off the bat." Bobby hadn't checked the trail for four days. Never told Buddy. Mostly he rode around in his truck. Just crossed his fingers and hoped everything was all right. When he finally made it to the edge, he had Aerosmith jacked up so loud on his iPod that he was barely aware of anything around him. He didn't want to hear the birds; he didn't want to hear the wind; he didn't want to hear the waves; he didn't want to hear anything that he had heard that morning. And when he got to the bluffs, he sat down on the jagged finger and cried.

"No, that's fine. I'll take the trail."

"Okay, remember, I'm just a call away if you need me," said Bobby.

Bobby started off in the other direction. Clancy watched him, noticing for the first time that Bobby wore Air Jordan's instead of the standard issue work boots. His jeans were shredded at the knees, and he loped when he walked, like a young deer.

"Hey, Bobby," said Clancy. Bobby turned around. "Thanks, okay?"

"Sure." Bobby held his smile until he turned away. It was the longest conversation he'd ever had with Clancy.

Truth be told, Clancy wasn't ready to go out on the bluffs. He wanted to take Bobby up on his offer, but then he thought, *How long are you going to let this thing run your life?* He snarled at himself. *You've got to snap out of it.*

He walked down the path and disappeared into the woods. At first, the caws and chirps and skittering sounds felt sharp and piercing, but soon he felt at home; he breathed in the air's damp dirtiness and stood for a moment at the gnarled feet of the tall trees. Up ahead, he could see the bend in the path, the bend that turned north towards the open air where only the bluffs stood tall. He unzipped his jacket and pulled the little green bear from his inside pocket.

Clancy reached the sign that warned all hikers to go no further. He inched out on the finger, worn down from the investigators' tracks. The wind swept up from below and chilled his neck and chin. He looked out across the great, green expanse that turned pale grey at the horizon. Not a boat in sight this early in the morning. He looked west to Sodus Point, its bay hidden by a jutting hillside. The ever-present chimneys of Oswego sat on the northeastern shore, plumes of white smoke lingering.

He leaned forward and looked down, relieved that nothing was there: no sacks, no bodies; just some driftwood, a hollowed log, and the water caressing the sand, continuing the work begun so many thousands of years ago when the ice began to melt—patient, unyielding, unimpressed by the human events that littered its shore.

Clancy looked at the little stuffed bear. "Well, here we are," he said. He thought about the hands that had held this bear and how senselessly his life had ended. "What should we do now?" He put the bear back into his jacket pocket and zipped it up again.

Clancy turned back to the woods again. He didn't notice Bobby sitting on the hillside nearby, looking after him. When Bobby saw Clancy talking to the little bear, he felt a chill run down his spine.

Chapter 12

Bobby must have driven past John Dan's a dozen or more times before he saw Clancy's truck. He went by a few more times before he pulled in, not wanting it to look like he'd been waiting for Clancy or following him. Bobby thought it was odd that Clancy was carrying a stuffed animal in his jacket pocket. He was worried that something was wrong, that Clancy was still a mess but didn't want anyone to know.

Bobby's father had slept in Mark's room for weeks before they'd taken him to the hospital. He'd believed he could talk with Mark, and that Mark was talking back to him through his picture on the dresser. Bobby's father had carried something of Mark's wherever he went—a shoe, a shirt, a toy; it hadn't seemed to matter what. No one had thought much of it until his mother found a bunch of Mark's clothes and stuffed animals in the trunk of the car. She worried but didn't say anything to Bobby's father. They just didn't talk about it. Bobby didn't know what to do. At the time of the accident, he had been barely six.

His brother's room had been so quiet; all his brother's things just sat there, and no one was allowed to touch them. Once his mother had found him in Mark's room playing with his brother's LEGOs, and she had beaten him hard. And then she had cried. Bobby stayed away from the room after that. Only his father went in. Bobby had figured it must have been haunted or something and that's why his daddy had to go away to the hospital for a while. He had wanted to ask him about it when his father came home, but somehow he knew that he shouldn't— not because of anything anyone had said, but because no one had said anything. Finally some neighbors helped his mom get rid of Mark's things.

When Bobby had seen the bag of toys at the bottom of the bluffs, it all came back. And when he saw Clancy holding that stuffed animal, he knew he had to do something. But what? He figured he could at least watch Clancy, keep an eye on him.

When he opened the door to the bar, he scanned the room and saw Clancy sitting at the end of the bar talking to John Dan. He stood for a few minutes, unsure whether to approach Clancy. Even though Clancy'd been friendlier since he'd come back to work a week earlier, Bobby could never tell what his mood would be like. He decided to take a seat at the other end of the bar, hoping Clancy might notice him. After a few minutes, he did.

Clancy was surprised to see Bobby; usually he heard Bobby coming before he saw him—always talking, always joking, always playing the fool. Bobby had been quieter since Clancy had come back to work—quieter and more courteous, not interrupting so much, leaving Clancy alone and not hounding him with stupid stories. The more Bobby kept a little distance, the more Clancy felt comfortable being around him. He walked to the other end of the bar.

"Hey."

"Hey, Clance, how's it going?"

Clancy slid onto the stool beside him and ordered another Blue Moon. He stared into his glass, not speaking. But it was okay. Bobby felt Clancy was letting him know that it was okay that he was there. But soon he couldn't stand the silence.

"So, you always drink Blue Moon?"

Clancy looked at Bobby and almost smiled. "Yes, I do."

"Not sure about that slice of orange," he said, nodding at Clancy's glass.

"I guess that's why you don't drink Blue Moon."

Bobby drank his beer and stared at the bottles of liquor lined up behind the bar like so many Christmas nutcrackers, wondering how he was going to ask the question: Why are you carrying a stuffed animal around with you? *Has to be the kid's*, thought Bobby. But he didn't want to push it because Clancy didn't like people pushing him. But he also didn't want to ignore what he'd seen with his own eyes.

"So, Clance, I noticed you've been carrying that bear around with you." Not exactly tactful, but to the point.

Clancy looked at Bobby. He put his glass to his mouth. He put the glass down. He looked at Bobby again. "What about it?"

"Nothing, I guess," said Bobby. He tilted his bottle of Molson to his mouth. There was another long silence. He looked at Clancy, who was staring into his glass.

"My dad did the same thing," said Bobby, surprised at the words that came out of his mouth.

Clancy looked at Bobby.

"Yeah, after the accident. He carried things with him all the time.

Not just stuffed animals. Lots of things." Bobby shifted his weight, the stool suddenly feeling too small. He put the bottle to his lips again.

"What accident?" said Clancy, clueless.

Bobby's face turned red. He forced a laugh and took another drink.

"Can I get you guys anything?" said John. Clancy shook his head and then turned back to Bobby, waiting.

"You know," said Bobby. "When my brother died."

Clancy put his glass on the bar and turned on his stool. He squinted a little at Bobby. "You had a brother?"

"Yeah, I told you this, didn't I?" said Bobby, hoping that Clancy had heard the story and he wouldn't have to tell it again.

"No. What happened?"

This wasn't what Bobby had planned at all. He didn't want to get into this. But Clancy's eyes were full of questions now.

"It was a long time ago. I was just a kid." Clancy waited. "I was six, and I my little brother was three. Mark. That was his name. He was my little brother. Of course. And we were all in the car going to my father's boss's house for a cookout or something. It was a sunny day. A Saturday. It was in October and it was sunny and the trees were turning color. I remember because my dad kept telling Mark and me to look out the windows at all the colors. Mark was too little; he didn't know what Dad was talking about. He was just so little." Bobby stopped talking. He looked around, wondering if anyone else was listening. Clancy was still looking at him intently. "He kind of looked up to me, Mark did; at least that's what my mother said. She said I was his hero; I mean, he was only three, you know."

"What happened?" said Clancy.

Bobby could feel the fire in his cheeks, and there was nothing he could do about it. He put the bottle down and wiped his hands on his jeans.

"I don't know exactly; I mean, I know, but it happened so fast." Bobby paused, collecting his thoughts. "We were going down this road and a car was coming and my dad started saying, 'What's this guy doing? What the hell is he doing?' and I didn't know what he was talking about. And then my mother started yelling at my dad to do something and the car started swerving and before I knew it, I felt something punch us as hard as could be; I mean, that's what I thought; I thought someone had punched the car and knocked us right off the road. There was a screaming sound from the metal and I heard my mother cry out and my father groan and fell over in the seat and then I didn't hear anything."

Bobby could feel a single drop of perspiration on his forehead. He hoped it wouldn't move; he hoped it would stay right there and evaporate as quickly as it had formed, but it didn't; instead it rolled slowly down between his eyes and along the side of his nose. He wiped it away before it reached his mouth.

"It was quiet. The car stopped and was totally still and I thought it was all over and I was relieved. But my mother kept on crying, and I saw that there was blood on her face; and my father said he thought for sure his leg was broken. They asked if I was okay, and I said I was. I had hit my head on the window, but I was okay. The only one who didn't make a sound was Mark. I looked over at him in his car seat. He was still strapped in tight, like nothing had happened at all, but he was leaning over, his head hanging down. My dad called to him, 'Mark! Mark!' Then my mother leaned back to shake Mark's arm and she said, 'Oh no!' And Mark, he never made a sound. That was it." Bobby sniffed once and wiped his right eye. "He was just so little that his brain couldn't take it; it couldn't take the crash; his brain shook too hard is what my mom told me later; it shook too hard and Mark couldn't take it. And so he died. Just like that, he died on the way to the cookout."

Clancy's chest felt tight. He realized he had been holding his breath as Bobby talked. He looked at Bobby and noticed for the first time that there were lines on his forehead that shouldn't have been there, lines that shouldn't have creased his face for another twenty years. Bobby looked down at the floor.

"Jesus, Bobby," said Clancy. Clancy almost reached out to pat Bobby's shoulder but was afraid that if he did, Bobby might shatter right before his eyes.

Bobby looked up, a smile on his face. "It was a long time ago."

They looked at each other, neither knowing what to say. Bobby looked down the bar and waved. "John," he called, "Clancy could use another one."

"You don't have to…"

"No, I want to. You're my friend," said Bobby.

Clancy shifted in his seat, feeling uncomfortable again. Bobby leaned forward on both elbows and looked at Clancy's face reflected in the mirror behind the bar. He could see that Clancy was watching him, that he was, in fact, leaning towards Bobby. He waited for Clancy to speak, but he didn't.

"After Mark died, my dad started carrying Mark's things with him. He did it for years. He had to go into the hospital because of it." Bobby shrugged his shoulders. "Everything about my father changed after that guy ran into us; after Mark, my father just kind of slipped away, and he never made it back." Bobby thanked John for the beer and tossed a five on the bar. "I know that little boy down on the beach wasn't your son, or nothing like that, but I've seen what can happen when someone holds on too hard. After a while, the thing you're holding onto starts holding onto you. And it never lets go. And before you know it, your life is half over and your other son is all grown up and you never even seen it happen." Bobby drained the last of his bottle. "I know it's not the same, Clancy. But in a way, it is."

Bobby stood up from his stool and hitched his thumbs in his belt. "Sorry to have bothered you with all this," he said and turned for the door.

Bobby's jeans sagged in the back—not like a punk kid, but like an old man. He looked like an old man who had come by to drop something off, something he'd been carrying for a long time. Clancy reached into his jacket pocket and felt the stuffed bear.

"Hey," called Clancy. Bobby turned. "Thanks," he said. "See you in the morning, Bobby."

Bobby smiled and walked away.

Clancy circled the rim of the glass with his thumb and forefinger. He looked down the bar at four other guys, all hunched over their drinks, no doubt sorting things out, things you'd never imagine. John dried another glass, put it on the rack, and came down the line to Clancy.

"Bobby was telling you about it, wasn't he?"

"Yeah," said Clancy.

"Thought so. Did he tell you that the old man told Bobby he wished Bobby had been the son who got killed?" Clancy looked at John. "Yeah, that's right. Guy's a real asshole if you ask me." John turned to another customer.

Bobby had always seemed like a cartoon character to Clancy, someone you didn't have to take seriously. He shook his head. Everyone has scars. He thought about Bobby's old man. He thought about what it must have been like to lose a son that way. Did he blame himself for not being able to keep his promise, the promise to protect his son until he was old enough to protect himself? Jesus. He thought about that little boy in the sack at the bottom of the cliff. He thought about poor old Bobby, just a kid who had never asked for any of what life had given him—and what's his old man do but tell him he wished he was dead. Clancy felt like he could smash Bobby's father's face in with his fist.

When Clancy stepped out into the evening air, he had to turn up his collar, it had gotten that cold. He walked to his truck, shuffled through his keys, got in, and started her up. He didn't notice Bobby's truck in the far corner of the lot. And he didn't notice Bobby's headlights in his rearview mirror all the way home.

Chapter 13

On the fourth day of Danny's hospitalization, Kate was awake long before dawn, long before the doctors came, long before Mitch woke. She stood beside Danny's bed, looking at her little boy. She reached out and touched his soft cheek. She bent over and kissed his eyelids. She rubbed his earlobe gently between her thumb and forefinger. She would gladly go on like this forever if she had to. If this was the only way she could have her son, she would accept it without complaint. She leaned over and kissed his eyelids again.

"Good morning, sweetheart."

She took Danny's hand in hers and looked at his tiny fingers. His nails needed to be clipped. Usually she had to bite them off since Danny wouldn't sit still for the nail clippers. That was fine; let them grow; let the blood course through his body so his nails could stay alive, so his hair could stay alive, so that everything that was in him could stay alive, even if he didn't appear to be alive at all. *I will love his nails and his hair and anything that I can have of him.* Kate's eyes filled with tears.

"What were you thinking?" she said out loud. *Why didn't you call the doctor earlier? Just one day. Maybe you wouldn't be standing here.*

And maybe Danny wouldn't be lying there. While we live our lives in large chunks—days, weeks, month, years—the really important things often happen in minutes or seconds or even in the blink of an eye. Chances come and go so fast, and we have no idea. This moment's earache is the next moment's meningitis. There's no going back. There is nothing to rewind; there are no second chances.

"Good morning," said Mitch, placing his hand on Kate's shoulder.

"He hasn't moved at all in so long," Kate said.

Mitch removed his hand, his whole body tensing. He looked at Danny. His arms and hands were stretched out on the sheet exactly where they had been hours earlier when Mitch had gone to the waiting room, where he had fallen asleep. He didn't want to admit what he was seeing. It just couldn't be.

"But who knows what's going on inside him," he said. "Who knows? Maybe he's hearing everything we're saying? Maybe he's just in a deep sleep," he said, unconvinced of his own words, yet unable to doubt.

Kate folded her arms and looked away. *Why can't he just say, "Yes, I see"?* thought Kate.

And so the day began.

Mitch got coffee and bagels, and they watched while the nurse went about her daily routine. Mitch visited the chapel. Kate took a walk to the lobby. They sat alone. They sat together. They watched Danny for any sign that he was coming back. They waited—for what, they were no longer sure.

The specialist came late. This time he only had one other doctor with him. He sat down and took his time and asked Kate and Mitch if they were eating, if they were sleeping, and how they were holding up. Usually distantly calm, the doctor looked haggard and worried and depleted. He rubbed his hands together and looked at them and inadvertently laughed; he blushed and said he was sorry and that he needed to talk with them.

"I think at the beginning we explained that we would have to be aggressive if we were to have any chance at all of beating this." This was not the way Mitch and Kate remembered it. All they remembered was the importance of hitting this illness hard so they could knock it out. Mitch took a breath as if he were going to ask a question, but then didn't. Kate sat silently, expectantly. "And that's what we've done. We've used every antibiotic available to us; we've consulted with experts in the field from around the country; we've explored every protocol." He looked at his colleague and then at Mitch and Kate. "But Danny's body just isn't responding."

"But it's only been a few days," said Mitch.

"Yes, that's true…"

"Maybe we just need more time, more prayer," said Mitch.

"We hoped that time would be our ally, that Danny's body would fight back." He took the chart that was lying across his knees and laid it on the bed. "But I'm afraid that we are not seeing any change."

Kate's face withered.

"What do you mean?" said Mitch.

"I'm afraid that Danny has gotten steadily worse rather than better." The specialist shuffled his feet and took a deep breath. "Danny's body is barely alive." He paused. "There's nothing more that we can do."

With that, Kate slipped out of Mitch's grasp and slid down the side of his leg onto the floor. Mitch knelt beside her. She looked up at the doctor.

"I'm so sorry," said the specialist, his face white, his eyes moist.

Danny lay still, unaware, the machines moaning. Mitch took Kate in his arms and tried to help her stand, but she said, "No. Please. I can't."

Mitch stood up. He looked at the doctor. "What do we do?"

"You can take Danny home. The social worker can make the arrangements. Hospice will make sure he's comfortable." He realized he was saying more than Mitch cared to hear. "You can take your son home."

On the way back home, the ambulance stopped at all the red lights and stop signs. No sirens, no flashing lights, both of which would have delighted Danny, who loved noise and all forms of wildness. Mitch and Kate followed closely in their VW van, looking out the windows at all the life about them, wondering why everyone wasn't stopped dead in their tracks.

"Well, we will just take care of him," said Mitch, answering some question that hadn't been asked.

"Yes," was all Kate could say. How cruel was life that an innocent mistake could lead to this, that she could cause the death of someone she loved more than life itself? She wished she was the one in the ambulance, that she was the one whose life was about to end.

"What?" said Mitch.

"Nothing," said Kate.

Mitch watched Kate closely, unable to read her face. He looked back at the road and the red and white ambulance ahead of them. There would be no miracle. He couldn't imagine how this had happened. How God could have looked away while his son was dying. He tried to find solace in his friends' comments that the outcome wasn't what mattered; it was your faith that would see you through. But right now, what mattered was Danny, his family, and what was about to happen to them. It just couldn't end like this. There had to be a way for them to stay together. Surely God would want that, too.

The ambulance slowed down and pulled to the side of the road so Mitch could turn into the driveway first. At the top of the driveway near the garage was Danny's blue tricycle, resting exactly where he had left it five days ago, the morning he last went to pre-school.

The house, usually alive with the sound of Danny's sneakers tramping across the kitchen floor, his voice calling out to his mommy and daddy, was as quiet as a pair of empty shoes. And Danny's room, where he lay unconscious in his bed, was the quietest place of all. Kate watched Danny as he lay motionless; she counted the seconds between each breath, her stomach knotting when it took too long and her fingertips tingling in triumph when he drew each new breath.

The sun crossed the narrow passage of Danny's window and cast light on him throughout the afternoon and then was gone, followed by the evening shade. Kate and Mitch got into Danny's bed and covered him with their arms. They kissed his cheeks and spoke to him in low tones and let him know that they were there and that he had nothing to fear. The doctors were right. Danny was already gone and had left any fear behind him days before.

They watched and they watched and they watched and they breathed with his every breath and they held theirs when Danny took his last. And they wept. And they lay in bed with Danny, never wanting to leave, hoping that now that this awful thing had happened, somehow he would come back and be their little boy again.

"No," Kate whispered through her tears as she hugged her son.

"God bless you," said Mitch as he kissed Danny's forehead.

They lay there holding each other, Danny between them, for an hour or more until Kate said, "We should call someone."

But as she moved to get up, Mitch said, "Wait."

She didn't understand why he said it. The waiting was over. Everything had passed away. Their lives had left the station without them. And there was no other life to catch. Wait? Why wait?

"We are a family," said Mitch. "And families should never be separated, no matter what happens. They should never be pulled apart, not even by death. We don't have to lose Danny. I'm telling you, Kate, the Bible is clear on this. We can all be together in the blink of an eye."

Kate looked at Mitch, mouth open, arms limp at her side.

"Endless years of waiting would be cruel. For us and for Danny. It would be cruel and unnecessary. We can't leave him alone. And we don't have to."

A shadow crossed Kate's face; her eyes grew dark. "But what about…"

"Look, Kate, it would be wrong to suffer when the end of suffering is so near." Kate looked at him, curious and confused.

"Kate," he said. "Can you imagine a lifetime without Danny?" At this, Kate began to cry inconsolably, hugging Danny, hoping that he would lean against her on his own, hoping he would feel her. Mitch kept talking. "Do you remember when I asked if you believed in an afterlife?"

Kate looked at him but didn't answer.

"You said, 'Doesn't everyone believe in heaven?' And I thought, Thank God, because that's how important it was to me—important that you believed and I believed, not only for our sake, but for Danny, who was too young to believe a thing. Right then and there I knew that if anything ever happened..." Mitch's voice cracked. He took a breath, trying to find words again. "If anything ever happened, I knew we wouldn't have to worry, because we would be together again in the next life, and we would never face another surgery, another earache, another worry, another sleepless night, another loss, another anything; we would just be together forever."

"What are you saying, Mitch?" said Kate, sitting up in bed, looking down at Danny, her hand on the top of his head.

"I'm saying we can end all this. We don't have to wait." He took Kate in his arms and held her. "I love you," he said.

Kate got up and walked into the bathroom, closing the door slowly behind her. She sat on the edge of the bathtub and wiped her face with a cool cloth. She felt a calm come over her, a disinterested serenity, a tranquil, empty feeling of floating that briefly replaced the free-falling terror of losing the only thing she'd ever truly loved. For the first time, she realized she wouldn't have to go on. She wouldn't have to pretend. She wouldn't have to tightrope-walk the deep chasm in her heart just to get up in the morning and go to work, just to show up each day as the front end manager of the local Wegman's grocery store and watch people buy milk and bread and bacon and bagels and donuts and toilet paper.

Could it be that Mitch had found the way for her to do the one thing that made sense? Who was she to go on living, given the mistake she had made, given the unforgivable error in judgment, the inexplicable lapse? Danny wasn't waiting for them. That was the horror. Danny was gone forever, and there was no way to change that —no amount of belief, no amount of grief, nothing. She wished she could have died instead of him, but now, at least, she could die for him. The pain, though, of giving up the memory of Danny, the one thing that would survive his death, the one thing she could treasure for all her life, took her breath away.

"Oh my God," she said, collapsing to the bathroom floor, her hands gripping the toilet seat, the calm gone.

When Kate opened the bathroom door, Mitch was standing in the hallway, his eyebrows raised expectantly. She stopped before reaching his outstretched arms. When he finally caught her eyes, he whispered, "Chimney Bluffs."

"Okay," was all she said.

Chapter 14

Kate stood at the hospital exit, facing a cloud of leaves caught up in a gust of wind. Carrie Goodwill stood by her side. The world beyond the exit waited.

"I don't think it's a good idea to go back home," Carrie Goodwill had said at the discharge meeting. "With no family support and few friends, well, it may be too painful to do at this point." It was the psychiatrist who had suggested that a "better plan might be to begin anew." Kate remembered those words, "begin anew." They sounded quaint, like something an English nanny might say with a clap of her hands.

The apartment manager was standing at the door when Kate arrived. "I'm afraid we didn't have time to paint the place, but we cleaned it pretty good," he said, picking up bags of trash as he walked into the kitchen. "I think it's kind of homey myself," he continued, pressing a loose tile back into place with his toe. Kate looked around. "If you'd like to paint it, you can, any color; I'll provide the paint free since we didn't quite get everything done." With that he smiled and fanned his arm out in a grand gesture. "So, welcome to your new home, Mrs., uh…"

"Duncan."

"Mrs. Duncan, of course."

Kate walked through the kitchen to the dining area. The green shag carpet was worn in four spots where the former tenants' table had been. There were a few dead flies in the corner. Beyond the dining area to the right was a living room with wood paneling on one wall that someone had decided to paint white. Her landlord, Mr. Griffin, came around the other corner from the kitchen.

"Bedroom's right through there," he said, pointing down a short hall. "Bathroom's on your left. Hope you like showers; doesn't have a bathtub. Most people like showers more than baths nowadays anyway."

Kate didn't answer. She walked down the hall, glanced briefly into the bathroom, its tiled floor looking like a collection of decaying teeth. There was a window high on one wall of her bedroom. Hollow wooden doors slid roughly as she opened the closet.

Mr. Griffin looked uncomfortable standing in the bedroom alone with a young woman. "Well," he said, "is there anything I can do for you? Anything you need?"

"No, that's fine," said Kate, still not looking at him. "Thank you."

"I can give you a hand with your boxes, if you'd like?"

"No thank you; really, I'm fine."

"Okay then," said Mr. Griffin as he headed toward the front door. "You know where to find me." He stopped, turned around with a smile, and said, "I hope you'll be happy here." Then he was gone.

Kate stood in the living room with its yellowing white walls and forest green carpet and nail holes where the last renters' pictures had hung. She walked to the window and pulled back the wide vertical blinds. Where she would have seen a garden, she instead viewed a parking lot and another grey building. Where she would have seen the VW van, she saw a 1986 Honda Civic, red with a white replacement door, the cheapest thing on the neighboring lot. Where she would have seen Danny's tricycle and Mitch's tool shed, she instead saw nothing.

Later that week, Kate met with her boss. "I'm sure we can work out a transfer, Kate," said Ronny. "Geez, you've been one of our best employees." He asked if she was sure she didn't want to come back to the store again. Everyone was thinking about her. Everyone wanted to help. But Kate didn't want to go back. She didn't want to go back to their sympathetic words. She didn't want to go back to their sad smiles. She didn't want to go back to the lunchroom, where everyone would fall silent each time she walked in. She didn't want to go back to anything. There was a new Wegman's out on 104 near Williamson. She told Ronny that would do just fine, even though all they had were cashier positions. He wished her luck as she left the store.

Kate pulled into the parking place in front of her apartment. She opened the hatch to the car and gazed at a half-dozen Dole pineapple boxes filled with clothes and towels and sheets and pillowcases and a shower curtain and a few dishes and glasses, some hand soap and dish soap and laundry soap—there was a laundromat nearby—Kleenex and toilet paper and just enough silverware, pots, and pans to cook a meal every once in a while and maybe eat it. Once inside, Kate tossed her jacket on the kitchen floor and placed one small box on the counter. She unpacked a snow globe with a tiny Empire State Building in it that Mitch had brought back for her from a trip to New York when they were dating. "Here you go," he had said. "A little something from the Big Apple." He'd bought it right in Times Square. "Never seen so many strange people, so many neon signs in my whole life. And don't plan to again!"

She shook it and watched the snow swirl and then settle, a few flakes on the highest spire, but most on the plastic base where the liquid looked thick as mucous. She thought of Mitch's hand reaching out to her, a smile on his face, this tiny globe in his palm. When she closed her eyes, she could still see his soft hand, but his face was cloudy and his voice was faint as a whisper.

She took the Plexiglas framed photo of Danny out of the box and wiped it on her sweatshirt, trying to rub away the scratches. This was the picture she had kept on her nightstand, the last picture she had taken of her little boy. He was sitting on his tricycle in the driveway, wearing a pair of jeans, a striped cotton jersey, and cowboy boots. And for once, he wasn't mugging for the camera. His smile looked just like Danny. He was waving at his mother as she took the shot. When she went to bed at night, it was the last thing she looked at, and when she woke up in the morning, it was the first. She held the picture within six inches of her face, counting the teeth in his smile, examining the folds in his neck, the redness of his round cheeks. She gently pressed her lips to the photo. She had thought of packing more, but she couldn't bring herself to go into Danny's room. She had stood by his bedroom door and listened, much as she had always done on the mornings when she awakened before him. She had loved listening for his first sounds, his stirring and then his babbling and then talking in his little boy voice to Little Green Bear, and at some point she would call in softly,

"Is Danny Duncan home?" and he would answer, "Mommy!" She listened, but there was nothing left—not a laugh, not a cry, nothing.

She brought all of her boxes into the apartment and put them in the living room in one great pile. She wasn't inclined to do more with them. She could live out of the boxes for a while. She had managed to pack one goose-necked floor lamp that she would use in her bedroom. A sleeping bag and a pillow would be her bed. Kate slept fitfully that first night; when she woke up and looked across the surface of the carpet at Danny's photo, she thought she heard water lapping behind her. She sat up and rubbed her eyes, trying to remember a pre-dawn dream. But it vanished like a vapor, leaving behind only a feeling of fear.

Kate's first day at the new Wegman's was easy enough. It was about a week before everyone figured out who she was. In the beginning, no one paid much attention to her when she arrived for her shift—no one except her neighboring cashiers. Soon, though, she noticed that her coworkers looked at her when she walked by—not directly, mind you, but in that sideways manner that seems nonchalant but is heavy with intent. Then they'd turn back to their work, but not before glancing at each other as if to say, "We know about you." And her neighboring cashiers chatted with at her more than they had before, nervously, sounding like songbirds around a feeder: talking, talking, talking so they wouldn't say what they were thinking. But Kate knew what they were thinking. They didn't have to say a word:

They must have been crazy, she and her husband—what was his name? They both must have been out of their minds. Look at her, acting like she's just as normal as any of us. But you can't do something like that and then just go back to normal; it's not like she was in some trance, under a spell, and someone snapped his fingers and now she's back to normal. No, she hadn't been hypnotized; she had known what they were going to do. She had known and she had agreed and she had gone up to that cliff and she had stood there with her son in a sack, of all things, his toys, too, and she had watched as her husband threw himself off the cliff to certain death. But she didn't have the courage of her own convictions; faced with it, she couldn't honor the pact she'd made; instead, she had pretended to jump. What in the world had she been thinking? That no one would notice that she didn't have a single scratch? That almost every bone in her husband's body was broken and she did not have so much as a mark on her? Now, that was almost as crazy as the idea of jumping to begin with. Better watch her; better watch her closely, because people don't bounce back from these things. They may look like they do, but they don't. You read about it all the time. Everyone thinks a person's doing fine, and then all of a sudden, they're walking down Main Street naked, or they're talking gibberish in the middle of a church service, or they're trying to finish what they couldn't complete to begin with: killing themselves.

Yes, Kate knew what they were thinking, because she was thinking the same things. When Kate went to bed each night, she shook the globe and patted Danny's picture and then lay for hours, waiting for the morning. When she did sleep, she would awaken in the deep night, feeling like someone was watching her—not watching *over* her, like a guardian angel might watch over someone to make sure she was safe, nothing like that at all—just watching her, like someone watching a specimen in a jar. She would turn, expecting to catch a glimpse of who it was, but only the dark corners of her room loomed back. She felt those eyes when she woke up in the morning, and when she closed her eyes, she could see a face. It was a face that seemed as big as the sky, with eyes as round as saucers, brown as dirt, and a mouth fallen open in a silent scream. Staring eyes that didn't blink, that looked at her coldly and steadily and uncaringly, as if they were looking at a bug that was seeking shelter. And then the mouth closed and the lips turned thin and white, and the eyebrows gathered like a storm across its forehead. And the dirty brown eyes, once full of shock, were now on fire, and she thought that with a single glance they might destroy her. And then the mouth opened and spoke words that cut like razors: "You killed that little boy. You did. I hope you burn in hell." Kate opened her eyes. She looked at her hands and touched her face to see if she was bleeding, and when she realized she wasn't, she began to weep.

Chimney Bluffs

Chapter 15

Clancy woke up early, made some coffee that he didn't drink, took a long shower, got dressed, brought the paper in from the front stoop, and rinsed—but didn't wash—the previous night's dishes. He changed a light bulb in the front hall and put a load of clothes in the wash. He sat down on the couch and reached for the remote. But then he put it down, got up from the sofa, and pulled his jean jacket out of the closet. He grabbed his keys as he went out the front door. Got into his truck, sat for a minute trying to think, sighed, and started the engine. He drove down Five Mile Line Road to 104 and turned right, heading for Williamson. The apartment complex was nestled between a used car dealership and an abandoned strip mall. Colorful flags waved from each car's antenna, and weeds grew tall in the mall's parking lot. The grey clapboard boxes placed at odd angles tried to look homey and welcoming but instead oozed exhaustion and poverty.

Clancy looked at the napkin—132 Ravenwood Oaks, Apartment 24. He looked at the number beside the screen door. There was a "2" and the shadow mark of a "4" that had once hung beside it. The screen was torn at the bottom, and the front door had a deep gash. He looked around the lot for a VW van, but all he could see were a couple of beat-up Caravans, a junker up on blocks, and several motorcycles. A little boy ran across the parking lot, his mother yelling after him, "When I get hold of you, I'm gonna beat your ass!" Clancy started to open his door but then thought better of it. He wondered if Bobby and John were right about meeting "this woman."

"Why go down that road, man?" Bobby had said. "I mean, what's it gonna get you?" He leaned back on his stool. "I'm telling you, you're just inviting a lot of hassle."

"I have to agree with Bobby on this one, Clancy. Just let it go," said John Dan.

Clancy pulled up the collar on his jacket.

"I thought you'd gotten this thing out of your system, Clance," said Bobby. "I thought you got rid of that stuffed animal."

Bobby thought of his father, how he had become addicted to Mark's death—no other word for it. Bobby's father didn't talk much at all anymore. He sat in his recliner and watched the History Channel all day. He ordered video sets about World War II and Hitler's henchmen. Bobby's mother brought his father his beer, his ham sandwiches, his newspaper and coffee. He seldom looked up from the TV. Bobby used to say "Goodbye" in the morning, "Hi" when he got home, and "Good night" when he went to bed, but he didn't even do that anymore. His father should have been the one to die in the accident. Bobby's mother smacked him on the cheek when he had said this. "How dare you talk about your father that way! How dare you!" But she knew he was right. She knew he was a dead man who sat in his recliner all day long, waiting for everything to be over. Didn't have the courage to kill himself, so he just waited to die.

It had taken Bobby a long time to stop blaming himself. Why hadn't he been sitting on that side of the car? Why hadn't he reached for Mark, protected him? Why hadn't he been a good enough son for his father? Why couldn't his father love him? He had before the accident. Or had he? Bobby couldn't remember. "Of course your father loved you," his mother would answer dismissively. But she wouldn't talk about it any further. "Just give him some time," she'd say. And he had believed her for a long while. He believed that time would heal all wounds, unless the wounded got up each day and tore off the scabs one by one. One year, two years, five years. Bobby knew it would never change. He knew that his family would never make it past Mark's death.

In high school, Bobby drank and smoked weed and skipped his classes. He was arrested once for beating up another kid at McDonald's. The charges were dropped. And he came home. And life went on. And his father sat in his chair. Bobby was like glass to his father; the man looked right through him.

"Look at me!" he had yelled on the day he left for Oswego State. Bobby vowed he'd never come home again, not to this mausoleum; he was gone for good. But he never stood a chance. He did well the first week or so, but then he started skipping classes and avoiding work and drinking—at first on the weekends, but then starting on Wednesdays, and finally seven days a week. He had never felt so free. At least, until the administration suggested he not return after the first semester for academic and "behavioral" reasons.

When Bobby and his mother had pulled into the driveway, his belongings packed in the trunk, his father was standing at the living room window. But when he walked through the door, his father was in his recliner, newspaper in front of his face. They didn't speak. Bobby vowed he would get his own apartment, but days turned into weeks and months passed and the well-worn pattern of living at home took over. His mother asked him from time to time if he had plans. In the beginning, Bobby would say he was figuring that out. Soon, though, he'd shrug his shoulders, and in time his mother stopped asking. And so they went along under the shadow of Mark's death.

Bobby feared that somehow Clancy, like his father, had been drawn into that inescapable inertia that brings all time to a standstill, that turns a single moment into the definition of all moments. So when Bobby glimpsed the stuffed bear in Clancy's pocket as he stood up from his stool at the bar and heard Clancy say he wanted to meet "this woman," Bobby felt like he was in one of those dreams where the only thing keeping you from preventing a disaster was that you were paralyzed; your legs were like lead and your arms were made of stone and everything happened just beyond your reach.

Although he could tell Clancy wasn't interested in anyone else's suggestions, Bobby couldn't help himself. "I mean, it *is* your call, but I've seen what this kind of thing can do…"

"What do you mean 'this kind of thing'?" snapped Clancy.

"I don't mean anything, Clance. It's just that my old man went through this and he never got out of it…"

"Jesus Christ, Bobby, I'm not your old man, okay? I know you went through hell with him, but I'm not your old man. This isn't the same thing. It's not."

Bobby looked away and then drained his beer. John looked at

Bobby and then at Clancy.

"Look, I think both of you are making a mountain out of a molehill," said John. "Here, have another one on me. No need to fight over this damn woman."

Clancy and Bobby took brief refuge in their frosty glasses.

"Is it so odd that I'd want to meet this woman?" said Clancy. "Is it? Considering what they did on *my* cliff? What am I supposed to do with that? Write a report and then go on like nothing ever happened?" He lifted his beer and then put it back on the table. He looked at John and Bobby and then at his beer again. "I don't know why this is so important, okay? Is that what you want me to say? I don't know why I can't let go of this, but I can't, and just walking away from it isn't the answer." He turned to Bobby. "I'm sorry that your old man got so messed up over your brother. And I'm sorry he's been such a bastard to you. I really am. But this is something I've got to do. Don't ask me why. It just is."

Bobby didn't follow Clancy when he left John Dan's bar. Instead, he drove straight home and went to bed. Had he followed Clancy, he would have seen him drive to the hospital, where he sat in the parking garage for half an hour before going to the front desk.

"Excuse me. Do you have a Duncan in the hospital? I think it's Kate."

"Duncan, Duncan, let me see here," said the receptionist as she scanned her computer screen. "Are you sure she's here?"

"I think…"

"Oh, wait, she was here, but she's been discharged."

"Discharged?"

"Yes, actually several days ago. Are you a family member?"

"No."

"Friend, then?"

"No," said Clancy. He stood at the desk as if he didn't know what to do next.

"Well, can I help you with anything else?"

"Do you know where she went?"

"No, I don't. Actually, if I did know, I wouldn't be allowed to tell you. Sorry," she said with a smile.

Clancy turned to walk away, but stopped and then sat down. He looked at the people coming and going, visiting their loved ones, some with balloons for new babies, some in a hurry to leave, some with tears in their eyes as they searched their pockets for their car keys. Clancy reached into his pocket for the stuffed bear. When he took it out, he noticed a little boy sitting across from him with his grandmother smile and walk over. The little boy stood in front of Clancy and looked intently at the bear. Clancy held the bear out to the boy, who reached to pat it and then tried to take it in his arms. Clancy held tight to the bear, feeling embarrassed. The little boy's face clenched into a grimace, and he began to whine. The boy's grandmother noticed the tug-of-war.

"Sammy, no, no, that's not yours. You mustn't try to take things that don't belong to you. I'm sure that man's little boy would be very unhappy if his daddy gave you his bear. You wouldn't want that, now would you?" Sammy grudgingly let go and walked back to his grandmother. She smiled at Clancy. "Sorry. He's just a little boy."

Clancy's throat closed and his eyes welled up. He smiled at the woman. "That's okay. I don't have any children. This belongs to…it's someone else's. I'm trying to..." He stood up. "I'm sorry," he said and walked quickly to the door.

It was a week before he went back to John Dan's. This time he didn't go there to drink.

"I'll try my best," said John without any expression on his face. "But I can't promise you anything. Jimmy's like stink on a skunk with his scanner, but I don't know if he has any real police connections." John went back to wiping the counter. There was disapproval in his silence.

"I got something of hers, John. That's all." John raised his eyes to Clancy but didn't speak. "Let me know if Jimmy learns anything more," said Clancy.

Later that same night there was a message on his phone: "132 Ravenwood Oaks, Apartment 24. Williamson, I think. Look, Clancy, I hope you know what you're doing."

Clancy clicked off the light, climbed into bed, and lay on his back, studying the ceiling fan. *When was the last time you felt like you knew what you were doing?* He worked at Mott's because it was there. He married Darlene because she was available. He let her go because he was tired. He came to Chimney Bluffs because it was easy. Each time, he felt like he knew what he was doing, but in retrospect he didn't know why he had done any of it, why he'd made the decisions he'd made. *Does anyone know? Or do you just do each thing as it comes along?* Standing on the cliff that morning, looking down at two bodies and two sacks, he had felt like a drunk who had suddenly been slapped stone-cold sober—like the goggles had come off and whether he wanted to see it or not, he was forced to look at life in all its bone-chilling starkness. *You live, you die, and in between, you better figure out what you're doing and why you're doing it, or none of it matters. Is that what happened to them? Did nothing matter anymore? Did they give up on life? Did life give up on them? Or did everything matter too much? Did everything matter so much that, in the end, dying was the only part of living that had any meaning?* Clancy shook his head and rolled over. He threw his covers off and then pulled them back up to his chin.

He and Darlene had led a careless life together; they'd barely given a thought to what they were doing and what it could have meant; they'd played a long and weary game that had ended in a painful draw. They could have had so much more, but they hadn't even tried. He hadn't tried.

Maybe that was why he had to meet her. Some people try. Some people make every effort, no matter how desperate. Some people go right to the edge, trying to save something even when it can't be saved. That had to be the case. He had cursed this woman without knowing her desperation, without understanding what drove her, without caring that she had committed herself in ways that he could only imagine.

In all his life, he had never stepped out onto any cliff for any reason. But on that morning, whether they knew it or not, that woman and that man had drawn him over the edge with them. He had to meet this woman. He had to give her what was hers. He had to let her know that he understood.

The door to 24 opened and a small, thin woman with narrow, dark eyes and sunken cheeks appeared. She was putting on her jacket. Her nose was flattened and her nostrils were flared, making her look like she was wincing. Her hair: thin and mousy brown, straight and careworn. She shook her head, loosening her hair from her collar. She buttoned her brown corduroy jacket slowly, never looking up.

Even from his car, Clancy recognized her eyes, deep-set, hidden from the light, so deep that he couldn't tell if they had color at all. When he had stood over her, they hadn't moved, hadn't blinked. When he had spoken to her, when he had damned her, they hadn't flinched. He wondered if she had heard him at all.

Kate stepped out the door, closed it behind her, and then looked up. She stopped. Her eyes met Clancy's through the windshield of his truck. He opened his door and stepped out onto the pavement. He took one step forward and then stopped, putting his hands in his pocket.

Kate stood at the door, expressionless. Clancy tried to smile, hoping it would put her at ease. She did not return the gesture.

"Hello," said Clancy. "You don't know me, but…"

"I know," interrupted Kate. "I know who you are."

Chimney Bluffs

PART 2

Chimney Bluffs

Chapter 16

"But we haven't *really* met," said Clancy. He closed the door of his truck and took a step forward.

"I think we have," said Kate, standing in the doorway of her apartment. She crossed her arms and looked at Clancy. *Those are the eyes*, she thought. But his face looked softer, older, more tired. The righteousness, the ferocity was gone. He wore jeans and work boots and a denim jacket with at least one button missing, and his hair was wiry and hadn't seen a comb in a long while. She had always imagined that he was tall and rough-hewn, like an old log. She was surprised that he was of average height, actually average in every way, the kind of man who might come through her checkout a dozen times before she'd notice him.

"Well, I guess so," said Clancy. He had thought of her every day since that morning on the beach, and yet he hadn't always been able to remember what she looked like. She had lain so still, so defenseless, on the beach that it had been hard to imagine her doing anything more than cowering, and yet there she stood. He knew more about her than he probably should, and yet he didn't know her at all. She had been his constant companion since that morning, and yet she was a complete stranger.

A dog across the parking lot yanked on his chain and barked loudly, then whimpered. Both of them looked, glad the spell had been broken. When Clancy turned back to her, Kate's arms were unfolded; her hands were in her hip pockets.

Clancy tried to smile again. "Noisy."

"Yes," said Kate. "There's always something."

"I imagine so." Clancy took a deep breath. "Have you lived here long?"

"Do you have a name?"

"What's that?" said Clancy.

"I asked if you had a name. It seems fair that I should know, since I think you know a lot about me."

"Not that much."

"You were there," said Kate.

Sweat glistened on Clancy's neck. He turned and looked at his truck. His hands began to fidget. "Clancy," he said.

"Does Clancy have a last name?" Kate felt a tremor of anger rising in her voice that surprised her. She felt that somehow he knew her, that he was the only one who had seen her right through to the bone. She hated him for it, and feared him. And was drawn to him.

"Brisco. Clancy Brisco."

"Clancy Brisco. Is that Irish?"

"I guess it is. Never paid attention."

"What's Clancy short for?"

"Clarence. It's Clarence Brisco."

"Clarence Brisco." Kate looked at him hard, trying to balance things out in her mind. *Should you just tell him to go?* she wondered. *And if you do, would he go?*

"And you work there, don't you?"

"Yes, I do."

"How long?"

"Five, six years," said Clancy, unsure why this mattered.

Kate finished buttoning her jacket. She stepped out onto the stoop and closed the door. The sun came up over the neighboring apartment building, and she squinted to see Clancy's face. She was looking for what she had seen that morning on the beach, what she had only glimpsed, actually, since she had been too afraid to look directly at him. She remembered him as a Godlike tower leaning over her, calmly yet vehemently telling her what she had done and what price she would have to pay. She had felt his breath on her cheek, his words pelting her face, his loathing blanketing her. She had felt that she would never be able to stand on her feet again after that. That she would have to crawl through her life on her belly. He was her judge. He had sentenced her. But she would be the one to carry out the punishment.

Clancy looked away and shifted his weight from one foot to the other. "Worked at Mott's before that." Kate didn't respond. "But I got laid off. Chimney Bluffs was the only thing I could find."

"Do you have children?" said Kate.

Clancy blanched at this question. He felt a bead of perspiration running down the middle of his back. "Well…"

"You don't have to answer that, if you don't want to." Kate looked at him expectantly. *Does he know what it was like to love someone so completely? Does he know what it was like to have failed?*

"That's okay," said Clancy, his tongue dry. "No, I don't have children."

"A child can make all the difference."

Clancy looked at her again, this time catching her eyes in the partial sunlight; they looked like a child's eyes, like they had seen too much and understood too little, like they ached but couldn't be soothed. She looked away. "Look, Mrs. Duncan, I shouldn't have come. I'm sorry."

"Clarence Brisco. You were the one who found me, weren't you? I mean, you were the one who stood over me, weren't you?" She didn't wait for his answer. "You know, I heard you coming. I heard your boots crunching the stones and gravel. I heard you panting, out of breath, and then you stopped. You were gasping. I heard you moaning. I didn't know what to think. I didn't know what you would do. I was afraid." Kate took her hands out of her hip pockets and folded her arms again. "I was afraid of what you would think. I was afraid that you would forgive me, actually, that you would take mercy on me. You see, that's what I thought I wanted. Even though I knew I didn't deserve it. I knew that I was guilty. I was afraid you wouldn't see that. I was afraid that you wouldn't recognize me. But you did. And you hated me."

"Mrs. Duncan. I was in shock; I thought I knew what had happened, but…"

"No, you were right to hate me. What you said to me, your judgment, it was the truth." She looked at him, but his head was bowed. "I couldn't have said it better."

Clancy didn't know what to say, or if he should say anything at all. He was hesitant to move, let alone speak. He looked at her, and instead of a stranger lying on a beach, he saw a person without a world, a person who was absolutely alone, a person without defense. Clancy turned to face her directly, squaring his shoulders and taking another deep breath. He opened his mouth to speak and then stopped, not wanting something to come out that he would regret—something that, once it had been set loose between them, could not be retrieved. She watched him carefully.

Clancy reached into his jacket pocket. "I have something that belongs to you," he said.

Kate stiffened, unsure of what was coming.

"I found it on the trail. I found it and I kept it. I don't know why. I've had it with me ever since. But I knew I couldn't keep it." He smiled as if to reassure her that he was not the same man who had condemned her. "I guess that's why I came."

Clancy took the little bear from his pocket and held it out to Kate. She looked at him but then covered her face with her hands. She slumped onto the doormat, her body rocking slowly back and forth. Tears gathered at the end of her chin.

Clancy froze. "I'm sorry." She didn't respond. He didn't know what to do. He thought he should leave, but found himself unable to go. He took a few steps forward, still unsure how close he should get. "Are you okay?" Kate didn't answer. She wiped the tears from her face. Clancy moved closer, this time to the bottom of the steps. When she didn't pull away, he went up the two steps left between them and sat beside her. He reached out with the little bear and placed it in her lap. She took it in her hand and pressed it to her lips, kissing it gently.

Chapter 17

It was ten o'clock when Bobby pulled into his parents' driveway. He was tired. The conversation at John Dan's had left him feeling frustrated and helpless. *Sometimes people have to do what they have to do; who are you to stop Clancy?* He shook his head, though, because he knew the dangers of being obsessed with something.

The lights were on in the living room, where his parents spent each evening watching TV. Bobby entered the house through the back door. He looked in the refrigerator and, seeing nothing interesting, closed it and headed for the basement stairs. He called to his parents, "Good night."

His mother responded, "Okay."

Bobby waited for his father, but he didn't say a thing. He almost called out again, but then thought better of it. His parents were talking about something. He could hear his father's low grumbling and the placating tone of his mother's voice. They could have been talking about a commercial his father didn't like, for all he knew.

He headed downstairs to his bedroom. He pulled the string on the overhead light, grabbed a *Maxim* from the shelf, and stretched out on his bed. He flipped absently through the pages, but his eyes were weary. He tossed the magazine on the floor, drew back the covers, kicked off his shoes, and turned off the light. He rolled onto his left side and stared at the moon shadows on the wall. He turned over again, and just as he settled into a comfortable position, Bobby heard a gathering storm upstairs; he could feel the torque in his father's voice, that twisting vice-like grip that tore at you layer by layer, much as a hurricane might tear off the shingles and finally the roof of an unsuspecting house. Usually he and his mother would seek shelter until it passed, withdrawing to their respective bedrooms. Sometimes, though, his mother would finally say, "Stop!" and that would be it. His old man would piss and moan at her a little longer, but the danger would pass.

Over the years, Bobby had often said, "Why the hell do you take it?" His mother would fire back, "What do you want me to do? Look at him!" His father would go back to his recliner, like a wounded bull returning to his pen. But tonight was different. It went on and on. Bobby turned to the wall again, hoping to escape, but his father's rage reverberated through the house like a thunderstorm in the dead of night.

He listened for his mother's voice, but all he could hear was his old man thrashing away. Bobby turned over on his back and kicked off his covers. He stared at the ceiling, waiting. He reached for his baseball bat and thumped it against the ceiling. Finally he heard his mother cry out, "Stop it!" Then again, "Stop!" He heard a lamp fall to the floor, and then everything went silent. He listened. Nothing. He got up and stood by his door. Nothing. He called, "Mom, are you okay?" Nothing.

Bobby ran up the stairs. When he reached the living room, he saw that his father had pinned his mother against the wall, his forearm under her chin. She looked at Bobby, her eyes bulging, her face swollen and red. She kicked at Bobby's father, but her legs dangled like a marionette's. He was leaning hard, sweat pouring down the back of his neck.

"What the hell are you doing?" said Bobby. His father adjusted his weight, assuring that Bobby's mother would not be able to move. Her eyes were no longer focused, and her arms fell limp.

"Stop it! Stop it!" said Bobby.

Bobby threw himself at his father, trying to pull him away from his mother. But his father was steady as an oak. Bobby punched him in the kidney as hard as he could. He punched him a second and then a third time. His father groaned and buckled. Bobby's mother slid down the living room wall and lay on the floor, gasping for breath. Bobby's father straightened up and turned to face his son. Bobby noticed for the first time how old his father had gotten; the corners of his mouth and eyes were wrinkled, and his eyebrows were bushy and grey; his once squared chin was soft and jowly; the bottom of his eyelids pulled away from his milky grey eyes. Bobby couldn't remember the last time he had looked at his father's face.

Bobby's old man took a deep breath, arched his back, and bared his teeth at his son. "Do you really want to do this?" he said. Bobby didn't answer. His father looked at Bobby from head to toe. "You're still a little snot-nosed shit, aren't you?"

"Look," said Bobby, hands limp at his side. "Don't you ever touch her again."

"This is between your mother and me. Ain't none of your business." Bobby's father pointed at Bobby, his finger in direct line with his right eye, lifeless as a shark's. "You. Stay. Out of it."

"I'm telling you, don't touch her. You hear me?"

Bobby's father pursed his lips and narrowed his gaze. "Goddamn you to hell," he said in a whisper.

Bobby's mother stood up and held her throat; she leaned back against the wall, coughing and trying to catch her breath.

"Are you okay?" said Bobby.

Bobby's mother tried to speak, but his father stretched his arm out in front of her.

"She's fine," said Bobby's father. "Better worry about yourself." He took a step towards Bobby. Bobby flinched and stepped back. His father laughed. "Look at that," he said to his wife. "Fat lot of good he'll do you." He took another step towards Bobby. Bobby backed away. Then his father turned to Bobby's mother. "Go to bed."

"But..."

"Just get!"

He took a step towards Bobby's mother as she back-pedaled toward the bedroom door. Bobby lunged at his old man and grabbed him around the shoulders, his face buried in his father's chest. His father tried to pull away, but Bobby wouldn't let go. His father tried to shake Bobby off of him, but Bobby held on tight. They tilted back and forth in a menacing dance.

"Goddamn you," said his father. Bobby began to cry.

"Get off me!" his father yelled, his shirt damp with Bobby's tears. He pushed Bobby to the floor. Bobby got up and swung at his father, who laughed and pushed Bobby to the floor again.

"Stop!" gasped his mother. "Stop, both of you!"

Bobby lay on the floor, looking up at his father standing over him, fists clenched.

"Go ahead," said Bobby. "You've always wanted to. Go ahead and do it. Hit me. Hit me as hard as you can! Hit me and get it over with!"

His father stared at him. He drew his fist back. Bobby didn't flinch this time.

"Go ahead," he said calmly.

Bobby's mother grabbed his father's arm. "I said stop it!" She stepped in front of her husband and pressed her palms against his chest.

"Get out of my way," he said. "I should have taught your boy a lesson a long time ago."

"Is that what you're gonna do? After all this time?" Bobby laughed. "That's rich. You've never done a damn thing for me my whole life, and now you're going to teach me a lesson."

"You've always had a roof over your head and food on the table, so don't give me any of your bullshit," said Bobby's father, his breathing heavy with exhaustion, his eyes stricken.

Bobby's mother leaned against her husband, forcing distance between the two men.

"Bullshit? Well, here's some more bullshit for you. And you're not going to like it." Bobby choked up again. He struggled to find his voice. "He's dead, Dad. Mark is dead. He's been dead a long time. But guess what? Although you might regret it, I'm not. I'm alive. And I'm the only son you've got."

Bobby's father pushed his mother out of the way and punched Bobby in the face, leveling him. He stood over Bobby, ready to strike again. But he wavered, unclenching his fists. He began to cry. He leaned back against the wall and fell to the floor, his face in his hands. Bobby's mother went to his side. She knelt on the floor and clutched him to her.

Bobby stepped forward, his hand outstretched, his face contorted. His mother looked up at him, her eyes fierce.

"Bobby, goddamn you! Look what you've done!" said his mother, her husband sobbing in her arms.

Bobby couldn't speak. He looked at his father huddled on the floor, weeping like a baby. He wanted to hold him and tell him he loved him. He wanted to tell him that everything would be all right, that he didn't really mean it. He wanted to tell him that he understood what his father had gone through. That he missed Mark every day of his life. He wanted to tell him that he was sorry. That all he ever wanted was to be his son. To turn back the clock to the day before the accident, when he wasn't the enemy, when he wasn't the one who should have died, when he was just a six-year-old boy, his father's oldest son, the same son that his father had smiled on the day he was born. That's all he wanted.

Bobby knelt down beside his mother and father. He reached out to his father, placing his hand on his shoulder. "Dad…" he began, but his father brushed his hand away.

"Don't touch me," he said, his voice a whisper.

"Dad…"

"Don't call me that."

"But Dad…"

"Bobby, look what you've done," said his mother. "And for what? To prove a point?"

"But Mom, I…"

"You've said enough, Bobby. Just leave."

"What do you mean?"

"You've hurt your father bad enough. Don't hurt me, too. Now go. Leave. Get out."

You've hurt your father bad enough? How? I survived an automobile accident when I was six years old. Was that what hurt him? Was that the wound I inflicted on my father? Was that my crime? He looked at his mother as she turned her attention to Bobby's old man. *They are one,* he thought. He had never realized it. He had always thought his mother was on his side; that even though she stayed with his father, she would always stand up for Bobby when he needed it. But as he looked at them huddled together, a single person disguised as two, the truth of the matter came clear. When Mark died, his mother had cast her fate with her husband; she had accepted that he would never move on and that her life would orbit his. Of course, there was the problem of Bobby, the other son. She didn't exactly turn her back on him, but she never embraced him, either. She fed him and clothed him and helped him with his homework and went to meetings at school and tried to buffer the conflict between Bobby and his father, but she never abandoned her loyalty to her grieving husband long enough to love her remaining son. Bobby had pretended otherwise. But looking at her now, he knew that her love for him had also withered in the aftermath of Mark's death. In its place, she had been dutiful and tolerant. Now even that was gone. It was just the two of them, and there was no room for Bobby.

Bobby had stayed for her. He had stayed because he couldn't imagine what life would be like for his mother alone with this venomous man. But he had been wrong all along. She would never leave him. She would never choose Bobby. His parents weren't cut from the same cloth—they *were* the same cloth, a cloth so tightly woven that their needs were indistinguishable; their nightmares had grown comfortable, their bitterness had turned sweet.

His mother held his father in her arms and spoke low and gentle words of comfort. She rocked him as she might have rocked Mark. Bobby's father wept much as he had wept on that day so long ago when he had called for Mark and there had been no answer. Would Bobby's leaving make things better for them? Without Bobby to distract them, would they settle into the quicksand of their sadness, together taking ease in their suffering?

Bobby went to his room and threw some clothes in a duffel bag. He came back to the living room, where his parents were still clutched together on the floor. He took his bomber jacket from the closet and put it on. He headed for the door, then stopped and turned to his parents. They looked at him as if he were a stranger. He wanted to speak, but there was nothing more to say. He turned again to the door, opened it, and walked out.

Chapter 18

Lucky for Bobby, the nights were getting warmer. He had been sleeping in his truck ever since his mother had told him to leave. The first couple of nights were downright cold, but once he bought a sleeping bag and pillow at Walmart, it wasn't so bad. In fact, with the temperature rising, it was as comfortable in his truck as it had been in his bed. That first night, he just drove around, wondering whether he should go back home and apologize. But then he thought, *Why the hell should you apologize? They should apologize to you.* Then he rode around some more, hoping his mother would call him. In the end, his cell phone almost died while he waited. He wanted to tell Clancy the next day, but Clancy was so focused on his meeting with the woman that he didn't seem interested in anything else. Bobby was relieved to hear that Clancy had given the bear back, but Bobby was so worried about where he was going to sleep that night that he didn't hear anything that Clancy said, except that he wanted to meet with her again.

Bobby drove around again that night and finally came back to Chimney Bluffs and parked in a dark corner of the east lot. And that's where he stayed. He washed up and took care of business in the public restroom. He bought some Molson, Doritos, a couple of Snickers bars, and two ham sandwiches at the AM/PM Mini-Mart. He played his radio as long as he could that night and then lay on his back, looking through the windshield at the sky, his own planetarium. No need for an alarm clock; the sun woke him in the morning. And so it went. He worked all day, left the office with everyone at five, drove around the park until it closed, and then came back and settled in for the night. He was surprised how easy it was to get used to this new arrangement. In fact, he looked forward to coming to his spot near the trails—the soothing sound of the lake each night. No parents fighting, nothing to haunt his sleep. It was like he had moved far away, leaving everything behind.

One night, he drove past his parents' house. He could see through the front window that they were sitting where they always sat, watching what they always watched. Nothing had changed. He could have been dead for all they knew or cared. He couldn't believe it was so easy for them.

He came back later when the lights were out and pulled into the driveway. He walked up to the back door, cupped his hands around his eyes, and peered through a window into the darkened house. It looked like a stage after the curtain had gone down. Bobby closed his eyes and thought of Mark. It had been years since he had been able to see his brother's face or hear his voice. They had faded in the avalanche of time that had come and gone since the accident. Bobby shook his head as if to say, "What has all this been about? Here you are standing outside your own home like some thief, all because over fifteen years ago a car veered a few feet from its path, hit us, and killed us all."

146

The world is a very big thing, thought Bobby, *but a life is very small. We may pretend it's not, but it is; it's small and it can change completely in the blink of an eye. And there's no going back. There's no second chance.*

A glimmer of light shone in the hallway. His old man must have gotten up. Since his prostate had gone bad, he went to the john all the time, often coming down to the basement bathroom so he could take his time and avoid his wife's chastisement for not going to the doctor with his affliction. The toilet and Bobby's bed backed up to the same wall. Sometimes Bobby would listen for twenty minutes or more as his father stood like a statue, trying to take a piss. He was so close that Bobby could hear his heavy breathing. His father would say "Goddammit" under his breath when it seemed like nothing would come. Then he would groan and wait, sometimes leaning a hand against the wall, causing it to creak in Bobby's room. Eventually Bobby would hear a broken stream lurching reluctantly into the bowl. His father would sigh with relief. Then he would flush the toilet and amble back upstairs to his bedroom, never knowing that he had shared such an intimate moment with his son merely two feet away.

The light went out. The house was dark again, and Bobby left.

After a week or so, Bobby fell into a comfortable routine, sometimes getting up early and driving around before work so that Clancy wouldn't become suspicious about him always being on time. Bobby also found an empty storage locker in the main office where he stashed some of the clothes he had bought at the Salvation Army. Between the mini-mart, McDonald's, and Wendy's, he ate just about as well as he had at home. On cold nights, he ran the heater for as long as possible before shutting the truck down and pulling the sleeping bag over his head.

He tried to think of himself as away from home, but not homeless. He tried to think of this as an adventure rather than a disaster. He tried, but sometimes his situation got the best of him and he would lie in his truck at night, struggling with a feeling of emptiness that seemed to have no limits.

Jesus Christ, he thought, *is this it?*

Then, afraid that his personal darkness might swallow him whole, Bobby would strain to find a hint of light. He'd think about Clancy or his friends at John Dan's; he'd think of an old song or a good joke or the young cashier at the mini-mart and how she smiled at him special. He'd think about anything, sometimes made up things about how he had graduated college and made a name for himself and how he was someone that everyone admired and how maybe all of that could still come true. He fought hard against the thought that all his life amounted to was this—living in a truck in a parking lot. He fought hard, pushing those thoughts out of the truck cab, leaving them in the lot, where it was cold and damp and lonely. And then he would sleep.

It was a Wednesday morning, the third week of this new life; it was far too early for sunrise, and yet a bright light woke him. Bobby shielded his eyes with his arm and tried to get his bearings. He looked out the driver's side window, but couldn't make out a thing, although he heard laughter and shushing and the shuffling of feet. Just as he reached for the ignition to lower the window, he heard a dull thud and watched a pocket form in the middle of his windshield, the glass around it spider-webbing in every direction.

There were gales of laughter. "Jesus Christ, you nailed the shit out of that thing!"

Bobby buried himself in his jacket as the head of a sledgehammer broke through the windshield, thousands of pieces raining down on him.

"Holy shit, you did it, man!" called another voice.

"What the fuck!" yelled Bobby. For a moment everything went silent.

"Jesus Christ, Matt, somebody's in that thing."

"You've gotta be kidding me! You said it was abandoned, asshole. Let's get the hell out of here."

"Jesus Christ, is someone living in that thing?" They were laughing again as they retreated to their car. Bobby thought he heard three, maybe four teenage voices. Doors slammed and wheels tore up the pavement. He could still hear them laughing as they sped out of the lot and headed for 104.

Bobby didn't move. He didn't take the jacket off his head. He lay on the seat for a long moment, trying to figure out what had just happened. As he sat up, glass poured off him, tinkling onto the seat. He slid his jacket off and looked up. A few jagged pieces of glass still hung tight, like stalactites on the walls of a cave. He pressed his hand against the seat and felt the sting of a thousand needles. He held his hand up and watched the blood run across his palm and down his wrist. He looked through the windshield, now an empty frame, at the full moon sitting on a cloud, its light cast in a long shimmering line from horizon to shore.

Bobby scanned the parking lot. He listened closely, hoping they were gone for good. He wrapped his jacket around his hand and carefully swept some of the glass onto the floor. He shifted his weight onto the cleared spot. He reached for the ignition and then stopped. *Where the hell can you go?* he thought. He shook his head and started to laugh. *Perfect. This is absolutely perfect.* He looked up at the sky. *I mean, someone up there must have been bored all to shit tonight. And this was the best he could come up with—Hey, let's go mess with Bobby.* Bobby held his hand up to the moonlight and picked some of the glass out of his palm. He could see that he was fighting a losing battle. "Shit." *What are you going to do?* "Goddamn sonofabitch!" he roared, kicking the dashboard with all his might, pounding it until the last piece of the glass had been shaken loose from the windshield.

After Clancy arrived, he looked at Bobby with a mixture of concern and confusion. "I mean, what are you doing out here anyway? And why didn't you call the police? Or your parents? Jesus, they did a job on you," said Clancy as he leaned over the hood of the truck. He looked at Bobby quizzically.

Bobby didn't know what to say. He had thought of calling the police. But he knew he wasn't supposed to be on park property, and with all the worry about park security after the incident, and him being an employee, he didn't want to cause any more trouble. Plus, who would have thought this would happen? All he wanted was a place to stay for a while until he figured things out. He'd looked at apartments, but he'd never been one to save money, and there was no way he could afford a security deposit and the first month's rent, at least not now.

Bobby shrugged. "I don't know. Wasn't thinking, I guess."

A tow truck came and went. Bobby's hand was wrapped in a t-shirt.

"Let me see that," said Clancy. Bobby unwrapped his hand. "Jesus, Bobby, we better get you to a hospital."

At the emergency room, they pulled out a dozen or more slivers of glass and wrapped his hand in gauze. When Bobby came back to the waiting room, his hand looked like a giant snowball.

"Shouldn't take long to replace that windshield," said Clancy. He looked at Bobby's sagging face, his hair jutting out every which way, his clothes a mass of wrinkles. "Hungry?"

The parking lot at the Truckers Haven was full of moaning semis waiting to hit the road. Men browsed the latest DVD players and portable heaters while waiting for an available shower. Wrinkled hotdogs turned slowly under a yellow light. The glaze from day-old donuts flaked.

Clancy and Bobby slid into a booth, its seat patched with silver duct tape.

"Coffee, boys?" said the waitress, dropping two menus on the table.

"Yes," said Clancy. The waitress walked away as Clancy stared at his menu. He looked up at Bobby, who was wiggling the tips of his fingers and looking out the window. Clancy closed his menu. The waitress returned with their coffee and took their orders.

"So, Bobby, what's going on? I mean, what was that all about?"

"Nothing, really." Bobby felt himself shrinking as he sat across from Clancy, shrinking and fading away, ashamed that he had called Clancy to begin with.

Clancy shook his head. His hair was tangled and his eyes were sagging. He yawned into his coffee, looked at Bobby again, and waited for a better response.

The waitress returned with their orders. Bobby dabbed his toast into the oozing yolks and took a bite. Sipped his coffee and then his OJ. He looked at Clancy, hoping he wasn't looking back at him. But he was. Clancy tilted his head forward slightly and raised his eyebrows. Bobby chewed more quickly, wiped his mouth, and put his fork down.

"I don't know what to tell you, Clancy. I was sleeping in the park and these punks bashed in my windshield. I don't think they knew anyone was in the truck because they ran like hell when they noticed me."

Clancy's expression didn't change. He looked befuddled and tired and annoyed. He sipped his coffee again. "Why were you sleeping in the park?"

"Just thought it would be neat; I mean, it was a beautiful night; I used to camp there, so I thought it would be…"

"Goddammit, Bobby," Clancy growled. "You got me up at 4 a.m. Don't give me any of your bullshit. Just tell me."

Bobby leaned against the back of the booth, trying to catch his breath and clear his mind. He looked at Clancy. He wished he hadn't called him, but at the same time, he was glad Clancy was there; he had to tell someone, no matter how pathetic it would sound.

"I got kicked out," said Bobby, shrugging his shoulders.

"Kicked out of your house?"

"Yeah."

"By your old man?"

"Well, not exactly…"

Bobby told Clancy about the fight his parents had had and how he had tried to protect his mother. He told him about how furious his father had gotten, how he had punched Bobby and knocked him to the floor; Bobby told him what he had said to his father about Mark, about him being dead and how Bobby was his only son now, and how it wasn't going to change no matter how much his old man wished it would; he told Clancy how old his father looked and how he crumbled under Bobby's words, how Bobby felt awful seeing him like that, but when he tried to apologize, his mother told him to leave, told him to leave and never come back.

"I tried to find an apartment, but I don't have enough money saved. So. I decided to stay in the park." Bobby stopped looking at Clancy as he told the story. He spoke to the Formica tabletop and hoped that Clancy might be listening, too.

At first Clancy didn't say anything, but then he waved to the waitress.

"Yessir."

"More coffee for my friend here. And another for me, too."

"Sure," said the waitress.

Bobby still hadn't looked up.

"How long have you been sleeping in the lot?" asked Clancy.

"Not long, really. A few weeks."

"A few weeks," said Clancy, his eyebrows raised. "Where are you keeping your stuff?"

"Found an empty locker in the back room of the office."

Clancy took a deep breath, pursed his lips, and squinted just a little, as if he were trying to see something that was just out of range.

"Okay, Bobby. Take your time. Drink your coffee. Finish your breakfast."

Bobby looked up and caught Clancy's eye. Then he looked down again, picked up his fork, and began to eat.

Clancy watched. There was egg in the corner of Bobby's mouth, and when he drank, a little coffee dripped into his lap. He saw Bobby bite the inside of his mouth as he moved the egg whites around the plate. Bobby's hands were puffy like a small child's, puffy and soft on top, his nails dirty like he'd been playing all day and didn't have time to wash.

"After you're done, we'll go by the office and get your stuff. You can stay with me for a while."

Bobby put his fork down. He wanted to look up, but he couldn't. He put his elbows on the table and held his face in his hands while tears ran down his cheeks.

Chapter 19

Kate looked down at Little Green Bear on her nightstand, now safely in her apartment, and remembered all the times she had sewn him back together, all the repairs to his button eyes, all the times he had been in Danny's young arms and beside him in his dreams. Having Little Green Bear back had upended Kate. In her eagerness to punish herself, she had put her sadness aside like it was a trifling matter.

In the hospital, Carrie Goodwill had asked Kate if she had given any thought to what she wanted to do. "About your husband and son, that is."

Kate ignored the question at first. The second time her social worker asked her, Kate said, "I'm not ready to think about that."

At Kate's next appointment, one of the hospital chaplains was sitting in Carrie Goodwill's office. "A ritual often helps those who are left behind," he said. Kate imagined being left behind at the bus station, her husband and son leaving on vacation without her. "It can help you get some closure." He spoke in velvet tones.

"Do you have any religious affiliation?" he asked.

"No," said Kate.

"Any particular beliefs?"

"No," said Kate.

The chaplain looked discouraged as he shifted his weight from one hip to the other. "It might not matter to you right this very moment with all you've been through, but in the future you might be thankful that…"

"Thankful?" was all Kate said, and the three of them sat awkwardly for a long moment until Carrie Goodwill suggested that they meet again at a better time.

In the end, Kate decided that cremation was what she wanted to do. If Mitch was right, then there was no need for bodies, boxed and planted. No need for calling hours and lines of mourners waiting to tell her how sorry they were for her loss. The social worker and chaplain supported her decision; they told her it was a good step, a first step on the road to recovering from her loss. She listened to them. She nodded her head, though what they were saying made little sense to her. They spoke as if the future were coming quickly and that she had better be prepared for life and all that living in the wake of loss entailed.

The funeral director smelled of cologne and alcohol. His hair was slicked back, the part ruler-straight. He had a broad smile and an FM radio voice, but his eyes looked weary. He wore a blue suit with grey pin stripes, white-on-white striped shirt, French cuffs, navy tie with small white polka dots, tie tack. He had mud on his shoes. When he spoke, Listerine filled the air.

"Would you like a private viewing before cremation for invited family and friends? Or perhaps just a viewing for yourself? Even with cremation," he explained, "family members often like to have a final few moments with their departed loved ones before they are cremated, to see them as in life one more time."

He would accompany the remains to the crematorium. It would take time for the remains to be "processed," and then they would be returned to the funeral home or mailed directly to her if she preferred. She thought of two boxes, Mitch and Danny, sitting on a shelf at the post office, waiting to be sorted and delivered.

The funeral director, Mr. Campbell, leaned forward in his chair, elbows on his knees, hands folded. He finished what he had to say and waited. Kate appreciated this about him. He didn't need to fill the air with extra words to compensate for her silence. He had something to say, said it, and was done.

She bowed her head and rubbed her cheek with the palm of her hand. She looked up again at Mr. Campbell. He smiled. Not the broad have-I-got-a-deal-for-you smile, but a halting smile.

"Mrs. Duncan, I can't imagine what you're going through. It must be awful."

"I can hardly imagine it myself, Mr. Campbell," she said. They sat for another moment. He shifted his feet but didn't get up, didn't leave. She ran her fingers through her hair. She took another breath.

"I don't think I want a viewing."

"Are you sure?"

"I'm not sure of anything right now. But I don't think I want to see them like that."

"Okay, then," said Mr. Campbell.

A few days later, there was a message on her phone that the remains had arrived at the funeral home and that she could either pick them up or the funeral director would mail them to her. She wanted to call back, but didn't; later in the evening, she picked up a pen to leave herself a note to call him, but then thought it wasn't necessary, so she went to bed convinced that she would call the next day. The following day she forgot again and the next as well, and so it went. She stood at her register telling herself to call when she went on break. When her break came, she sat alone in the locker room, phone in one hand, Diet Coke in the other. Finally she put the phone back in her locker.

How could two lives fit into the same size canisters as the sugar and flour above her stove?

She carried the funeral parlor's phone number with her everywhere she went. She put it on a Post-It and stuck it to her dashboard. She memorized it. She just didn't call it. He left another message and another.

It was a Friday when she finally called. She left work a few minutes early, stopped at Walmart, bought some gas, came home, unpacked her bags, and stared at the white phone on the wall for a long time. Finally she dialed the number. She got the answering machine. She told the machine that she would come by to pick them up the following week. And then she hung up, lay down on her bed exhausted, and slept until morning.

It would have been easier to have had them mailed. But the thought of them being handled by strangers who were sorting Lillian Vernon catalogues and electric bills and *People* magazines and letters addressed to someone's Aunt Mary was too much. No, she would go to the funeral home, pick Danny and Mitch up, and bring them home.

That's where she was heading when she opened the door that morning, the morning when Clancy was waiting in the parking lot.

Clancy was older than she, maybe by a dozen years, although she didn't ask. He was quiet, unlike Mitch, who filled the air with talk and laughter. He sat at the kitchen table, his jacket still on, shifting his weight uncomfortably. She put water and coffee in the coffeemaker and watched until the hot brown liquid began to flow. She poured two mugs and put one in front of him. She apologized for not having anything else to offer him. He nodded as if to say this was plenty. She sat down in the chair opposite him, smiled, and took a sip.

"How long have you been living here?" asked Clancy.

"Not long at all," said Kate.

"I've been to the dealership next door, but I never noticed these apartments."

He asked if she had a job yet and she explained her circumstances. He shook his head. She looked down at her cup, watched the steam curl, blew on it, and took another sip. She looked at him again.

"I hope I'm not keeping you from anything," said Clancy. "I wasn't really thinking when I decided to come. You looked like you were getting ready to go somewhere."

"That's okay. I can do it another time," said Kate.

Chimney Bluffs

Chapter 20

Clancy stood in front of the bathroom sink. There was a swath of shaving cream on the mirror; wet towels were piled in the corner by the bathtub; stubble formed a ring around the sink; toothpaste stuck to his palm when he opened the medicine chest. Such was life with Bobby after the first week.

"Hey, Clancy! You want some eggs or something?"

Clancy lathered up, took out the double-edge razor, and drew it slowly from the base of his right sideburn over the slope of his jaw and down his neck, smooth as a downhill skier. He inspected his work with his index finger.

"Found them! You want coffee?"

Clancy stretched his upper lip across his front teeth, clamping it in place with his lower lip, and then carefully shaved the delicate skin beneath his nose.

"Hey, Clancy? Where's the coffee?"

Clancy swished the razor in the soapy water and wiped the steam from the mirror. He studied his half-shaved face, the lines at the corners of his mouth, the creases on his forehead. He looked into his eyes. They were ready for the day. His mouth was a straight line, almost smiling.

"Found it!"

Clancy soaked a towel in hot water and buried his face in it; the startling heat sent a shock down his spine, then he settled into the soothing, dreamlike warmth. He leaned forward, his elbows on the edge of the sink. He breathed in the heat.

"Clancy! Your eggs are getting cold and this coffee's turning into mud!"

"I'm coming; I'm coming, for God's sake!"

It was raining hard when Clancy and Bobby left for Chimney Bluffs. The highway glistened and swished as each semi passed in the opposite direction. It was cold but humid. Both men were sweating in their winter coats. Bobby rolled his window down. Clancy turned on the defrost as his side of the windshield began to fog. The trails would be muddy troughs today. Wouldn't be many visitors. Just a few hearty locals who came to the Bluffs no matter the weather. They thought the park was just for them, and they resented the intrusion of families with their portable grills and teenagers with their thoughtless noise and college students with their drugs and loud music; mostly these intruders made a mess and left it behind, never appreciating the beauty of the place.

At first Clancy didn't understand the hold that Chimney Bluffs had on the natives, but in time, he did. It took hold of him, too. Every day the headlines screamed; every day things seemed to get worse in the world; every day the news made your head ache; every day there seemed to be less promise in the world than there was the day before. But the Bluffs never changed. Of course, they eroded and trees tumbled and changes had to be made to accommodate the risks that nature created. But in another sense, it never changed. It was there longer than one thousand generations of Briscos and would be there for at least one thousand generations more. There was comfort in those majestic spires, the way they stood at attention day in and day out, as if responding to some call of duty.

On that morning when he had made his tragic discovery, part of him worried that the Bluffs would be changed forever by what had occurred at its peak and at its base, that somehow the basic nature of the place would crumble, so extraordinary was the assault on its integrity. He startled awake the very next day having dreamt that the Bluffs had been swept away in the night, erased, forgotten. He was relieved when he glimpsed its peaks that morning, so much did he need to know that something could withstand what he could not. The Bluffs remained steady, though he wavered; the Bluffs remained stalwart, though he doubted.

There was the occasional, undefended moment when he wondered if anything lasted, if anything could weather life the way the Bluffs weathered time. He thought of Darlene, how they had missed the point, how they hadn't understood that the life they could have borne was what mattered; instead, they played a game and nothing more. It would help to know this when you arrive in the world. It would help to know that, if you aren't careful, most of what you'll do in life will be wasted time, will be a bunch of nothing.

He had met the woman from the beach, the one whose eyes were still as death, the one whose matted hair had covered her cheeks, the one whose husband and son lay beside her. It had been simple that morning at the base of Chimney Bluffs. It had been easy to stand over her, to judge her, to hate her. The woman on the beach wasn't really a person, after all. She had no past, no future, no flesh and blood, no laughter, no tears, no sighs too deep for words. She was just a punctuation mark, a period at the end of a cruelty. It was easy and it was clear: What she had done was unspeakably wrong; he had every right to say whatever he wanted to say.

It was different, though, standing face-to-face with Kate Duncan, who, indeed, was a flesh and blood person whose face flushed in the sunlight, whose eyes were coffee brown, whose body grimaced, and whose hands were lined and dry and sorry. When he gave her the stuffed bear that she called Little Green Bear, he could see a fault open in her, so deep was her sadness.

He was convinced that Kate Duncan understood the importance of time, because she had seen it dissolve and disappear in the most chilling way; yes, she knew how precious time was; she knew that time sustained us, lifted us above the teeming waters, made everything possible, and she knew, as well, that it was no more permanent than the bottom end of a single breath.

"It's God awful out there today," said Bobby, leaning forward and looking up at the grey sky. Bobby opened the lid on his Dunkin' Donuts coffee. When his hand slipped and he scalded his finger, he shook it as hard as he could. He stuck his finger in his mouth, and then he shook it some more.

"Jesus, there ought to be a law about this." Clancy looked across at Bobby, who was still occupied with his throbbing finger. His Yankee's hat sat sideways and his Nikes were unlaced. His flannel shirt must have been in a ball for a month to have perfected the deep creases that zig-zagged its surface like a road map to nowhere. His hands were just a little stained and his clothes smelled musty. His Grateful Dead t-shirt barely covered his bulging middle. Bobby was getting doughy, no doubt about it. Clancy had written Bobby off at first, like he was just some dumb kid who didn't have a clue. But when Bobby told his story, Clancy took a second look. The real problem with Bobby was that he was unfinished, like a cabinet that had never been squared correctly or sanded smooth or stained properly. Whoever started the project had given up and had sent him out into the world as an odd collection of poorly fitting pieces.

"Wow, that stings like crazy," said Bobby.

Clancy looked at Bobby, deadpanned. "May have to amputate."

Bobby looked at Clancy. "What are you talking about?"

"Injury like that's pretty serious; might have to cut it off…all the way up to your mouth if you don't stop complaining."

Bobby studied Clancy's face for a clue. Clancy looked back at the road and then smiled. Bobby started laughing.

"You son-of-a-gun, you sure had me going!"

Clancy wasn't sure why, but it felt good having Bobby in the house. After Darlene left, he had continued to clean all seven rooms, keeping things in order, trying to make it a home. Soon, though, it didn't make sense to keep all the rooms open, so he turned off the heat in the upstairs bedrooms and converted the front sitting room into a bedroom, thus reducing the house by half. Even though it would have made sense, he couldn't get rid of the place. It was where he and Darlene had started; many of his own dreams still lingered there.

Funny thing about living alone, you don't notice what it's really like until someone else clutters up your loneliness with theirs. Suddenly you see it for what it is—visits to Walmart to avoid going home, pulling up to a house that is unlit, TV dinners with Katie Couric, watching late-night infomercials because going to sleep is impossible. When this makes you feel uneasy, you're still okay, because you know it's out of the ordinary, but when this feels normal, you have crossed the line, you have entered the world of one. Bobby, sleeping on the couch, must have gotten up five times the previous night. All the noise out in the living room annoyed Clancy, but it also made him feel alive.

"Hey, where do you want to go for lunch?" said Bobby.

"Jesus, Bobby, is that all you think about? How to fill that gut of yours?" said Clancy.

Bobby thought about this. "Yeah, I guess it is." They both laughed. "No, really, Clance, where would you like to go for lunch? My treat. I mean, you took me in, man; I want to at least buy you lunch. It's not much, but…where would you like to go?"

Clancy was about to say it wasn't necessary, but the look in Bobby's eyes made him think better of it. "Okay, well, how about McDonald's?"

"No, Clancy, I want this to be special." Bobby thought for a minute. "How about Friendly's?"

Clancy smiled. "You are a high roller, Bobby."

Bobby's expression turned serious. He cleared his throat. "Well, today's kind of special. I want to thank you."

Clancy put both hands on the steering wheel and settled his gaze on the pavement ahead. Bobby shifted in his seat and turned on the radio.

"Love their fishamajig sandwich," said Bobby.

Chimney Bluffs

Chapter 21

Several days after seeing Kate, Clancy read in the paper that Danny Duncan's autopsy report had come back and that he had died of meningitis shortly before the incident at Chimney Bluffs. He also read District Attorney Sewell's comment that he had "no intention of pressing any charges against Mrs. Duncan" and that "living with the whole thing would be punishment enough." He wondered if they had needed to include the DA's comment, although he had felt the same way when he came upon her that morning.

Later that day, Clancy drove to the Wegman's, where Kate Duncan worked, but she wasn't there. He drove by her apartment, but her car wasn't in the lot. He picked up his phone a couple of times, but couldn't bring himself to call her, even though they had talked about getting together again. He wondered if she had meant it, or if she was just being polite. In spite of his doubts, Clancy found himself in her parking lot again the next day after work. This time her car was there and lights were on in her apartment. He knocked on her door and listened for movement but heard none. He waited a full minute, was about to knock again, but thought better of it. As he turned to leave, the door opened. At first he thought he had knocked on the wrong door. Although she was petite, Kate Duncan looked like she had shriveled to a memory of herself since the last time he had seen her. Her eyes were dark clouds, and her clothes hung loose as if from a wire hanger.

"I'm sorry," he said. "Is this a bad time?"

Kate raised her cheeks as if to smile. "No, it's okay." She opened the door and Clancy walked in. "I have some coffee; would you like a cup?"

"Okay," he said.

Kate motioned for him to take a seat at the table in the dining area. She reached for two mugs from the dish drainer. She went to press the button on the coffeemaker. Then her arms fell to her side and she began to cry.

"Is there anything…?" asked Clancy.

"It's the coffee…"

"What?"

"It's at least a day old," she said. She leaned against the refrigerator and looked at the empty mugs as if she had no idea how to fill them.

Clancy got up and walked to her side. "Look, why don't you sit down and I'll make some fresh." Clancy smiled at her, but she wasn't looking. She stood in the middle of the kitchen examining the mugs in her hand. "Really, why don't you sit down and relax."

She put the mugs back in the sink and took a seat. She ran her hands through her hair and rubbed her face hard, as if trying to erase all the lines. "Thank you."

"Don't mention it," said Clancy. He put a filter in the basket, poured the water into the coffeemaker, and finally the coffee. He pressed the button, and both waited for the coffeemaker to announce the completion of its work. Clancy filled the mugs.

"Do you want anything in yours?"

"Black is fine."

He walked to the table, put one mug in front of Kate, the other on the table in front of his chair. He sat, sighed, and looked at her weary face. A roaring silence followed, twisting his insides and causing him to sweat. He picked up his coffee, took a large gulp that burned the lining of his throat. He set the mug down again. Kate had yet to touch hers. "Would you rather have something else?" he said. "Let me know, and I'd be glad to fix you anything you want."

She looked at him as if she just realized he was there. She turned slightly in her chair, placed her elbows on the table, the mug cupped in her hands. "No, this is fine. Thank you. I'm sorry that I'm not..."

"No need to apologize."

Kate put her mug to her lips, but it was hard to tell if she drank any of the coffee. Clancy gulped and spoke again. "I wanted to tell you how sorry I was. I mean, about your son. I didn't know he had been so sick." He waited as his words registered with Kate, her face turning red, her eyes moistening again. "I don't want to upset you. I just wanted to say how sorry I was."

"You read the paper," she said.

"Yes."

"So did I."

Clancy watched as Kate Duncan crossed her legs and tucked her foot behind her ankle. She ran her fingers through her hair again, the ends loose as string. "Don't be sorry," she said, her eyes hollow, her mouth open slightly. "There's already enough…sorry."

"But I am," said Clancy, to himself as much as to her. "I *am* sorry. I am sorry that you went through all of this. I am sorry that you were there for me to find. I'm sorry that I didn't know what I was doing." Clancy looked at his hands, sweat rising in his palms. He looked at Kate again. Her eyes were hazy and soft. "I wish that I could do something…"

"You brought me Little Green Bear, Danny's favorite thing," said Kate.

"He was there in the mud that morning, and I picked him up and thought of all the little kids who leave their favorite toys behind. We find them all the time. We put them in a barrel at the main office, and when no one comes for them, we throw them out." Clancy cleared his throat. "But I put him in my pocket and after…after everything, I kept him there."

Kate wiped her eyes with the backs of her wrists. She stood and took her mug to the sink, where she poured the remaining coffee. Clancy froze. He turned his head to look at her from the corners of his eyes, wanting to read her face, but she had her back to him. He waited for her to speak, and when she didn't, he stood as well, preparing to leave, believing his visit had been a mistake. "I was going to the funeral home," said Kate.

"I'm sorry, what was…?"

"I was going to the funeral home that day when you first came to visit. You had asked me if I was going somewhere. I was going to the funeral home, or at least that's what I told myself. I have gone to my front door many times, determined that I would go. That was one of the few times I even opened it."

Clancy sat down again.

"They're there waiting for me to come get them."

"Excuse me, Mrs. Duncan…"

"Just call me Kate. Only the hospital people called me Mrs. Duncan."

Kate took a deep breath as if she had to rewind in order to go forward. Clancy was still.

"Danny. And Mitch. I was on my way to the funeral home to get them." Her eyes fell. "It seemed like the right thing to do, cremation. But I hadn't thought about…" Kate placed a hand over her mouth.

Clancy's back stiffened. He sat bolt upright.

"There are two canisters waiting for me. One with Danny inside, and the other with Mitch. Everything I ever loved."

Clancy stood. "Kate. I can't imagine…"

"I know I have to go; I know I have to get them, but I can't bring myself…" Kate's lips quivered as her voice faded. "The district attorney was right," she said. "I know he was right." She looked up briefly at Clancy. "You know it, too."

"I don't think I know anything anymore," said Clancy.

He looked at Kate's hands then, her fingers long, her nails gone. They were the hands of someone who had held everything she had ever wanted. And now they were empty. They were empty, but clutching nonetheless.

"They call them cremains," said Kate, the corners of her mouth turned up in an almost-smile, her voice an echo. "Did you know that? I didn't." She rubbed her hands slowly together, as if feeling them for the first time. "There are names for everything. Someone must spend all their time thinking up names for things that no one wants to name."

Clancy felt a fist-like knot in his stomach that grabbed at each breath. Kate's brown eyes were wide now, wondering, asking.

"I just can't bring myself to go," she said with a fading smile.

Clancy stepped forward as if to catch her if she fell.

"But that's where I was going. If you wanted to know."

Clancy tried to swallow. He reached out with one hand but then let it drop. "I'll go with you," he said.

Kate's face twitched as he spoke. "Thank you, but no," she replied, gently but without hesitation. Her face was empty as the sky.

"You shouldn't have to do this by yourself."

With this, Kate straightened her shoulders, as if coming to attention. Her mouth drew taut and her eyes were tired but determined.

"No, this is something I should absolutely do by myself."

Clancy backed his truck away from the apartment and headed for the exit. But before he reached the street, he pulled over and sat, staring in the rearview mirror at a battered car with no hubcaps and tires that looked nearly flat. It was another fifteen minutes before the lights in Kate's apartment went out and Clancy headed home.

Chapter 22

Bobby was surprised that Clancy's house didn't look like Clancy at all. There was an antique-looking coat rack in the entryway and a flowered runner on the wood floor leading to the living room. The couch had ruffles across the bottom, and there were two rocking chairs, one with a large red cushion, at either end of the sofa. There were bookshelves with knick-knacks and two floor lamps with curlicued feet. The kitchen linoleum was worn in places from foot traffic, and the kitchen tablecloth was torn in one corner. The place smelled old and worn, but welcoming as toast.

"Darlene's doing," said Clancy with a shrug.

Bobby had never set foot in Clancy's house before. And he had never thought he would. He had hoped they would become friends when they started working at the bluffs, but that just hadn't happened, no matter how hard he tried. After a while, Bobby just decided Clancy was his friend even if there wasn't any evidence to support it.

"Hi, Clance. How's it going, buddy?" he'd say in the morning. More often than not, Clancy would grunt, finish the morning paper, and then go about his business, Bobby following close behind. Clancy never said much. His face was solid as oak, difficult to read. Bobby decided that it wasn't because Clancy didn't like him; it was more that he was private and often caught up in his own thoughts, thoughts that Bobby assumed were much deeper than he could comprehend.

"What are you reading?" Bobby would ask.

"Just the paper," Clancy would answer, barely looking up. But it wasn't the kind of stuff Bobby read, which was usually limited to the sports page, the comics, and, when he was feeling lucky, the horoscope.

"Hey, look at this, man; it says here that I might want to ignore responsibilities today, but the weather may change my mind." Bobby laughed out loud. "That's me, for sure. Says tonight I may teach a cooking class. How do they come up with this stuff?"

But Clancy would be busy reading about the war in Afghanistan or the budget problems in Albany. Clancy would sit there with a craggy, weathered, I-don't-give-a-shit look about him that Bobby both admired and feared.

You see, Bobby's skin was thin as wax paper; it didn't take much at all for him to tear—had always been like that. His father called him "baby-boy" even when he was mostly grown. After Mark died, Bobby was afraid of almost everything for a long time. Couldn't sleep without the light. Couldn't be at home alone. Couldn't sleep over at a friend's house. Couldn't stand up for himself in the gym locker room. Was afraid to ride a bike, swim in deep water, catch a baseball. For a long time, everything in the world seemed fragile, no matter what it looked like to everyone else.

Living with Clancy, even for a few days, made Bobby feel like he could be a different person. Not special, just better. Bobby wanted to be like everyone else, and as far as he could tell, Clancy was the best example of everyone else that he had met. Clancy shaved every morning and he washed his clothes twice a week and sometimes he made actual meals, and he always did the dishes—washed and dried them and everything. His house was kind of sorry-looking, but it was basically in order, even though it didn't need to be. I mean, it was just the two of them, so what did it matter? The fact that these things seemed important to Clancy, and other things, too, like getting to work on time and not taking shortcuts on the job, made Bobby think there was a whole new way to live, a more serious way, like things mattered.

It had never felt that way at home. They did all the regular things, but everything was done under a cloud. After Mark, you did things, but nothing really mattered, so after a while you did them less and less. Bobby's father used to go for walks, but then the walks were just to the mailbox, and finally he sat in his chair and Bobby's mother got the mail every couple of days. Bobby couldn't put it into words when he was growing up, but he understood in his skin that there wasn't any reason to try hard at life; there wasn't any reason to expect something better. How different things might have been if they had made it to the picnic that day, if those two cars had passed each other without any notice.

Bobby had tried an experiment once. He had driven down 104 and had turned the wheel just a notch toward the oncoming traffic, and in a few seconds cars were blowing their horns at him like crazy. Didn't take much to change everything.

Being around Clancy made Bobby think the steering wheel could be steadied again.

If Clancy knew how much he mattered, it would probably scare him off, so Bobby kept these thoughts to himself, and, in small ways, tried to show Clancy how much he meant to him. Like taking Clancy to Friendly's. And Clancy seemed to like it. He thanked Bobby when they slid into the booth, and his face looked lighthearted as he opened the menu and glanced up and down.

"Don't forget, this is on me," said Bobby. It made him feel older in a way, like he was the man and Clancy was the boy, and Bobby was doing something for him just because he wanted to.

"Got it," said Clancy, studying the menu.

"Make sure I get the check," he whispered to the waitress when she came with the water.

"Okay," was all she said, but she looked right at him, like he was in charge of the table.

Silence hovered as they waited for their meals. Bobby waved to the waitress, pointing to their coffee cups. She refilled them. Bobby put a couple packs of sugar and one creamer in. He stirred it and took a sip. His face flushed from the heat.

Clancy leaned his elbows on the table, folded his hands in front of his face, and watched the young family in the next booth. The mother cuddled an infant while the father struggled with a toddler, trying to get him to stay in his seat and eat the Cheerios that were scattered on the table in front of him. Bobby looked up at Clancy and then over at the young family.

"Kids," said Bobby.

"Yeah," said Clancy, continuing to watch.

The waitress approached, arms heavy with plates of food.

"You had the fishamajig, fries, Coke, and clam chowder, right?" she said as she laid the meal in front of Bobby.

"And you had everything else," she said with a smile, placing Clancy's burger, fries, and Coke in front of him.

The sound of chewing replaced the sound of silence. Bobby squirted ketchup on his fries. "Ketchup?" he said, sliding the bottle across the table.

"Thanks."

Bobby took another bite of his fishamajig and wiped the tartar sauce from the corner of his mouth. He looked at Clancy, who was still watching the little boy standing on the seat with his toy airplane, zooming it back and forth while his father watched closely, ready to grab him if he fell.

"Little boys are something, aren't they?" he said.

"Yes, they are," said Clancy.

Bobby took another bite. "Ever wish you had a kid?" said Bobby.

Clancy looked at Bobby. He finished chewing and wiped his mouth. "Yes."

"Awful lot of work," said Bobby.

"Yes, it is."

"And you never know what will happen," said Bobby. "I mean, I would be afraid of having a kid because no matter what you do, you can't keep things from happening, you know what I mean?"

"That's true," said Clancy, taking a drink of his Coke. Bobby had a grin on his face as he looked at Clancy.

"Never had the chance," said Clancy. He glanced again at the kids. "I guess it wasn't in the cards for me and Darlene." He picked up his burger. "I wish things had been different. But you can't change what you can't change."

"That's for sure," said Bobby. "Just like that little boy who died. Kind of like my brother, too, you know?" Clancy shook his head. "Like you said, things happen sometimes, and there's nothing you can do about it." Bobby sat back. "Seems odd, though, don't you think? I mean, people can be just living their lives, minding their own business, and then something happens." He shook his head and pulled at his jacket collar. He leaned forward again, about to pick up his sandwich. "I guess I don't know if I could be a father."

"I think I could have," said Clancy, reaching for a napkin from the dispenser.

"You do?"

"Yes, I do."

"Even with everything you know?"

"Yes. Somehow, that doesn't matter." He looked at the little boy again, who was studying his fingers and singing. His father leaned over and kissed him on the head. "Look at that," said Clancy, nodding to the neighboring family. "I could be wrong, but that looks like it's worth the risk."

"I don't know. So much can go wrong."

"Yes," said Clancy, "that's true." Clancy caught the little boy's eye and waved. The boy shrunk into his father's arm at first, but then waved back. Again Clancy wiggled his fingers at the boy, who smiled. Bobby watched Clancy, whose eyes had turned tender—his hand, gentle. Clancy winked at the boy. Bobby wiped his eyes quickly with his sleeve.

The waitress came by and removed all the plates and glasses, dropping the check in front of Bobby.

"Can I help with..." asked Clancy, reaching for his wallet.

"Your money's no good here," said Bobby with a laugh.

"Then thank you, Bobby." Clancy's face had a lingering softness as he smiled at Bobby.

"My pleasure, Clance. You know, I feel like you saved my life a little bit. I didn't have anyplace to go, and I fooled myself into thinking that it was okay. But..."

"Glad I could help you out, Bobby," said Clancy. "You'd have done the same thing."

"You think so?" said Bobby.

"Sure."

When they walked out of Friendly's together, Bobby felt about as much like a grown-up man as he'd ever felt before.

Chimney Bluffs

Chapter 23

The only thing that had changed in the weeks since Clancy's second visit to Kate was the weather. An early frost had killed off all the nuisance bugs and left the landscape glistening. Leaves fell like rain at Chimney Bluffs, adorning the ground like a rainbow. The lake was slate grey and the bluffs were hardening in the chill, preparing for the season of hibernation.

By the time Kate finished her shift, she had to scrape a thin layer of ice from her windshield before heading home. She started the engine and turned the heater on high, even though all it blew was cold air. She watched a tiny arc spreading across the inside of the windshield as the car began to thaw. The engine rumbled, sputtered, and stalled. She started it up again, and then again. She rubbed her hands together and leaned back in her seat, her right foot lightly feeding the gas. She closed her eyes and let the white noise of the fan drown out her thoughts. After a few minutes, she could feel her toes. She opened her eyes, and the windshield was clear. She pulled into traffic.

She was never eager to go back to the apartment in the late afternoon. Each evening was longer than the one before. The only furniture she had added was a blue bean bag chair that she bought at the Salvation Army. Every night she sat in her chair, feeling like a bird without an egg, watching her TV, which was perched precariously on a crate she had confiscated from Wegman's. Sometimes it worked, sometimes it didn't. The same was the case with the hot water.

Friends at work invited her out for drinks at the Oasis on Friday nights. She went once. But the longer she sat at the table, conversation swirling around her, the more she felt she should go home, even though there wasn't a home to go to anymore. She felt that, for Mitch and Danny's sake, she should leave. And never go back. She felt that way about a lot of things. She thought of driving to Rochester on a Saturday morning, just for something to do, and then she changed her mind. She pulled into the parking lot of the multiplex and then decided she didn't want to see the movie. She bought a book and didn't read it. She bought a new sweater and didn't wear it. All the new moments in her life were set aside like so many train cars in a rail yard, leaving only one track open—the one that led back to Chimney Bluffs.

The traffic ahead slowed to a crawl. Kate could see flashing lights at the next intersection. Someone was directing traffic around a fender bender. A man was yelling and waving his arms. A woman leaned against her car crying, another woman consoling her. Kate sighed as the traffic came to a stop again. She looked at her watch. She thought she would be able to get there by six-thirty.

"I look forward to seeing you," the funeral director had said brightly.

"Thank you," Kate had said.

She looked at Little Green Bear in the passenger seat beside her, now her constant companion. At the light, she reached over and picked him up. She sniffed what little was left of his fur. She closed her eyes, looking for Danny, but all she could see was Mitch's hand slipping away. She gasped when the driver behind her leaned on the horn. Her foot hit the gas and she lurched forward, almost crashing into the car in front of her.

A police officer came to her window. "Are you okay, ma'am?"

She was startled by his question, wondering how he knew.

"What?" she said.

"You almost hit that car. Gotta pay attention to what you're doing, okay, lady?"

"Okay," said Kate.

She pulled slowly forward, finally leaving the scene behind. She reached for Little Green Bear, who had fallen on the floor between her legs. She wiped him across her arm and laid him on the seat again, this time propping him up as if he were sitting, exactly as Danny had always done. The world forgets these little things too easily. The tide cleans the shore too quickly. Some things should never be forgotten. Some marks should last.

There was only one car in the Campbell Funeral Home parking lot. She pulled in beside it. She entered the front door to the smell of dying flowers. There was a lectern near the entrance, a small light over it, an open book with signatures and comments: "So sorry for your loss," "We'll miss him," "Never forget." She walked down the hall, large parlors on either side, one with an empty pedestal, the other with a closed casket. There were photographs on a large sheet of cardboard and a montage on the TV screen. Everyone in the pictures was smiling.

There were scenes of fishing and Thanksgiving and golf and one black-and-white photo of a little boy sitting on the front steps of a house; he wore shorts but no top, his soft belly, his placid face, his head turned upward and to the side as if looking to the future. "Hello! Hello, is someone there?" came a call. Kate slipped out of the room and back into the hall. A young man was heading toward the front door, but then turned and saw her. He smiled.

"You must be Mrs. Duncan," he said enthusiastically, as if greeting an old friend for the first time in years. He walked swiftly towards Kate, his hand extended. He looked and smelled like a younger version of the Mr. Campbell who had graciously sat with Kate as she struggled to decide what to do with Mitch and Danny.

"Hello," said Kate. "I have an appointment with Mr. Campbell. Reece Campbell."

"You must mean my father. He's Reece, Sr., and I'm Reece, Jr., although everyone calls me Campy. I'm afraid he's not here, but I'm sure I can help you." He let go of Kate's hand and gestured towards his office. "Why don't you come in?" The son had a tube of Pringles on his desk. He had pimples on his chin, and the sleeves on his brand-new suit were about a half-inch too long. "I am so sorry for your loss," he said, his voice turning syrupy. "Can I get you a cup of coffee? Or tea, soda, water?"

"No. I just…"

"I assume that you are…"

"Uh, I'm here to, I'm here…I have to pick up my son and husband."

"Pick up your son and husband," he said, his eyebrows raised slightly, one eye squinting as if he didn't know the answer to a question on *Jeopardy*. "Can you…"

"I was told that they were here," said Kate, fearing suddenly that they had been thrown out like day-old bread. Campy's expression didn't change.

"They were cremated…" said Kate.

"Oh, the cremains!" he said, the answer having come to him just before the buzzer. "I'm so sorry. You must think I'm an idiot. The cremains, of course." He stood. "Duncan, right? D-u-n-c-a-n, right? I'll be right back." She noticed that his shoes were black patent leather— not a scratch, not a hint of dirt. He offered a crooked smile and then left.

A clock on the wall behind the desk was the only sound remaining in the room. Kate breathed deeply, stretching her shoulders with each exhale. When Campbell, Jr. didn't return after several minutes, Kate stood and paced the room. There were plaques from the Chamber of Commerce, the Kiwanis, and the Elks on the wall; bereavement material stocked a bookshelf. Small bowls of mints and candy. And double-doors slightly ajar. Kate pushed them open. There before her were twenty or more caskets, tastefully lit, violins lilting in the background, displayed in an expansive showroom like so many shiny new cars at the auto show; the only things missing were leggy models waving their arms fluidly across the sleek hoods. When her mother had died, Kate had toured a similar showroom, and once the undertaker had realized she was not as financially set as he had assumed, he had led her to the back of the room where the wood boxes were—no finery, no angels, no nothing.

187

Kate heard the rhythmic heel-to-toe sound of the younger Campbell's footsteps and returned to the office. His faced beamed as he came through the door.

"Wow. At first, I couldn't find them anywhere, but when I looked in our books, I realized we'd had them a long time." He paused as if Kate might want to say something. "So finally I went back again and looked behind our new arrivals, and there they were!" He held two brown boxes, one under each arm, just large enough to hold five pounds of sugar or maybe five pounds of flour. He sat them on his desk and took a seat. Kate took in the boxes, surprised that they didn't look special at all. He opened each box, pulled out the canister, and checked the name and number on the side. "Can't be too careful," he said. Kate felt a wave of nausea. The canisters looked no different than the ones that filled row after row of shelves at her store.

He asked if there was anything else he could do for her. Kate looked at the floor. She wanted to ask if there was any way to get her son and husband back.

"What do people do…?" she asked.

"You mean with the cremains?" he said softly. Kate shook her head and the young man smiled. He explained that many mourners buy a cemetery plot for their loved one's cremains, or ashes if you prefer.

"Of course, one plot can hold several loved ones, depending on your preference. I know one family of six that bought a single plot, hoping everyone would fit." He chuckled at this. Kate's confused expression remained. He explained that they would set everything up for her with the cemetery, that she wouldn't have to do anything except bring the cremains for burial. If she'd like a small service, it could be arranged.

"How much would one plot cost?" she asked.

"They start as low as twenty-five hundred," he said, as if he had just made her day. This time Kate chuckled and the young man looked confused.

"There are other alternatives," he recouped. "Some folks put their loved one in a beautiful urn and place them somewhere in the house so that they have them always. Urns start as low as two hundred and fifty dollars." When Kate didn't protest, he went on. "We have children's styles, Mrs. Duncan, which might be nice for your son. Danny, right? We have urns shaped like lambs and baseballs and puppies and, of course, angels. I'm sure we could find one that fits your wishes." He stopped and smiled and waited, but Kate didn't speak. "Others," he continued, "scatter their loved one's ashes somewhere that was meaningful to the decedent, like a garden or the ocean or a forest, something like that."

"Thank you," said Kate, standing to leave.

"You're welcome," said the younger Mr. Campbell. "Feel free to call us if you need anything."

Kate carried the boxes to her car, where she put them on the front passenger seat, one on either side of Little Green Bear. She took them into the apartment and placed them on the table with the Big Apple snowball and the picture of Danny. When she got up in the morning, she couldn't bear to leave them behind, so she took them with her to work. They waited for her in the parking lot all day until she returned.

Kate didn't want to talk to them, but sometimes she couldn't help herself: "This morning we have to stop for gas" or "I've had such a day, you wouldn't believe" or "I'm here, don't worry." She'd put her hand on them when she rounded a bend, as if to make sure they were safe. She drove more slowly than she had before. She turned on the radio, not because she liked to listen, but because she knew how much Mitch and Danny liked country music. When she took them in the house, she carried them in a Wegman's shopping bag so they wouldn't look conspicuous. Sometimes she sat them on a pillow beside the bed at night.

One Monday morning when the alarm went off, Kate reached over and patted both boxes and then lay in bed another twenty minutes before getting up.

On Tuesday, she rolled over and accidentally knocked Danny off the bed; she jumped up and grabbed the canister, patting it; she kissed it with tears in her eyes and said she was sorry, then she went back to sleep, unable to get up again.

On Wednesday, she startled from a deep sleep when the phone rang. It was her boss. She acted surprised and told him she was sick and apologized for not calling in. She was so upset that he told her not to worry at all, to take care of herself and get better as soon as she could.

On Thursday, she made it to the front door, but went back into her bedroom when she realized she had forgotten the canisters; she put them in a shopping bag, went to the front door again, opened it, looked at the grey morning, and called in sick once more. Later, she got in the car with the boxes and the bear and drove west on 104 the whole way to Lewiston, just north of Niagara Falls. She stopped at a McDonald's there and bought a Diet Coke.

"Just got back from Toronto," said the customer in front of her.

"Talk funny up there, *eh*?" said the teenager behind the counter. They both laughed.

"We shouldn't laugh, you know; they say Canada is the best place in the world to live."

Kate sat in her car sipping her Diet Coke. She put her hands on the canisters and spoke to Little Green Bear. "I wonder what it's like to live in the best place in the world?"

The next day she called in sick again. She drove to the Carousel Center in Syracuse. It was a busy day at the mall. Williams-Sonoma was featuring a class on grains and legume preparation; the Girl Scouts were selling cookies; Mickey and Minnie were shaking hands with kids and parents alike outside the Disney Store; there was a blood drive at the Center Atrium. She bought a pretzel at Aunt Annie's, found a seat by a fountain, and looked up at the glass ceiling over six stories above her.

"Hey, look at the bag lady," said a teenage boy, nudging his friend.

"Hey, lady, what you got in the bag?"

Kate looked up to see who they were talking to when she noticed one of them pointing at her. She looked down at the canisters she held at her feet, now triple-bagged to hold the weight, a stuffed bear hanging over the side, her fingernails gritty, her knuckles dry and cracked.

The next day she drove to Chimney Bluffs. There were only a few cars in the lot. There was a fine, heavy drizzle, like fog, blowing across the lake in sheets, the wind tearing the last of the leaves from the awkwardly bent trees lining the shore. Kate parked in the middle of the lot. People came and went, scurrying with coats over their heads; others were soaking wet but didn't seem to care; everyone was going somewhere, living their lives. She looked at the tables on the grassy knoll where they had often picnicked. She felt calm, the calm that comes when there is nothing inside.

There were days she called in sick but didn't go anywhere. Didn't get up, didn't get dressed. And there were days she didn't call in at all. Her boss tried to check on her, but she stopped answering the phone. Soon the phone stopped ringing.

Kate had thought her mother was pathetic when she stopped living after Kate's father had run off:

"There's no point going on," she'd say. "You might as well accept the truth now."

"Not me," Kate would say. "There's got to be more than this."

"Ha," her mother would say with a snarl in her voice. "Wait and see, Katy girl, wait and see. Try all you want, but in the end, life's a losing proposition."

Kate would sneer back at her mother, but she never left her, and she never forgot. Now she understood how easy it was to stop, how easy it was to give up.

In the late dusk light, Kate sat at her kitchen table, two canisters in front of her. She picked up Little Green Bear and then walked into her bedroom. There was a crinkled slip of paper beside the lamp on the nightstand. It had lain there for days upon days. Several times she had picked it up, about to throw it in the trash, and then had put it down again without looking at what it said. This time she picked the paper up and looked. There was a phone number on it, printed in faded black ink. She went to the phone hanging on her kitchen wall and picked up the receiver, her hand trembling. She looked at the scrap of paper as she slowly punched in each number. When she was finished, she dropped the paper to the floor and waited while it rang over and over again.

Chimney Bluffs

Chapter 24

"Hello," said Clancy, but there was no response. "Hello," he said again, this time a little annoyed. All he could hear was breathing, but for some reason he didn't hang up. For some reason he knew. "Hello? Is that you?" No answer. "If that's you, it's okay. It's okay that you called." He waited. She sighed but still didn't speak. "I was thinking about you; I mean, I was wondering how you were, how things went with…everything. But I wasn't sure I should call. So, it's okay that you called me." He waited again. "How are you? Are you okay?"

Kate took slow, deep breaths, but she couldn't speak. She always lost her voice when she started to cry. Her mother had told her she'd better get over that or she'd never be able to stand up for herself; people would run right over her as soon as they saw the waterworks and knew she couldn't speak up for herself. "Never give them the satisfaction," she had said. Kate tried again to speak.

"I don't know how I am. I don't know anything right now. I'm here on the floor. I don't know what to do."

Clancy's throat went dry. He wanted to say something helpful, but he couldn't find the words. He tried to clear his throat as he listened to her crying in his ear. Darlene was right; he was no better at talking now than he had been when they were together. He could feel a rising frustration, red across his face. "I'm coming over," he said.

"Uh huh," she said, but he had already hung up.

When Clancy pulled into the parking lot, he could see a faint light in Kate's kitchen. He opened the front door without knocking. Kate was standing in the kitchen, as if she had been stationed there. Beside her on the counter were two boxes and one green bear. Clancy knew immediately what the boxes were. He started to speak, but she interrupted.

"Did you know that I didn't jump? Did you know that?" said Kate, her voice barely a whimper. "The doctors figured it out quick when there weren't any bruises, when there weren't any broken bones. But most people never gave it much thought, the fact that I was alive. I was in the hospital so long, they must have figured I'd gotten hurt bad." Kate's arms hung at her side. "You saw me lying there. You must have thought I had jumped. You must have. I mean, I was there, wasn't I? I was there at the bottom of the cliff, lying on the beach beside my husband and my little boy. And you were the first one to find me." She looked past Clancy, at the wall behind him. She was ramrod stiff as if she were in a witness box giving testimony. Kate placed one hand on the counter to steady herself. "I was going to jump. I was. But I couldn't."

"I understand," said Clancy.

"No. You don't. You think you do, but you don't. You think I wanted to live and so I didn't jump. But that wasn't it at all. I didn't want to live." Clancy was barely breathing. "I didn't. But when I stepped out to the edge, I became afraid—afraid that every memory of

Danny would die with me. That in no time at all, everyone would forget. It would have been like he had never been alive. But he had. He had four years. And that counts for something." Tears caressed Kate's expressionless face. "He was beautiful. His voice had the sweetest lilt and his hands were fat and his face was round and he had his own little dreams. And I loved him. No one should be forgotten so quickly." Kate wiped her eyes with the tips of her fingers. "So I walked down the trail to the parking lot and then up the beach to the base of the cliffs. And there they were," said Kate, pointing as she spoke. "So still. I loved them both so much. I lay beside Danny and listened to the water and waited for the sun. Someone has to remember. And someone has to pay."

"Pay?" said Clancy.

"Danny was sick, and I waited too long to call the doctor. And he died." She spoke with unsettling calm. The story defined her now; it was her signature, her scarlet letter. She wore it without flinching.

Clancy's lips parted, and he raised his hands in gesture, but he didn't speak.

"I'm sorry. You've never had a child," she said. "Someone has to pay."

Clancy lowered his arms. She was right. He didn't understand. He couldn't imagine what it was like to lose a child. But even worse, he couldn't imagine what it was like to have loved so dearly, so deeply. "I don't know that kind of love," he said, speaking to the floor. "I've never known anyone who loved anything that way—I mean, so much." He raised his head slightly to see if she was looking at him. Her face was grey and her brown eyes looked scuffed. His shoulders rolled forward, temporarily at ease. Clancy walked over to the counter, picked up the boxes and the bear, and then turned to Kate. She was still looking forward, barely breathing. "Come with me," he said.

It was raining and the windshield wipers' hypnotic rhythm was welcome. Kate sat with the boxes and the bear in her lap, a few plastic shopping bags full of clothes at her feet. She glanced at Clancy as he turned a bend, checking to see if this was indeed the same person who had stood over her on the beach. Clancy clenched the steering wheel and drove slower and more carefully than ever before. He didn't once look at his passenger. "A friend of mine, a co-worker actually, is staying at the house for a while," said Clancy. "He may not be there, but I wanted you to know. He's kind of young in some ways."

Clancy had developed a grudging affection for Bobby. He grew on Clancy like a vine that had never had never before had anything to grip onto. But in many ways, Bobby was still as unformed as a newborn. You just never knew what was going to come out of his mouth. Bobby was pretty clear how he felt about "that woman" and all the trouble she had caused. Complained all the time about the little bear and how holding on to it was going to ruin Clancy. He was more than a little happy when Clancy got rid it. When he found out that Clancy had met her, he asked Clancy what he thought of "that woman," but Clancy hadn't answered. Bobby shrugged, as if to say, "Good riddance."

"His name's Bobby," said Clancy.

"Okay," said Kate.

"Sometimes he rubs people wrong, but he doesn't mean to," he said, now looking at Kate to see if any of this was registering. "Like I said, though, he probably won't be there."

When Clancy pulled into his driveway, Bobby was standing at the front door waving. He bounded down the front steps and started running to the truck, and then he saw that Clancy had someone with him. He slowed to a walk and put his hands in his pockets. He nodded to Kate and winked at Clancy.

"I didn't know you'd be bringing home company," he said, louder than necessary. "Maybe I should go for a walk or something," he said, nudging Clancy in the ribs.

"Bobby, this is Kate," Clancy said, staring hard at Bobby, hoping he would get the drift.

"Hi there, Kate," said Bobby, opening the door for her. "Nice to meet you." Bobby was smiling ear to ear now. "I don't get to meet many of Clancy's lady friends."

"Jesus, Bobby, she's not a 'lady friend.' This is Kate, Kate Duncan," said Clancy, this time more forcefully, as if by turning up the volume he might get Bobby to understand.

"Okay," said Bobby. "So, hello, Kate Duncan." He stuck out his hand. Kate looked at Bobby from the corner of her eye. She took his hand gently and then let it go. Bobby grinned, but the look on Clancy's face told him that grinning wasn't what he should be doing. Clancy stared at Bobby and opened his eyes a little wider. All the muscles in Bobby's face went slack and his neck turned red. "Oh, *that* Kate Duncan," he said. He stuck his hand out again and then let it fall to his side. "I'm sorry. I didn't…"

"That's okay," said Kate.

The only sound in the room was a fly attacking a light bulb.

Bobby rubbed his hands on his pants. He looked at the bags and the two small boxes that lay in the entryway.

"What's all this?" he asked.

"Bobby," said Clancy.

"What? I'm just asking. All these bags and boxes." Clancy glowered at Bobby. Kate stood in the entryway, again at attention.

"Come on in," said Clancy, his face softening. Kate took ginger steps into the living room. She looked back at Clancy as if waiting for more directions.

"Bobby, would you mind taking Kate's things into the bedroom?"

"Yessir, boss, sir," said Bobby. He yanked at the bags and juggled the boxes.

"Just be careful, okay?" said Clancy.

"Whatever you say," said Bobby, stomping off to the bedroom. There he looked at the bags full of women's stuff. He held the boxes, one in each hand, and shook them. He carried them back to the living room.

"What's in the boxes?" he said.

Kate opened her mouth, but Clancy stepped forward. "Put those down!" said Clancy. His voice had a cutting, metallic edge to it, something Bobby hadn't heard in a while.

"Didn't mean nothing by it," said Bobby with a huff. He looked at Kate, whose face was wringing. Bobby put the boxes on the couch. Kate moved like a shadow across the room and took the boxes in her arms.

"I'm just saying, they're not yours," said Clancy.

"I know they're not mine," said Bobby. "You think I'm an idiot?"

"Stop it!" said Clancy.

"Don't tell me to stop it," said Bobby "What's going on, Clancy? Why are you doing this?"

Clancy spoke through clenched teeth. "This isn't the time, Bobby. I'll explain everything later."

"Maybe this isn't a good…" said Kate.

"Everything is fine," said Clancy, struggling to find a calming voice.

"Fine for you," said Bobby.

"Bobby!"

"Why are you doing this, man? What is she doing here?" Bobby pointed at Kate.

Kate carried the boxes into the bathroom and closed the door.

"What the hell are you doing?" said Clancy, squaring himself to Bobby.

"What the hell am *I* doing? What the hell are *you* doing?" Bobby rocked back and forth, his ears red, his breathing short.

Clancy drew in a deep breath and let it out. He pursed his lips and leaned one hand on the back of a rocking chair. He wiped his face with his other hand. Bobby's hands trembled.

"Bobby, just give this a rest. You and I can…"

"Don't tell me to give it a rest! You're the one who should give it a rest. What are you doing? Can't you just let it go? Why are you doing this? This isn't your mess; it's hers. Why bring it home?" he said.

Clancy didn't say a word. He took two steps towards Bobby and then waited, reloading. When Clancy spoke, his voice was laser-steady. "Bobby, who are you to tell me what I can and cannot do in my own house? Do I have to remind you that this is my house? You are my guest. Do I really have to remind you of that?" Clancy was leaning forward, his eyebrows raised, his lips taut. "I don't think I do, do I?"

Bobby could feel the heat radiating from Clancy's face while his own rage crumbled into cold ashes. *Don't tell me to leave*, he thought. *Not that*. He started to cry, but when he opened his mouth, the defiance was back. "You want me to leave? Go ahead, kick me out!"

"That's not what I said."

"I'm used to it! I've been there!"

"Bobby."

"Don't 'Bobby' me; you're not my old man." Bobby covered his face with his hands. Clancy reached for Bobby, but Bobby swatted his arm away. "Don't touch me! Don't you dare touch me!"

"Listen, Bobby, this is crazy, c'mon."

"Crazy?" said Bobby. "This is crazy? I'll tell you what's crazy. That's what's crazy," he said, waving his arm at the bathroom door. "And you should know it. I've told you a hundred times…"

"Stop it!" said Clancy as Bobby turned and ran to the front door, slamming it as he left.

Chapter 25

In the wake of Bobby's eruption, Kate had remained in the bathroom for another hour, wondering what she should do. When she finally came out, Clancy was standing in the hall waiting for her. "I should go," she said.

"Look…"

"No, really, I should go. You were being nice to me, I know. But it's clear that this isn't a good idea." Kate leaned against the doorjamb, her arms crossed.

"It will be okay," said Clancy, trying to convince himself as well as her.

"I don't know what okay is."

"Okay is okay, I guess," said Clancy, feigning a smile. "Look, it will work out."

Kate wanted to believe Clancy, but she didn't know his eyes well enough. "Watch the eyes," her mother had always said. "That's where the lies come from." Mitch's eyes didn't lie. It was just that sometimes Kate didn't like what they had to say.

"You know, when I called you, I didn't expect you to take me in like this. I didn't."

"I know."

"Then why did you ask me to come?" Kate was taken aback by her own question.

Clancy tilted his head to one side, hoping he could find an answer. He avoided her face and any expectation written upon it. "I didn't know what else to do," he said. When Darlene had walked out, Clancy hadn't said a word, hadn't raised a finger to stop her, even though he had desperately wanted her to stay. When the door had slammed shut behind her, he cleaned up the kitchen and put all the dishes away as if nothing had happened, as if the next day everything would go back to the way it was. "I didn't want to just leave you there in the kitchen. It would have been wrong."

"It would have been wrong?" echoed Kate, trying to solve the riddle before her.

"Yes, wrong."

"But why do you feel you need to do right by me? You don't know me. You don't owe me anything."

The wind caught the outside frame of the bedroom window, sending howls across the first floor.

"The wind," said Clancy. Kate waited.

"I think I do owe you," he said.

Before she could respond, Clancy turned to the refrigerator and then spoke again. "You haven't had anything to eat. If you don't mind eggs, I can at least make you some dinner."

Kate sat at the kitchen table and watched Clancy move fluidly from the refrigerator to the cupboard to the stove. With one hand he cracked three eggs into a shallow bowl, wiping his fingers afterwards on his pants. He poured a little milk into the bowl, added some salt and pepper, lit the burner, whisked the eggs, and tipped them into the pan, turning them slowly with a wooden spoon while she listened to the sizzle and breathed in the toast. Despite her ambivalence about being there, Kate thought she could sit in that chair for a long, long time, watching Clancy crack eggs and mix in salt and pepper and milk; she didn't even have to eat it; just watching someone else doing simple things would be meal enough.

Clancy brought the skillet to the table and spooned the eggs onto Kate's plate. He put the diagonally-cut wheat toast on the borders. He stepped back and, realizing he had forgotten coffee, took a mug from the cupboard and poured. He stood in the middle of the kitchen watching Kate nibble at the corner of her toast.

"Now. I owe you an apology," said Clancy, putting the skillet into the sink.

"I get it. He was upset. No need..."

"No, I don't mean about Bobby. Although I'm sorry for that as well." Clancy pulled a chair out from the table and sat down. Kate's eggs began to cool.

"Well, you don't need to apologize to me for anything," said Kate.

"I think you're wrong," said Clancy. The words rushed out too quickly. "I didn't mean to say you're wrong; it's just that..." Clancy looked at his feet, hoping to find some words. "I said some awful things to you that morning..."

"You don't have to say a thing about that," said Kate, putting her hands on the arms of the chair as if she were about to stand.

"But I *do* need to say something."

"Please don't," said Kate.

"I didn't know you. All I knew was what I saw on that beach, and what I saw made me think some things I shouldn't have thought. It made me feel like I was right to say anything I wanted to say. I was right to hurt you. In fact, that's exactly what I wanted to do." Clancy reddened as he spoke. Kate's head was bent now, her hands back in her lap.

"Look, I still don't know you well at all, but I think I know you some. And what I know is that you are hurting like no one I've ever seen before." Kate began to squirm in her seat as if it had caught fire. "And you are hurting because you gave yourself completely to your son and your husband; you spent everything you had, like nothing else mattered; you loved them in a way that I can't even…" Clancy shook his head. "And then you lost them. I mean, you lost it all and you lay on that beach with nothing left."

"Stop! Please stop. I can't listen to this," said Kate. "You can't pretend that I'm something I'm not." Clancy's mouth hung open. "The first thing you said was probably the truest—you don't really know me. If you did, you wouldn't be saying these things about me." She looked at Clancy, her eyes unblinking.

"Like I told you, the illness took my son in just four days. Four days. And I wasted one of them. I wasted it and with it, I wasted any chance that he might have had to survive. That's what I did." Kate took a breath and swallowed hard. "If it weren't for me, Danny and Mitch would still be alive, and I wouldn't be here in your house. We wouldn't be having this conversation. Maybe I'd see you at Chimney Bluffs when we were on a picnic. And you might say 'Hi' to us, and my son might say 'Hi' back and we might laugh because he was so cute, but we would just be strangers to each other, living our own lives." Kate stood, her back straight again. "I'm not the pitiful woman who has been wronged by life. I am the reason that the two people I love most in the world were found at the bottom of that cliff. Dead. It was me. I'm the one who should be gone, not them."

Clancy paused, looked at the eggs, and then looked at Kate. "But you decided to live. That has to count for something, doesn't it?" Clancy looked past Kate like he was trying to figure this out. "I mean, for some reason, you didn't kill yourself. No matter how you look at it, you chose to stay."

Kate couldn't look at Clancy. Her stomach was churning, and her legs and arms were weak. It was what she had feared most—being seen as noble, as a remarkable sufferer, as someone to be emulated because she had lost and she had endured.

Kate took a step towards the bedroom, then stopped. "You know why I didn't jump?" Clancy looked up but didn't speak. "I didn't jump because it would have been wrong of me to escape; it would have been wrong of me to have been relieved so easily of what I had done."

With these words, Kate ran out of breath. As she slowly tried to reinflate herself, she could see that Clancy's expression hadn't changed. He looked at her as if he still believed his own version of her story.

She didn't know what else to do, how else to convince him. His mind was set. She was moved by his determination, his insistence that she was someone other than who she was, and in spite of herself, she felt some measure of relief that Clancy seemed so blind. She tried to smile, but couldn't. It was dark out. She was exhausted.

"You have been so good to me. I thank you from the bottom of my heart. I really do. But right now all I want is a glass of water to take to bed with me. And then I'll be leaving in the morning."

Clancy took a glass from the shelf, turned on the spigot and let the water run cool, then filled the glass and handed it to her. "I'll see you in the morning," was all he said.

Chapter 26

Bobby worked out his anger at Clancy by stopping at the AM/PM Mini Mart, buying a twelve-pack of Molson, driving to the Chimney Bluffs parking lot, drinking the twelve-pack in rapid succession, throwing up on the dashboard, and falling asleep. He woke up a little after midnight and got out of the truck just in time to throw up again. He wobbled into the nearby woods and took a piss. Bobby sat on the front fender of his truck, the doors wide open to let in some fresh air. *Jesus, Bobby*, he thought. He heard the sound of someone pulling into the lot and turned in time to see a familiar truck. Bobby stood and then thought better of it and sat back down, this time on the pavement. He rubbed his eyes and looked away as Clancy closed the truck door and walked slowly towards Bobby, pebbles crackling under his shoes. The footsteps stopped, and Bobby could hear Clancy breathing. Bobby leaned forward and pushed himself up with his hands. His legs wobbled but held him. He still didn't look at Clancy.

"Bobby?" asked Clancy.

Bobby didn't answer. He wanted to disappear.

"Bobby?"

Bobby turned to Clancy, whose face was shadowed by the

streetlamp.

"Yeah," he said, haltingly.

Clancy stepped forward and leaned into the truck cab. "I like what you've done to the place," said Clancy.

"I do my best," said Bobby.

"Yes, you do. And yes, you did." Clancy's smile looked more like a grimace than he had intended.

Bobby leaned against the side of the truck, rubbing his eyes.

"My God," said Clancy, waving his hand in front of his nose.

"Like I said, I do my best." Bobby looked at Clancy, who had already found rags behind the seat and was starting to clean the dashboard. "You don't have to…"

"Jesus, Bobby, I'm doing it out of self-defense."

Bobby put his shoes on, threw his jacket over his shoulders, slid a stick of gum in his mouth, and threw the wrapper on the truck cabin floor. By then, Clancy had most of the dash cleaned. Bobby watched, embarrassed. "Look, Clancy, let me finish this up. It's my mess."

"Yessir, boss, sir," said Clancy.

The corner of Bobby's mouth pinched into his cheek as he looked at the running board. "Look, Clancy, I'll find someplace else to stay. You don't have to worry about me. Don't go by this," he said, gesturing to the truck. "I can take care of myself. Really."

"Uh huh," said Clancy, carefully wiping the gear shift and steering wheel. He dropped the rags on the pavement and wiped his hands on his jeans. He looked at Bobby from the corners of his eyes. Bobby looked like a little boy who had made a wrong turn and didn't know his way back home.

"Come back to the house," said Clancy.

"You're just doing this because I don't have any place to go. I appreciate…"

"That is true," said Clancy. "You don't have any place to go." He raised his eyebrows in agreement. "Look, Bobby, you can't live in a truck, and you can't go home. I've got a big house. Stay until you can go on your own terms."

"What about *her*?"

"What *about* her?"

Bobby shook his head disapprovingly. Clancy bit his lip.

"Bobby, you know what the inside of your truck looks and smells like?" Bobby looked at Clancy, a frown across his face. "Well, it's nothing compared to what her life is like right now. She's got nobody and nothing. And if she wants to stay, she stays. If she wants to go, she goes." Clancy shrugged his shoulders. "You've got to make your own decision. But for now, my door is open."

Chimney Bluffs

Chapter 27

Clancy didn't sleep much at all, and when he did, he might as well have been awake. He dreamed that he was standing over Kate as she lay on the living room floor. He couldn't open his mouth to speak, so he pounded hard on the floor with his hand, hoping that she would understand, but it only scared her. The harder he hit the floor, the more upset she got. He wanted to say that it didn't matter, that she would be okay. But even in the dream, he wasn't sure that would be the case.

He was brewing coffee when Bobby rolled off the couch and walked into the kitchen, looking sheepish. Clancy looked at him and then turned back to the coffeemaker.

"Do you want some coffee?" Clancy asked.

"Yeah."

Bobby stepped lightly across the kitchen floor. Clancy pulled a mug from the cupboard, filled it, and put it on the counter.

"There you go," he said.

Bobby picked up the mug and stood, waiting for directions.

"Have a seat," said Clancy.

Bobby pulled a chair out from the kitchen table and sat down. He sipped the coffee and put the mug down. A finch flew into the window over the kitchen sink. Clancy poured himself a cup and leaned against the refrigerator.

Bobby looked around. "Is she here?"

"Yes, she's here for now."

Bobby drank his coffee and watched Clancy put bread in the toaster. "Are we okay?" said Bobby.

Clancy pushed the knob on the toaster. He turned to face Bobby and took a sip of coffee.

"Yes, we're okay."

"Man," said Bobby, "I am so sorry. I don't know what got into me last night."

"Look, Bobby, it's forgotten," said Clancy. "At least by me." He said this as he looked past Bobby. Bobby turned, and Kate was standing in the bedroom doorway, her Wegman's bags in her arms.

"Morning," said Kate in a whisper, as if meeting a stranger. She hadn't realized that Bobby was back. "Am I interrupting…?"

"No, come in," said Clancy, walking towards her with his hands extended as if she might fall.

Bobby stood up suddenly, his chair screeching along the linoleum. "Good morning." He tried to smile.

Kate looked at Bobby, but didn't respond. Clancy poured Kate a cup of coffee and invited her to sit. She moved in a perfect arc around Bobby and sat at the table, mug in hand. Bobby sat down again, this time pushing his chair back a few feet from the table. Clancy stood. "I can offer you toast for starters," said Clancy, noticing his ring on the ledge above the sink and feeling for the circle on his finger that had finally disappeared.

"No, thank you," said Kate as she placed her bags on the floor beside her, watching to make sure that they didn't tip over.

"Clancy makes some mean toast," said Bobby, forcing a smile.

The corners of Kate's mouth worked on a grin but then grew weary. Bobby thought about his truck, how surprisingly warm it had been.

"Look, Kate," said Bobby.

"Bobby, maybe it's not..." Clancy began, but Bobby's searching eyes stopped him.

"I'm sorry. I am. I don't know what got into me, but..."

"It's okay," said Kate, looking over her shoulder, as if the refrigerator beckoned.

"No, really; it's not okay. I know that."

"Thanks," said Kate.

"'Cause you've been through a lot, I know. I mean your son and..."

"Really," said Kate "It's okay." This time the corners of her mouth succeeded. Bobby nodded.

It was quiet in the kitchen. Clancy opened the cabinet under the sink and tossed an empty coffee can into the trash.

Bobby noticed Kate's bags. "You're not going anywhere, are you? I mean, you're not leaving?"

Kate didn't answer.

"There's room for both of you," said Clancy. "If you'd like."

Kate studied Clancy's back, his rolled shoulders, his sagging jeans, his stockinged feet. His was a different sort of kindness. Her mother was kind when she wanted something. Mitch was kind when you wanted what he wanted. Clancy, as far as Kate could tell, was just kind. She had learned how to handle the first two, but not this one.

"You didn't really believe anything I told you last night, did you?" she said to Clancy. He turned as he wiped the previous night's skillet clean. He opened the bottom cupboard drawer and slid it back under several others. He tossed the hand towel onto the counter top.

"Not so much," he said.

Her arguments, her explanations hadn't mattered to him at all. Her words were not nearly as important as Clancy's perception of who she was.

"Blind, are you?" she said.

"Maybe. Or maybe you can't see a thing clearly when you're standing right on top of it. Maybe you can't see it clear until you look at it from one angle and then another."

Bobby looked on like a checkers player trying to make sense of a game of chess.

"You should stay," said Clancy. "You should stay, if only for a few more days. There's no reason for you not to. Just a place to stay until you're a little more on your feet. Then you can go and do whatever you want. There's no reason to be in a hurry."

Although Clancy was ready to counter Kate's next argument, when she didn't respond, he decided it was best to move on to something else, and by doing so, close the curtain on the question of whether Kate was staying or not.

"More coffee?"

"Yes," she answered.

Clancy poured her another cup. Bobby got up from his seat and walked to the sink, where he rinsed his mug. He turned as Clancy leaned over the table, pouring coffee into Kate's cup, as if he were pouring balm on a wound. She looked at Clancy as he poured, her eyes examining him, hoping he was who he seemed to be.

Chimney Bluffs

Chapter 28

"Okay, watch this," said Bobby, tapping Kate's arm. "Here comes the gay guy who's in charge. I love this guy! He always puts people in their place without them even knowing it. Watch!"

Bobby had introduced Kate to his favorite guilty pleasure, *Say Yes to the Dress*, which he watched religiously. The real draw for Kate, though, was watching Bobby argue with the families on the show, who were consistently overbearing and insensitive about their daughter's or sister's or whoever's selection of a wedding gown.

"Look at this! Look at her sister's face. I can't believe it! She should be telling her how beautiful she looks no matter what!"

Kate felt like she was sitting on the couch with an Irish setter puppy, full of unbridled enthusiasm and completely unaware of the broken dishes and furniture left in his wake. She looked at his beaming, clueless face and had to smile.

"Jesus, five thousand dollars for that! This time I agree with Grandma: It's too slutty."

Clancy stood in the hall, shaking his head.

"If they don't get the mom on board, she's never going home with a dress, I'm telling you," said Bobby, leaning forward to see how the mother would respond.

"Oh. My. God. Definitely a no sale," said Bobby. "Look at the fiancé's face! He's gonna kill her, I'm telling you."

At least once per episode he'd turn to Kate and say, "Isn't this just about the dumbest show you've ever seen?"

And Kate would raise her eyebrows, and tilt her head, and grin. "Ya think?"

It helped, though, to be reminded that there was still something to laugh about, that there was room for foolishness, that not everything was life and death.

Kate didn't leave. And in the days that followed, she felt her insides slowly cross the divide between numbness and feeling. It wasn't exactly a pleasurable sensation, but it was a sensation. The mornings remained the biggest challenge. Usually she got up and went to the kitchen table while Clancy and Bobby got ready for work.

"Here's some toast and cereal," Clancy said. "Coffee?"

"Yes, please," said Kate. She listened to the hum of these two men, appreciating activity, appreciating noise, and yet when they left, the toast and cereal sat and she went back to bed.

It was a week before she went outside. She sat on the front steps and counted thirty trucks before going back inside. Another morning, she took her coffee with her and listened to three woodpeckers in the trees across the road. She tried not to think much about anything; instead, she focused on the smallest details of daily living: the dampness of newsprint on her hands, the coldness of linoleum on her feet, the way hot water made her skin crinkle, the rhythmic pulsing of her heart against her fingertips when she laid her hand on her chest—

each made more notable for being recognized and named as they happened.

"I'm so sorry about this," she said to the apartment complex manager when she asked about breaking the lease.

"Normally, I wouldn't be able to do that. It's against the rules, you know," he said in a whisper as if they were conspiring together. "But to be honest, I have so many people on the waiting list that it doesn't matter. I can put someone in there in no time."

"I've never done anything like this," she said, needing to apologize, though it wasn't necessary.

Her boss was just as understanding, saying she should take as much time as she needed and that if she decided to come back, he would gladly rehire her.

Kate was wholly unprepared for more kindness.

"Everyone has been too nice," she told Clancy.

"What do you mean, 'too nice'?"

Kate shook her head. "Just too nice, that's all."

Kate's mother had taught her to be wary of easy kindness, unexpected compliments, and back-slapping smiles from people you hardly knew, or even from people you knew well: "Excuse my language, Katy, but it's all bullshit and don't you forget that. I learned that from your old man," she said, as if blaming her daughter for not having raised a better father. "Usually they want something from you, something you don't want to give them."

"It's not the way I learned things," she said to Clancy.

"Okay," said Clancy, not wanting to pry.

She appreciated Clancy's respectful silence on most things. He made her feel comfortable, as much for rarely imposing himself on her as for his watchfulness over her.

"Thanks," she said.

Clancy turned and looked at her as if he had missed something, which of course, he had. "You're welcome. Can I get you something to eat?"

How odd that he would be such a person, the grizzly recollection of his curse still lingering in Kate's mind. She struggled to reconcile these two Clancys, much as she struggled to reconcile most things every single day, not the least of which was the fact that she was here and they—Danny and Mitch—were not. If there was any justice, this would not be the case. They would all be in one place or the other without this separation, this enormous gulf.

"No, thank you. I'm not hungry," she said, glancing at the canisters on the table in the hall. She knew she should do something with them. Some days she felt remarkably rational about the whole thing, reasoning that the containers held only the shadows of what was, and that she should give them a final place of loving remembrance, wherever it might be. But on other days she felt that the canisters themselves *were* Mitch and Danny, merely transformed, veiled, and that it was her job to care for them and preserve them and devote her life to them.

She got up from the table and walked towards the bathroom, pausing briefly to touch them both. "Morning," she breathed.

"Is there anything I can do?" said Clancy.

"No," she said lightly, pointing to the bathroom. "I'll be back in a minute."

There was a plainness about Kate that Clancy liked. Although her face seemed shuttered most of the time, when she smiled, her eyes danced and her teeth shown top and bottom and her whole face came to life; then the smile would leave just as quickly as it had come, as if by smiling, she was breaking some rule she had set for herself, something Clancy came to understand was true. And every time she withdrew, whatever the reason, he wanted to tell her not to go; he wanted to tell her to stay, to sit and eat and drink some more coffee and maybe even smile again. But he didn't. He feared that his desire for her to smile, to be happy, if only fleetingly, was more for him than for her. There were still the two canisters after all. And Little Green Bear, once his constant companion, had become hers.

He was ashamed that he resented the canisters, the dust that clung to everything. She would be better off, she would have a better chance at life if only she'd get rid of them, if only she'd let them go the way of all things. Clancy tried to rid himself of these thoughts, tried to rid himself of feelings that arose unbidden, like morning fog—feelings he did not understand. Taciturn by nature, he sometimes found himself even more silent around Kate, not because he didn't have anything to say, but because he had too much. He wanted to tell her about his life, about Darlene, about how he had wasted so much time and didn't want to waste any more; he wanted to tell her that the only thing he had ever wanted in life was something she had had and then lost.

To Clancy, Kate had survived the awful truth that there was nothing certain about life, not one thing. Because of that, you have to make your choices with either precision or with abandon, but never with the assumption that it doesn't matter, never believing that what doesn't work out today can be fixed tomorrow. There is no tomorrow, really; there is only a dream of it, a mist that we believe is true because we wake up so often and find it there. And perhaps the startling thing about it all is not that terrible things happen, but that usually they don't; usually the dream of tomorrow comes true over and over again until we believe tomorrow is a right, rather than understanding that it is a gift.

Each time he inched out to the precipice, hoping to share these thoughts, he shrunk back from the edge, unable to take the leap, unable to speak his own small truth.

Chapter 29

No one talked about the canisters, even though it seemed to Bobby that they called out to him every time he walked past. In the beginning, he understood that it was probably too difficult to talk about. Kate seemed half-dead when she first arrived and Bobby had gone off the deep end and Clancy had tried to hold it all together. It was such an odd situation for a while, like they were all away at camp, so busy trying to figure out how to build the campfire and where they were going to stow their stuff that everything else took a back seat; everything else was left hanging in the air, waiting for someone to take notice and do whatever needed to be done. But after a few weeks, it seemed odd that no one mentioned them—the canisters, that is—and everything that had happened.

Bobby lay awake on the couch, Clancy already snoring in the portable bed beside him. He pulled himself up on his elbows and looked across the darkness at the two shadows on the table. It scared him a little to think that his life could end up on a table somewhere with people who had loved him being too busy to do anything about it.

Kate's bedroom door slid open slowly, not a squeak. It stood open for a minute or more before Kate appeared, bending forward, looking out from her room. It was another minute before she stepped into the hall and tiptoed to the table where the canisters stood. She caressed each one. She laid her hand on top of them as if feeling for a pulse.

"Hushaby, don't you cry, go to sleepy little baby," her voice as soft as a vapor. "When you wake, you shall have all the pretty little horses…"

Bobby held his breath.

When Kate finished, she patted the canisters and then leaned over, kissing them.

They weren't "nothing," after all; they were still everything to Kate, and that's why they were still there. Not because she had forgotten but because she couldn't forget. Bobby shook his head, thinking about his father and his brother and the problem of remembering and forgetting. Maybe it wasn't about forgetting at all; maybe it was about finding ways to remember differently, remembering sideways so it didn't hit you full-force, or remembering in bits and pieces so that you could choose what to remember and when to remember it. Maybe it was all about finding a way to remember that didn't make you die a little each day.

Worried about Kate, Bobby brought the whole thing up with Clancy during lunch break one day. They sat at the picnic table outside the main office watching swallows, their fighter-plane wings cutting the wind as they dipped and turned and soared. Bobby and Clancy popped their Diet Pepsis and opened their lunch bags. Bobby looked at Clancy and smiled as Clancy chewed his tuna fish sandwich and leaned forward on his elbows. They had fallen into a routine of meeting for lunch, though neither of them ever mentioned it in the mornings before they left the house. It just happened. Bobby was glad, and he assumed Clancy was, too, or he wouldn't have made himself so easily available. Sitting at the picnic table, Bobby felt the distance between them shrinking. When he opened his mouth, his words came more easily:

"What do you think she's going to do with those things?" he said.

Clancy had just taken a bite of his sandwich and, never being one to talk with his mouth full, waited a full minute before clearing some space to speak. "I don't know what she's going to do," said Clancy. "I guess it's up to her."

"Yes, that's true," said Bobby. He tilted his head back and took a long drink of his Pepsi. Wiped his mouth and squinted into the sunlight. "It is up to her," he said. "I just worry, you know…"

"I do, too," said Clancy.

Bobby was pleased that he and Clancy were on the same wavelength, like they were brothers who had the same thoughts at the same time.

"She eats like a bird. Have you noticed?" said Bobby.

"Yes, I have."

Bobby studied Clancy's face, which usually looked to him like the grey walls of the bluffs at dusk. But Clancy's face definitely looked different when Kate was around. Every capillary in his face opened wide, and his skin turned pink and alive and supple. Against that canvas, his eyes actually glistened. As they talked about Kate, he watched the transformation again.

"I told her she ought to eat more," said Clancy, "but she has a mind of her own about those things." Clancy took another bite and chewed slowly, as if it helped him think.

"Yes, she does," said Bobby, smiling with recognition. Clancy sipped his soda.

"I don't think she's going to eat right until she…" Bobby hesitated.

"Until she what?"

"I don't know. Those canisters, they—I don't know."

"It's up to her what she does," said Clancy, like he was speaking from rote.

"I know that. It's just, if they were gone, I think…" Bobby stopped, wanting to gauge Clancy, whose eyes were fixed on the ground just beyond the end of the picnic table.

"I'm not sure what to do about the remains." Clancy rolled the rest of his sandwich back up in the cellophane. "Sometimes she seems like she's coming back to life. But then she falls back. It's only been eight months, I know." He shook his head and tossed the sandwich into his bag. "But I'm afraid she's going to give up. And I don't know how to stop her."

Bobby saw a deep crease of sadness cross Clancy's face.

"You know," said Clancy, looking away, "my life hasn't really amounted to much. I mean, my chances came and went, and I missed them all. I was kind of stupid about life. I didn't understand that this is *it*, if you know what I mean." He paused, clenched his mouth shut as if trying to hold the words back. "There isn't going to be a do-over; if you don't get at least some of it right, then what was the point?" He looked at Bobby, not like he wanted him to speak, but like he wanted to know that Bobby was listening. "I feel like this whole thing with

Kate, this may be the last chance I'll have to get something right—I mean something absolutely goddamn right." There was a deep rumble of fear and determination in Clancy's voice. Bobby didn't say a word. "You know, I've lived a lot of life, but I've just been sleepwalking through it like it didn't matter at all, but it does." He looked hard at Bobby. "I think you know what I mean, Bobby."

Bobby's eyes welled up. He never imagined that Clancy thought about him, about his life, about Mark, about the things he'd gone through.

"You care about her a lot, don't you?" said Bobby.

Clancy looked Bobby in the eyes and then looked down. He cleared his throat and his face went flush. "I don't know if I've ever cared for anyone. I thought I had once, but that was different. I mean, with Darlene, I hate to put it this way, but I fell in love with her outsides. I didn't know any different. I thought that was the way it was." Clancy took a deep breath. "With Kate, it's different. It's hard to explain. I don't know exactly how I feel about her." Clancy picked up his drink and then put it down again without taking a sip. "You know when you're standing up there on the bluffs sometimes, with the wind and the sky and the water and nothing else, you feel peaceful in a different way—a way that makes you feel things are good?"

"Yeah, I think I do," said Bobby.

"That's what I feel sometimes when she's around," said Clancy with an embarrassed shrug.

Bobby smiled. "Are you going to tell her?"

Clancy gave a low, grumbling laugh. "I'm not crazy. I wouldn't put that on her with everything she's dealing with. It just wouldn't be right."

"Why not?"

"She's barely on her feet. I mean, she still loves that little boy and his daddy more than anything. And that's the way it should be, I guess." Clancy shifted his legs and stretched them out so they were under Bobby's side of the table. "I don't think what I'm feeling would do her much good right now."

"How do you know?" asked Bobby.

"Well, I don't. But it's what I'm inclined to believe." He shook his head. "Anyway, the timing's just not right."

"I don't know much about timing, but it seems to me that if that's how you feel right this very moment, that's got to mean something." It suddenly got quiet, and Bobby wasn't sure what to do or say. Clancy sat still as could be. He looked at Bobby, and then he looked toward the lake. He breathed deep and arched his back, but then his posture slumped into confusion again.

"Wind's kicking up," said Bobby.

"Yes," said Clancy. The trees on the edge of the woods bent over in unison, crows leaping from their branches.

"Tell you what. I'm gonna fill my tank before I go back to work. Wanna come?"

Clancy didn't look up this time. "No thanks."

As Bobby drove away, he looked through the rearview mirror at Clancy, still sitting at the table.

Chapter 30

Winter insinuated itself onto the bluffs in late November, grey dragons lumbering across the horizon, a whirling dervish of snow surrounding the peaks. Only the hearty came to the park when winter set in. The trails became nearly impassable, and the trees were bleak and creaky. The water was dark as hot chocolate, a whipped cream froth along its edges. Deer congregated in the hollows where "No Hunting" signs were posted, assuring their safety from the explosive presence of orange-vested men in middle age.

Clancy lingered in the office, having a private conversation with Buddy. Bobby stepped out the door and into a wind that slapped his face numb. He pulled the collar up on his bomber jacket, raising his shoulders to further protect his neck, if not his ears. He walked stoop-shouldered to his truck, Kate and Clancy on his mind. Clancy was close-lipped as ever around Kate, talking mainly about the weather, the morning headlines, and the menu for dinner. Sometimes he asked how she was doing, but in a way that showed he wasn't sure he wanted to know the answer: "You doing okay?" She always answered, "Fine." They smiled at each other more often, but that was about it. Kate's canisters sat in the same spot on the same shelf where Bobby had witnessed her tenderness that one night, dust settling in around them. It was like the three of them were passengers in a plane stacked over a busy airport; it felt like they were going somewhere, but all they were doing was perfecting a circle.

Bobby decided to take 15 back to Clancy's so he could buy cheap gas at Lou's Sunoco. He turned the heat on high, yet opened the window a crack to avoid a fogged windshield. The cold shaft of air felt good on his face, and the warm air felt good on his feet. There was a brown pasture with a half-frozen pond on the right and thick woods on the left where the snow was falling lazily. The guy in the Taurus in front of Bobby must have been a hundred years old, he drove so slowly. Bobby popped the horn once to encourage him along, but the man's foot was immoveable.

There were two hawks circling above Bobby as he came round a soft curve, the woods closing in a little on one side of the road and tall grass and brush closing in on the other. Just beyond the bend, a deer stepped out of the brush on the left side. Not just any deer: a thick, barrel-chested buck, eight points by Bobby's quick count. *My God*, thought Bobby, *he's beautiful*. The buck held his head high; his nostrils flared, his eyes dark and piercing. "I'll be damned," whispered Bobby. He watched, expecting the buck to retreat as the Taurus picked up a little speed coming out of the bend into the straightaway. But he didn't. Instead, the buck took a few steps toward the road and raised his head. Then he began to run.

Bobby could tell that the old man either didn't see the deer coming or was too startled to slow down. The deer was hitting his stride, and so was the Taurus. There was no doubt what was going to happen. Bobby leaned on his horn now, hoping to scare the buck or warn the old man, but it didn't matter—the buck was a goner. Bobby didn't know what to do. He slowed to a crawl. The Taurus didn't slow down at all. *Why the hell can't he drive like a snail now?* thought Bobby. Bobby held his breath and winced as he watched the Taurus take dead aim at the buck. He didn't want to see it get killed, but he couldn't help himself—the animal was so magnificent, so perfect in its way, that he had to watch; he had to witness. He hoped it would be quick, that the deer would take a good hit and be dead, not like some he'd seen that lay on the road, their heads up, their bodies mangled, waiting for the state cops to come and put a single bullet in their head. The buck was at full-speed as his front hooves hit the pavement. The car was only feet away, and neither it nor the deer was going to relent. What came next was so unexpected, so serendipitous, that Bobby had to pull the truck off the road, stopping it dead in its tracks. Had he actually just seen what he thought he'd seen? His hands were shaking. He turned off the engine and sat in the quiet aftermath. His shoulders relaxed and his hands fell from the steering wheel. He smiled.

When Clancy reached the front door, he could see Kate through the window. She was standing in the hall, near the shelving. She reached for one of the canisters but stopped, her arms falling to her side. Clancy opened the door.

"Oh," said Kate, raising one hand to her chest. "I didn't see you." She smiled. "I was just looking..." She turned to the shelves again and ran her finger across the surface, leaving a streak behind. She wiped her finger on her jeans. "Maybe I should do a little cleaning," she said sheepishly.

"No, no, really, I'm usually a better housekeeper," said Clancy, taking off his jacket and hanging it on the rack. "I guess I just haven't stayed on top of things lately." He cleared his throat.

Kate's smile faded as she glanced back at the canisters. "I didn't mean for you, I mean, I wasn't suggesting that you should…," she said.

Clancy walked over to the shelves. He took a handkerchief from his back pocket and quickly ran it across the surface, hesitating at the canisters, not wanting to touch them.

"Here, let me," said Kate, picking them up.

"I'm sorry," said Clancy. "I've never…"

"Touched them. I know," she said. Clancy ran his handkerchief over the perfect circles left by the canisters. Kate then put them back into place.

"I guess I haven't," he said. Kate's face looked ashen.

"I wasn't sure if…I mean, I didn't want to disturb…" He nodded solemnly toward the cremains of two people he knew only in death.

"I'm sorry," said Kate. "I've made a little cemetery right in your house."

"No, you haven't. It's not that at all," said Clancy, wanting to go back outside and knock before entering again. "I know what they meant, what they *mean*; I know they are important and that you still…"

"It's taking a long time," said Kate, her posture stiffening. "I know."

"That's not a problem. I mean, it's okay. You can take all the time…" Clancy stopped, feeling his words veering dangerously off-course.

"All the time," said Kate, lifting her hand and touching one canister gently as if brushing aside a hair from her son's forehead.

"I just wish I could, I don't know," said Clancy, swiping the top of the shelf one more time with his handkerchief.

"I don't want you to..." Kate turned to the kitchen. "You don't have to do anything. You've done enough."

"I wish I could make this go away," said Clancy. "I wish I could empty those things for you." His face winced at his own words. "I didn't mean..."

Kate went to the cupboard and took down the dishes. She stacked them on the table. She pulled out the drawer beside the kitchen sink and took out a handful of utensils. She looked at them as if they held a riddle she couldn't discern. She dropped them on the table beside the plates, as if they were now on their own.

Clancy stood under the dangling kitchen light, a shadow across his face. "Look, Kate, what I mean is, I wish those were just two empty cans; I wish they'd never had anything in them, that they were just a couple of cans that I needed to take out with the trash, like they didn't belong to you at all."

Kate leaned on the table, her shoulders bowed. She looked up, glimpsing the moisture in the corners of his eyes. She walked to his side and took his hand, holding it tight and then letting it go. She turned back to the table, setting the plates, arranging the utensils, folding the napkins, moving from task to task, gently, quietly as a mother while her baby slept.

Clancy started breathing again. "I guess I'll start dinner. Bobby will be here in no time." He slid by her to the stove.

The macaroni and cheese was just coming out of the oven when Bobby burst through the front door smiling like a schoolboy on the first day of vacation. He unzipped his jacket but didn't bother to take it off. He clomped into the kitchen, his hands raised above his head. "I gotta tell you what just happened!"

Clancy put the casserole dish down, tossing the oven mitts onto the stove. Kate was bent over the drawer looking for a serving spoon.

Bobby proceeded without waiting for a response. "So, Clancy, when I left work today, I took old 15 to Lou's to buy some gas." He smiled at both of them. "Well, I never made it."

Clancy rinsed his hands off in the sink. Kate dipped the spoon into the casserole.

"You know why?" he asked. "Of course you don't! Look, I'm driving along behind this old guy who was going like twenty miles an hour. I honked my horn once, but he didn't seem to hear. I'm stuck, so I just chug along behind him. In about five minutes we came to that long curve, you know where I mean, Clancy?"

Clancy nodded.

"Yeah, you know where I mean—where the woods close in on both sides and in the summer the air is always cool no matter the temperature. Just as we come out of the turn, wouldn't you know it, he starts speeding up. As he speeds up, I see this great big buck step out from the bushes alongside the road. I mean, he was eight points at least. I'm thinking, *Wow, that's something!*"

"Eight points," said Clancy with a nod of appreciation.

"So I'm thinking, *Take a good look, 'cause you're never going to see that again.* But would you believe the buck didn't budge even with two cars bearing down on him? Instead he takes a couple of steps *forward* and starts running towards the road as determined as anything, his head up, almost like he doesn't care what's coming. And the guy, well he acts like he doesn't even see the deer. He never takes his foot off the gas; in fact, he's speeding up and so is the deer, and I'm thinking, *Jesus, he's going to kill this buck.* I could just see it. I mean, how many deer are killed along that road each year, Clancy?"

"A lot."

"A lot, for sure, and this buck is going to be the next. There's no doubt. I could barely watch. In fact, I slowed down and started pulling over just as the buck reaches the road. Now the car is on him and I close my eyes a little, but not the whole way. I just couldn't stop watching. I brace myself for the collision, and you'll never guess what happens." Bobby stopped, savoring the moment. "I'll tell you what: That buck leaped right over the car! I mean it. He leaped over the car, his flank muscles pulling his hind legs up so high that there were several inches between him and the roof of the car. I mean, he was *airborne*. And when he hit the pavement on the other side, he didn't miss a stride. In no time, he disappeared into those woods. I don't know if that old man ever saw what happened. But I sure did."

Bobby grinned as he shifted from one foot to the other. He looked at Clancy and Kate, raising his eyebrows. Kate and Clancy looked at each other, their faces shrugging.

"That's something," said Clancy, meaning "What does that have to do with anything?"

Bobby was perspiring along his forehead as he spoke. "Here's the thing, though, here's the thing." He paused, gathering his thoughts, his grin evaporating. "You know, if that deer crosses that road one hundred times like that, he's going to get killed ninety-nine times. But that one time he made it. That one time, he leaped and made it and lived another day. One time out of a hundred."

Bobby swallowed hard. He looked at Kate. "Kate, once upon a time I had a little brother who was three years old. His name was Mark and I was his hero. We were driving to a picnic on a sunny day and some guy coming from the other direction swerved about three feet, just three feet, and hit us head on. My mom, my dad, and I, we all made it. But Mark didn't." Bobby wiped the perspiration from his upper lip.

"Sitting there in my truck after the deer had made it to safety, I thought about that accident so long ago. And I realized that while I got to go on living, I was left with a great big hole inside. And that hole bled and hurt and ached for years, and I couldn't figure out how to get rid of it. And people told me that it would go away, that time heals these things, but they were wrong. Time didn't close it up. I mean, it just wouldn't go away no matter how much I wanted it to." Bobby took a deep breath. "And after a while, because you've lived with it so long, it's like you say to yourself, 'You know, that hole isn't going away; in fact, maybe it shouldn't; because if it did, you'd stop remembering your brother'—and you don't want that to happen. And then you think, 'Life doesn't go away either, and you want to keep living, you know, because sometime you might be in the right place at the right time to see a buck jump over a car—or, even better, you might see yourself jump over that hole, even if it's one time out of a hundred. And you think, 'That just might be enough to keep me going.'"

Bobby wiped tears on his sleeve.

"Kate, I hope you don't take this wrong, but I think you have a hole inside you. And I'd like to tell you that's it's going to go away, but it isn't. You can't love someone and lose them and not have a hole for the rest of your life. But, you know what, you can learn how to jump over that hole; you can learn how to jump over that hole when you need to; you don't always have to fall in. It may take ninety-nine tries before you can do it, but once you do it, you'll be all right—not all better, but all right."

Kate stepped forward and put her hands on Bobby's shoulders. She leaned in and embraced him delicately, as if he (or perhaps, she) might otherwise break. She stepped back.

"Thank you," she said.

"That's okay," said Bobby, glancing at Clancy, who looked different, like the scaffolding had been removed from the facade and all that was left was his real face.

Chimney Bluffs

Chapter 31

The shrill silver-grey of winter, its howling jet streams, was no match for the spunky, green crocus shoots coaxing their way through the early March ice, trumpeting the advance of a freshly-scrubbed new season and, with it, other changes as well.

The content of Buddy and Clancy's talks was revealed. Buddy's wife's breast cancer had reawakened, tearing through her body, forcing Buddy to keep his promise to retire. Clancy took over, supervising ten full-time park employees and twenty part-timers, not to mention countless volunteers. Never one to stand in the light, Clancy took the stage reluctantly, but soon fell into the routine of leadership, unglamorous for its paperwork and reports and staff meetings and budget talks and boredom. The pay raise made it tolerable. He still scheduled himself for shifts in the park, something Buddy hadn't done in years. Clancy was loathe to give up his place on the bluffs where the light shone in ways that defied language and the spires soared with unsettling confidence.

One day Kate walked into the house, hung up her coat, took a seat on the couch as Bobby channel surfed and Clancy puttered in the kitchen, and announced she had gotten her old job back. Much to

Kate's surprise, her former boss was happy to see her. In fact, he promised her that if she lasted six months, she could take over as front end manager. "The cashiers keep quitting," he had said under his breath. Bobby ran to the mini-mart and bought an ice cream cake and plastic spoons to celebrate. Clancy congratulated her, though he barely smiled.

Bobby ordered a course catalogue from Oswego Sate. He even took it out of its manila mailer and sat it on the TV, where it reminded him daily of his intention to read it. The future couldn't be far away.

For the first time in months, Bobby went to visit his mother and father when he learned she had been hospitalized for gallbladder surgery. When Bobby arrived in the hospital corridor, his father was sitting in the family waiting area reading the paper. Bobby stood in front of him for almost a minute before his father looked up.

"She's down the hall in twenty-nine, sleeping," he said, as if they'd just seen each other that morning.

"Is she going to be okay?" asked Bobby.

"Yes, she'll be fine. Not that it matters much to you."

Bobby decided to ignore this. "Has she been sick long?"

"No. It came on sudden. Ambulance took her, and that was that."

Bobby's father looked back at the newspaper. Bobby was about to turn away and then decided to sit. He took a chair across from his father. His father looked up again.

"How have you been, Dad?" he said.

"What do you mean, how have I been?"

"I don't mean anything except—How have you been?"

"I've been fine."

Bobby thought his father might ask how he'd been, but instead, he just looked at Bobby. Bobby studied his father's face: red and puffy and downcast. His jaw was as set as it had been on the night of the big fight. It was as if time had stopped, which Bobby had come to realize was true. Since Mark's death, his father had been stockpiling disappointment and living off bitterness. Without even realizing it, he had made a decision on the road that day to hate everything that was associated with that accident, which is to say, all of life. He had been dying ever since.

"Look, Dad, I'm sorry for what happened. I'm sorry that things didn't work out," said Bobby.

Bobby's father's jaw went a little slack. He looked down at his feet and then up at Bobby again. "Go see your mother. It will make her happy."

When Bobby entered his mother's hospital room, he saw that her eyes were closed. Her hair was disheveled and matted on one side. Her face was spotted, and the skin under her lower lids seemed to pull away from her eyes, unable to resist the urging of gravity. The chin below her chin had grown since he'd last seen her. Her arms, resting on her stomach, were baggy, and her hands and fingers gnarled. Had she changed that much? Or had he never looked at her before?

Bobby took another step closer, and she opened her eyes. "Bobby," she said in a whisper, and began to cry. Bobby sat beside his mother and held her hand. He had almost forgotten what her voice sounded like. Her face came to life, and the signs of aging receded slightly, making room for moments of relief and happiness. Bobby laughed as she described thinking she had indigestion from his father's chili until she felt so much pain that he grudgingly called the ambulance, muttering, "There's nothing wrong with my chili." She explained how different the surgery had been from when Bobby's grandfather had had it. Not nearly as much cutting. Amazing what doctors could do nowadays. Of course, it still cost like crazy, but she liked the nurses and felt they were doing a good job but, just the same, she was eager to go home again. She knew how hard all this was on Bobby's father. He didn't like to leave the house at all, let alone go to the hospital. She gave Bobby a knowing look when she said this. She worried that it might be too much for him, all the trips back and forth and all the reminders. And for what? She wasn't even sick. She told Bobby's father not to come, but he came nevertheless and stayed as long as he could, poor thing. She reminded Bobby of how hard things were for his father and hinted that Bobby's leaving hadn't helped and that she hadn't thought Bobby would stay away so long. Surely he had known that she hadn't meant anything by what she had said. People say things they don't necessarily mean. It was just that Bobby and his father needed to get away from each other, and she couldn't ask Bobby's father to leave. She wasn't sure why Bobby had felt the need to stay away so long. She worried about him all the time and hoped he was doing okay. She'd thought of trying to contact him, but with looking after his father, time just had a way of slipping by.

Bobby listened and said little. Soon she was tired again and feeling uncomfortable. The nurse came with pain medication and suggested she might need a nap. Bobby leaned over to kiss her and she said, "I love you."

"I love you, too," Bobby whispered.

As he passed the family waiting area, his father looked up.

"I'll see you," said Bobby.

"Okay. She should be home the day after tomorrow," he said, his way of inviting Bobby to visit.

"Okay. I'll remember."

They hadn't changed a bit. They had sealed over what had happened between them and had stamped it "Case Closed." Bobby stood in the parking lot expecting to feel lost or sad or angry. But all he felt was the wind on his face. He was glad he had come to see his mother and father, if only because it had helped him recognize how far away he had moved. When he had looked at his father, he understood that he could never be the father Bobby had wanted. He was Mark's father, and anything else he had to offer had died with Mark. He almost felt pity for his father, although he couldn't help but also feel his father had chosen his path and was now suffering the consequences.

He smiled when he thought about his mother. He loved her, but for the first time he realized that he was just a sounding board, someone she could complain to about her husband and her life, someone she could bounce her misery off of. Bobby had mistaken that for love, and who knows, maybe his mother had believed it was.

Bobby would go by to see his mother from time to time after that. His father would sit in his chair. He would speak to Bobby if Bobby directed something his way. Nothing more. And his mother would wonder aloud why Bobby was staying away, although she would never ask him to return. It was a while before Bobby realized that what he had felt on his face in the hospital parking lot that night wasn't just the wind—it was freedom, not the running-around-crazy freedom of high school or the totally-messing-up-your-life freedom he felt when he was drunk or stoned, but the freedom from being burdened by all that had been and all that would never be. The change had occurred sometime between the fight with his father and seeing his mother in the hospital a few months later. How it had happened, he couldn't explain. He had lived in his truck, moved in with Clancy, fought about Kate, and eventually befriended her; he had seen a buck jump over a car, and he'd lived in the shadow of the canisters and all that they meant. Every one of them was important, but taken individually, none of them explained how differently Bobby felt. Perhaps the explanation could be found in the combination, the unique ingredients that, when blended and stirred, became a saving potion—because that's how it felt to him, like he had taken a potion, almost unknowingly, and had been saved as a result.

Even Kate had noticed, commenting to him one morning as he headed off to work:

"Something's different about you, Bobby. You look taller or something. I don't know, but you look different. Sorry, I don't mean it in a bad way; it's good, but I can't put my finger on it."

"New cologne," Bobby joked and didn't think anything more about it, at least not until after his trip to the hospital. He knew he was still five feet nine and one half inches tall, no matter how hard he tried to reach five feet ten, yet he felt taller.

Kate felt it was time to get her legs under herself again, and going back to work was one way to do it. Clancy was pleased for her, although Bobby thought he saw fear on Clancy's face for days after

Kate went back to work. He didn't know if Clancy was afraid she couldn't do it or if he was afraid she could, and by doing it, would realize she could move out on her own again.

After a while, he didn't look quite so preoccupied, perhaps because he had gotten this new job and was busy trying to be the boss, which wasn't his style at all. If anything, Clancy liked being on his own without having to bother with anyone else's business. Bobby was surprised when Clancy took the position, although there was no doubt that the extra income helped.

"*Boss* Clancy. I guess I don't quite see it," he said.

"I guess you'll have to look a little harder," said Clancy.

Everyone pitched in, although Clancy still felt it was up to him to be the breadwinner. Bobby could tell that Clancy assumed they'd go on like this—living together, that is—even though Clancy never said so. He cleaned out a back storage area and made it into a passable bedroom for himself, all but announcing that his old bedroom was his no more.

"Do you like moonglow?" he asked Kate.

"Moonglow?" she said.

Clancy lifted the paint can to eye level. "Yes, moonglow. Yellow. Pale yellow. I'm going to paint the bedroom and figured I should get something that..." Clancy's face turned maroon. Red. Dark red. "I wanted something that you could live with."

"You should pick something *you* like," said Kate. "It's your bedroom."

"But I'm back there now," he said, gesturing to the storage room.

"Paint lasts an awful long time, Clancy. I mean, who knows how long I'll be..." Kate's voice trailed off when she saw Clancy's mouth sink into his chin.

"I know; I just thought..."

"No, that's fine. Really. Moonglow, pale yellow is fine. I like yellow." Kate's smile twitched in the corners.

Clancy opened a plastic bag. "I bought this, too," he said, unfurling a bright, flowered border.

"Never figured you for a daffodil man," said Bobby, laughing.

"Bobby," said Kate. She turned to Clancy. "Thank you so much, Clancy."

Kate appreciated everything Clancy did for her. She spent less time in the bedroom, and she lingered longer in the kitchen after dinner, helping Clancy with the dishes or sitting with him over a second cup of coffee. She would take him a cold drink when he was working outside or walk with him to the mini-mart down the road when he needed to buy some bread or detergent. It was clear to Bobby that Kate liked Clancy, but how that fit with the sadness she felt was hard to tell.

There were some nights when Bobby would hear her crying, nearly moaning, and he would go to her door and listen until she stopped. Once, he told Clancy about this. The next day, Clancy made her a special breakfast and he sat beside her and was gentle with her in every possible way, even patting her shoulder as he walked by, but he didn't ask how she was doing and she didn't offer, although she looked him straight on and said, "Thanks," in a way that was more than a thank you for breakfast. Her grief was deeper than the average person could recognize by looking at the surface, which was often all she showed. Bobby knew it; Clancy did, too.

Bobby noticed that over the months they had all lived together, Clancy had gradually become a different person. He smiled more often, he talked more freely, he laughed more loudly, he listened more closely, he seemed more at home in his skin, especially when he was around Kate. "More" was the best word to describe what was changing in Clancy. He was *more* Clancy than perhaps he'd ever been before. There was no way to tell if Kate knew any of this. She had nothing to compare it to.

How and why paths crossed the way they did was difficult to understand. Maybe it was just happenstance. Or maybe it was part of some Grand Plan. Happenstance seemed like an easier explanation to swallow, mainly because if this was part of a Grand Plan, some pretty awful things had to happen for it to work out. Two canisters sitting on the shelf seemed like an unreasonably high price to pay just to bring two reluctant strangers together.

Bobby felt obligated to help things along. His opportunity came one night when Clancy was out at a planning meeting with some of the big bosses and Kate was home with Bobby watching *Entertainment Tonight*. They had just finished a segment about whether that actor, Gary Busey, was crazy or just colorful. When they went to commercial, Bobby took a deep breath and started in.

"You know, that's something about Clancy," he said.

"What's that?" said Kate.

Bobby smiled to himself. "He's just so different."

"How's that?" said Kate, taking a bite of a chocolate chip cookie.

"Well, I guess you wouldn't have noticed."

Kate turned her head and stared at Bobby, chewing her cookie more slowly.

"You never knew him before," he said.

"What are you talking about?" said Kate, wiping her mouth and hands on a napkin.

"Well, he's always been this serious guy who never really talked much to anyone, except maybe me or John Dan. But even then he didn't say all that much. Kind of stayed to himself, private-like. He never seemed all that happy." He looked at Kate, hoping again that he might have piqued her curiosity.

"Is there something wrong with Clancy, Bobby?" said Kate.

"No, no, there's nothing wrong," said Bobby. "It's nothing like that. It's just that he has been so much happier lately. I mean, you see it, he talks more and sometimes he cracks a joke; he laughs. He just seems like a different person, that's all."

"Okay," said Kate. The commercial was over and *ET* was now taking its daily look at Charlie Sheen. Kate shook her head as Sheen screamed "Winner! Winner!" at the camera.

Bobby cleared his throat and shifted his weight so he was sitting on his hip, looking directly at Kate instead of the TV. "I think it's because of you." Bobby's eyes were wide, surprised by what he had said.

Kate turned back to Bobby, her eyebrows bent over her eyes, her head tilted slightly. "What do you mean, you think it's because of me?" she asked, quizzically.

Bobby tried to put the car in reverse. "I don't know what I mean, exactly. I thought Clancy seemed different and maybe it was because

250

of you, but I could be completely wrong. Maybe it's me who's different, and that's why Clancy seems different; maybe he's not different at all and you don't have anything to do with it. Would you like another cookie? Or some milk?"

"What do you mean, he's changed because of me? What are you talking about, Bobby?" said Kate, looking worried.

Bobby froze, his eyes now as big as saucers.

"Bobby? What are you trying to tell me?" said Kate.

"I don't know if I'm trying to tell you anything. I'm just making an observation, that's all." Kate didn't say a word, but she also didn't take her eyes off Bobby. It was clear that she wasn't accepting his answer, that she was expecting more.

"Look, Kate, you're a special person—at least I think you are— and Clancy, well, I think Clancy thinks so, too. And because you are a special person, Clancy's, well, different. That's all I mean."

All the color drained from Kate's face.

Clancy came through the front door just then, a bag of groceries in his arms. Bobby jumped up. Kate didn't move. Despite the nattering on the TV, it seemed oddly quiet to Clancy.

"What?" said Clancy.

Kate's face was ashen. She got up, her eyes glued to the floor. She headed towards her room, trying her best to be invisible.

"Kate? Is something wrong?" said Clancy. By then she was in her freshly moonlit room, having closed the door quickly yet silently behind her.

Clancy trained his eyes on Bobby. "Bobby?"

"It's nothing," said Bobby. "Everything is…I don't know; it's just that I…"

"What? What did you do?" said Clancy, thunder in his eyes.

"I didn't do anything. Really."

"Something happened. What was it? Did something happen at Kate's work?"

"No…"

"Is it something about what *happened*, you know?"

"No…"

"Bobby."

Bobby's Adam's apple had grown three times its normal size, and his tongue was thick and his mouth was dusty. "It's just that I was trying to help, that's all. I didn't mean anything by it. I was trying to help Kate understand…"

"Understand what?"

Bobby shuffled and put his hands in his pockets.

"What were you trying to help her understand, Bobby? What?"

Bobby looked at Clancy sheepishly.

"What did you say to her?"

Bobby shrugged his shoulders. "Nothing much, really."

Clancy got up in Bobby's face as Bobby tried to avoid his eyes. "Look at me," said Clancy. "What did you tell her?"

Bobby didn't say a word, but when his eyes met Clancy's, Clancy knew.

Clancy stepped back. "My God, Bobby, you didn't. Tell me you didn't."

"I didn't mean to…"

"Jesus Christ, Bobby," said Clancy. "I was just talking. I was just talking to you. That's all. Did I say, 'Hey, Bobby, feel free to tell Kate what I said'?" The hook was in now, and Bobby was squirming. "Did I ever once say it was okay for you to say anything to her or to anyone, for that matter?" Bobby shook his head. "No. That's right. I didn't. So, explain to me why you did. Explain to me what part of 'don't tell anyone' you didn't understand." Bobby didn't answer. "You know, Bobby, I told you some things that I wasn't sure I could even say to myself." Clancy stepped back from Bobby and turned away, rubbing his face with his right hand. He looked shaken, like someone had taken his only private thought and posted it on Facebook.

"I'm sorry, man," said Bobby. "I didn't mean to cause any problems." Clancy didn't turn to face him. "I thought I was just helping things along."

Clancy turned. "How? How were you helping?" Bobby stuttered and fumbled for the right words, and then they just came out.

"She should know. She should know how you feel about her. She, in particular, should know. She lost everything and blames herself for all of it and more. She's waiting for the whole freakin' world to come down on her. She hates herself, Clancy. She hates herself. She feels to blame for her son, her husband, and God knows what else." He paused, expecting Clancy to say something, but he didn't. "It's like every day some new part of the world gets hoisted onto her shoulders. For no good reason. She thinks she deserves the worst and, if she has it her way, she will get the worst. She will find every black hole, every dark cloud, every cut and bruise and wound and make it her own. And you know I'm right." Bobby was feeling his strength returning; his face was throbbing; his heart was running wild. "She, of all people, deserves to know that even one other person, just one, would move the whole world for her if that would make things better."

Bobby sighed. His voice softened. "You know, man, some people never have that happen, not even once in their lives—not even once do they have someone tell them 'I love you,' not as some bullshit way of saying hello or goodbye, but as the real honest truth about how they feel."

Bobby made one swipe with his shirtsleeve across his eyes and his tears were gone. "I told you I was sorry, but you know what? I'm not. You're the one who should be sorry—sorry that someone else had to do it for you."

Bobby stopped. He was breathing deep, but he was breathing even. He looked at Clancy, and this time he didn't shrug, he didn't joke, he didn't do anything to minimize himself.

Clancy's eyes were wide. His breathing was shallow. His arms hung low; his hands, like weights, pulled at his wrists. Bobby's words spun round Clancy's head, like bees around a nest. He looked at Bobby, who looked as steady as the peaks at Chimney Bluffs. He opened his mouth, but the words were a jumble in the back of his throat. He looked out the kitchen window at the maple trees across the road, bending in the wind, and even they seemed to know. He leaned back against the refrigerator and covered his face with his hands. He took a deep breath and his shoulders settled. He walked across the kitchen and through the living room to Kate's door. He knocked and waited.

Chapter 32

Kate leaned against the bedroom door. The room was dark except for the glow from a streetlight on the corner. She reached for the switch on the wall and then decided against it. She walked to the bed and sat down, her feet curled to one side.

On Kate's first day of school, her mother had knelt beside her, holding her close as the bus pulled up. "Go ahead, then," she said. "Don't worry about Mommy; I'll be all right." As the bus pulled away, Kate waved, but her mother turned and walked back to the house as if she hadn't noticed. Kate felt it then, even though she couldn't define it until years later: a pang in her chest, an empty tingling in her arms, like she'd done something wrong but couldn't figure out what it was. That old empty feeling had never really gone away; even the contagious optimism of Mitch could not erase it, his butterfly confidence, his belief that the air itself was all they needed to sustain them, that the ground below would never harm them. Now, so many years, so many losses come and gone, she still wasn't sure what was safe and what wasn't.

She held Little Green Bear in her hands. She looked out the bedroom window at the silhouette of trees against the last hint of day.

She would have cheered Danny when he got on the bus his first day of school, and she would have waited all day at the bus stop for him to come home.

The voices of men vibrated at the bedroom door.

All Bobby had said was that Clancy had changed and that she was the reason. She studied this notion, unsure what it meant. No one had ever changed because of her. She had always been the caboose on someone else's train. Perhaps she had heard him wrong. Bobby liked to tell a tale. Perhaps he was just being Bobby, saying things. This argument seemed flimsy even to Kate. Bobby had been clear. Clancy's change was *because* of Kate. A had led to B. Kate looked at the canisters on her dresser. After the first few weeks of living in Clancy's house, she had moved them from the hallway, which had seemed too public, too ornamental, too shared. They held her as surely as they held the ones she loved. Had she done something to make Clancy feel whatever he was feeling? How could she entertain anyone else's feelings when she could barely manage her own?

She wept each night for all that she had lost. Yet recently she struggled with other feelings, feelings unencumbered by anything more taxing than scheduling her cashiers. Sometimes she felt empty, not in a burdensome way, but in a way that made her light and even gave her pleasure. Sometimes she felt like she was just another person, no different than the stay-at-home moms, the retirees, the pimpled teenagers, the busy business women in their powersuits who came through the store each day and spoke to her in friendly voices like they knew she was no different than anyone else. There were times when Kate wanted to tell them that if they really knew her, if they knew the whole story, if they knew Mitch, and if they knew Danny, and if they knew what had happened, what she had done, they would also know that she was different, that she was not like them.

But there were other times when she liked it, when she just plain liked the feeling of fitting into the crowd, of fitting almost invisibly into the landscape of daily life, where she could come and go as she pleased without feeling that fingers were being pointed or stories were being told. There was no doubt that Bobby and Clancy were the reason for this. As far as she could tell, they hadn't even tried to change her. They'd stopped talking to her about the canisters and what she should do. They'd stopped trying to convince her of anything.

There was a no-big-deal quality to the way Clancy handled things that was just what Kate needed. Mitch's everything-is-a-big-deal optimism both attracted and repulsed her; she wanted it for herself, but it was always several sizes too big. She smiled, thinking of him, though, thinking of how much he expected out of this life. And the next.

So many months had come and gone since Chimney Bluffs. There was a part of her that still lay on that beach, that still sat in her apartment alone, trying to make it through the next hour, living a nightmare and trying to make it through even if she didn't know why. And yet here she was, farther down the road by more than just time—pleased and saddened that she had been able to do it, that she had been able to press on with her life despite her doubts about whether she even deserved to live. Life had its ways; it took her up in its arms and delivered her to another place before she even knew what had happened, before she even made the choice to go along. She couldn't say whether that was good or bad; all she knew was that it was true.

How did she feel about Clancy? She had avoided this question many times recently, putting it on the back shelf of her mind, unable to throw it out and unwilling to take a closer look. How dare she look? Was there a point to feeling anything after Chimney Bluffs? And yet she couldn't deny that there was something about Clancy that had taken hold of her heart, perhaps just a small portion of her heart, a portion that she had opened to the world. At times, the guilt associated with this feeling hit her like the cold wind off the highest bluff, leaving her gasping for air, but at other times it made her smile to feel something for someone else, to care deeply for another person.

Her mother would have curled her lip and shaken her head. "How could you!" she would have said. "It's just not proper; it's not allowed!" Maybe "allowed" was a word that didn't apply to what was happening to Kate. Did the sun have to get permission to shine, the moon to rise, the rain to fall? Did that deer wait for a signal before leaping? It seemed like something else was at work, something she couldn't see or name or explain, something she wasn't sure of, something she wasn't prepared for—and yet there it was.

She took Little Green Bear in her hands and squeezed it gently. She held it to her nose and breathed deeply, no longer able to smell her little boy yet always hoping she would. Kate got up from her bed and walked to the dresser. She lay the bear down and placed her hands on top of the two canisters.

There was a knock on the door.

Chapter 33

The ash trees, their lance-shaped leaves a brilliant yellow, their velvety stems swaying in the autumn breeze, clustered around the entrance to the forest path. Tall chestnut trees with their distinctive upright oval leaves and downward hanging branches reached out to every visitor, while dazzling sugar maples, all afire, filled the forest floor. Nature strutted its golden plumage on the ridge above the stark, soaring chimneys of glacial till that were the Bluffs. The azure blue lake, speckled white caps rising and falling with the wind, stretched to the horizon and beyond.

Clancy left the office and walked the short distance to the parking lot. No one had arrived yet. He looked up as a wedge of Canada geese, their mournful honking filling the air, cut a path south, their journey just begun. He squinted at the horizon, trying to see the CN tower in Toronto, and much to his surprise, there it was, a tiny spike sitting on the water. He smiled. His first sighting this season. It had been a long, rainy summer, but the fall had been crisp and cool and sunny each day, allowing the world to wind down luxuriously. *What will the winter bring?* he wondered. He could bet there would be a hundred inches of snow or more before the first crocuses broke through the semi-frozen ground again in late winter.

He looked at his watch. *They're late*. Bobby, coming from Oswego, had the longest drive. It had been about six weeks since he'd moved on campus and had begun his first semester at college. He didn't know what he wanted to do yet, but he'd gotten the notion that ther was the best place to start over, and unless he tried, he'd never be able to take a reasonable step forward. He took out loans that he would be paying off forever, but he didn't care. On the day he resigned from his job at the Bluffs, he told Clancy, "You know, I can't get that old buck out of my mind. Never seen anything like that. I feel like I've been standing on one side of the road for a long time, when I actually needed to be on the other. I wish there was an easier way to get there, but I guess leaping is the only way for me to go."

About a week after he moved into his dorm room, he got a letter in the mail from his mother and father. In it was a check for one hundred dollars. The note from his mother said, "I know it's not much, but I figured you could use it for something." Usually she signed both names, but this time Bobby could tell that his father had signed the letter, too.

Bobby usually stayed at Clancy's on the weekends. Everyone at school was too young for him, Bobby insisted, although Clancy thought Bobby was afraid he'd get into his old habits if he stayed on campus. Whatever it was, Clancy was happy to see him. They'd go to John Dan's and have a beer, play some darts, shoot some pool.

Clancy had gotten used to his new job. It wasn't what he had expected to be doing, but it was better money than what he had been making before, and that made life considerably easier. He had an office and a desk and a chair, and people treated him with respect, and everyone said he was doing a good job. He found that he was skilled at solving problems and making decisions—either that or everyone who worked under him was dumber than dumb. Whatever it was, people counted on him, and the park was doing well; attendance had been up that summer, despite the weather, and they had added a new path that made fall hiking even more inviting. He liked the idea that he was taking care of a living thing, which is exactly how he thought about the park. It was as much a living thing as he was, and it deserved the kind of attention you'd give to anyone you cared about.

He looked towards the parking lot entrance. Nothing. He walked closer to the hedgerow dividing the picnic area from the beach. The lake was calm, and the water lapping the shore barely made a sound. A piper cub buzzed down the shoreline so low that when it got near, the pilot tipped his wings and Clancy waved. Just then he heard something pull into the lot behind him. He turned, expecting to see Kate's old clunker, but it was an SUV. A family got out and headed down the upper trail. Clancy hoped Kate hadn't run into car trouble.

Since she had moved to her own apartment, she called Clancy almost every week to come and help her out because the battery was dead or a tire was flat or the carburetor was sputtering. He had to stop and think how long ago she had moved. *Let's see, Bobby was still living at the house; it was about six weeks after she and I had talked; must have been seven months ago. Where has the time gone?* he thought.

It seemed odd that they had all lived together for all those months. Two years ago they hadn't had a single thing in common and no one would ever have predicted that their paths would have come together as they had. Clancy shook his head at this. *Why do some things happen and others don't?*

Darlene had called a couple of months back just to tell him she was moving to Springfield, Massachusetts. She had met a trucker who'd stopped at the bar. They'd hit it off and after a few months decided to marry. She said she would have told Clancy about the wedding in advance, but she felt funny after their last conversation and wasn't sure he'd want to hear her news. But when she decided to move, she just had to call because, who knew, they might never see or speak to each other again. When Clancy hung up, all he felt for Darlene was happy. He hoped she had found the thing she'd never had before— someone to deep-down love her. It was the only thing that counted, after all, and even if it took the better part of a lifetime to find it, finding it was what mattered. He moved his wedding ring from the saucer near the sink to the back corner of his bottom dresser drawer.

Clancy heard a horn blow, and when he turned around, it was Bobby in his old truck, blinking his bright lights and waving his arm out the window. When he got out of the truck, he was laughing. Bobby stood straight and held his head up when he walked. When he first told Clancy about his plans to go back to school, Bobby cried like a baby because he felt like he owed Clancy more than just leaving him. Clancy told him not to think anything of it. He told Bobby he should go and do whatever he had to do; there wasn't any reason to wait. Anyway, Clancy said, he'd leave the porch light on just in case Bobby ever needed a place to crash, which, of course, he did.

What an odd thing, this friendship with Bobby. Before everything had happened that morning long ago, they had worked side by side for a few years and Clancy had never given him the time of day; worse, he hadn't even wanted to; he'd written Bobby off the first time he met him as a young punk kid who was on the fast track to nowhere. In a sense, Clancy had been right. But when he saw Bobby hurting, when he saw that he was completely lost in the world, Bobby became a real, live, three-dimensional, flesh-and-blood human being, and Clancy couldn't turn his back.

"How's it going?" said Bobby.

"Good. How'd your test go?" said Clancy.

"I think I aced it."

"Good," said Clancy.

"Where's Kate?" said Bobby.

"Good question."

"Thought she'd be here by now," said Bobby.

"Me, too."

Kate saw the entrance to the park about a half-mile up the road. This wasn't the first time she'd been there since that dark morning when she came with Mitch, but it felt like it, nonetheless. So much had changed; so much had stayed the same. She was now the assistant manager at the new Wegman's with promises that one day she would manage a store herself. How could this be? Somehow she had moved forward even though she hadn't had a destination in mind. Getting up and going had been accomplishment enough.

She looked at Little Green Bear on the dashboard. The first time her and Clancy's paths had crossed, Kate's life had just ended, and he had showed up to condemn it. The second time their paths had crossed,

Kate took her first steps towards an unknowable tomorrow, and he was there to help her. The events that had taken her to Chimney Bluffs and the events that had brought her back from the brink were equally puzzling.

When she had opened the door to her bedroom that night in his house, he had not said a word, as if his knock was explanation enough. She had stood at the door, not ready to look at him, holding the doorknob and waiting. He had cleared his throat and had taken a deep breath but then had hesitated. She had wanted to help him say whatever it was he wanted to say, but she couldn't. It was not hers to do. He would have to rummage around and find his own voice. And finally he did.

"Kate, I don't know…I've never felt this before…so I don't have the right words. They just don't seem to be in me. But I want to say something…I have to."

Kate had let go of the doorknob, and her arms fell to her side, a small door inside her beginning to open.

"When I'm around you, I feel like nothing else matters; all my yesterdays and all my tomorrows, they just don't seem important. All that's important is right now." Clancy couldn't speak and look at Kate at the same time.

"Look, I know that you probably don't feel the same way, but I want you to know something: You are a beautiful person. You are the most beautiful of all. I don't know how else…" He paused and looked at the ceiling. "You know, sometimes I find a tree on the cliff near the bluffs and it's tilting over the edge, its roots a little exposed, but it's holding on tight, and it's green and tall and strong, and it's not perfect like all the trees around it, but it's perfect, if you know what I mean. Beautiful, I guess." He turned red at this, but didn't try to hide.

"I guess that's how I feel about you." He didn't wait for her to respond. "I hope I'm not offending you. I know that you love Mitch and you love Danny in a way that I could never…well, in ways that could never…" He could feel his words thinning. He put his hands in his pocket and creased his face with what he hoped was a smile. "I guess I just wanted to be sure that you knew how I feel."

Kate looked at the two canisters on the seat beside her. She reached out and patted them gently. She thought again of that morning long ago, before dawn, when she and Mitch had pulled into the lot, parking their old white van wherever it happened to stop. She thought of the sacks that lay in the back of the van, that held so many of her dreams. It seemed so long ago that it was fuzzy in a way, yet so clear in her heart that it could have been yesterday. She pulled over to the side of the road and closed her eyes for a moment, trying to hear Danny's voice. But all she could hear now was what she hoped his voice had sounded like.

Bobby had been right. No one else could see it, but there was a hole inside her. It was a ghastly hole torn across her soul that oozed pain and anguish and memories. And the suction of that hole had been inescapable in the beginning and, at times, still was. It drew her into darkness, where there was no hope, where there was only guilt and fear and sadness. In time, she was able to stand apart from the hole, at least a little, her eyes always on it, yet falling in less often. More recently, she could come and go from the hole as she wished. She was glad, in a way, that it was there. She wanted it there where she could tend to it and honor it and not forget. It was true that sometimes she dove into the hole because she felt so lost that it was the only way to find herself. Then she would come out again. Sometimes she would leap over it to other things: to work, to Bobby and Clancy, to other thoughts and feelings, to the morning rain and the late afternoon sun, to tomorrow and to what it might bring after all. But even when she did that, she knew the hole was still there, full of the gnawing comfort that often comes with memories of loss. Some things, even when they were gone, were not meant to be buried; they were, instead, meant to be lived out the best you could.

"There she is," said Clancy, eagerness in his voice. Bobby waved, and they both stood up straight.

When Clancy had knocked on that bedroom door, he had no idea what he was going to say. And he had no idea whether Kate would even open the door. But when she opened it, he knew he had done the right thing. She was so quiet after he had spoken that at first he thought maybe he hadn't said anything at all; maybe he had thought the words but they hadn't made it out. But then she spoke.

"I don't know what to say. I don't have any breath, any words."

He was certain he had made a mistake. He should have kept his foolish feelings to himself.

"I've only ever loved one man. And I loved Danny even more. And when they died, my love went with them to wherever love goes when there's no one left to love. And that was fine. It was for them and no one else. It was all I had left to give. I can never really let that go."

When Kate got out of the car at the Chimney Bluffs parking lot, she smiled, but her eyes were red and her face was pale.

266

"Do you need some help?" said Bobby.

"Thanks," said Kate.

Bobby opened the passenger side door and gently picked up the canisters and cradled them, one in each arm. He pushed the door closed with his foot.

Kate took a deep breath and looked at Clancy.

"Are you ready for this?" he said.

"Yes," said Kate.

Together they headed toward the opening in the woods that was the Garner Point Trail. They leaned into the slight grade that brought them to the Bluff Trail, the path well-worn from all the summer traffic, the grass drying, the leaves turning, the world readying itself for that glorious transition, that exquisite passageway to the sleep of winter. A chipmunk here, a squirrel there, noisy on the cluttered floor of the forest. No one spoke. They walked with purpose, the sunlight catching their faces, the lake receding below them as they went higher, higher.

When Kate had told him about her love for Mitch and Danny, Clancy had understood that there could be no end to the love she had for them—that it was a love that went from everlasting to everlasting. He understood, and yet he hoped.

Kate had looked at Clancy as they stood together in the bedroom, her lips parting into an almost-smile, her eyes warm. "Life had color. And then it didn't. And I didn't want it to. I didn't deserve it. I would just go on without it. That's what I believed. That is what I wanted."

Kate stepped back from Clancy as if she needed more room to say what she had to say. She sat on her bed and took Little Green Bear in her hands. "But then you showed up with him. And you kept being there." She stood up again, holding Little Green Bear to her chest. "I woke up one morning and looked out my apartment window and found myself watching the sun come up. The sky was gold. And I didn't cry."

A small pasture of waist-high ferns surrounded them as they made their way up the first slope. Here the trail turned abruptly away from the woods and towards the open space near the edge where the path wound like a snake towards the bluffs. Below them, one hundred and fifty feet or more, the water came and went in slow motion. Clancy stopped and looked out through an opening in the trees, feeling, as he always did, like he was in flight, nothing but the wind holding him up.

Kate had told Clancy that, at first, she had been afraid of the changes, that she tried to stay away from them. For a while she convinced herself that she could divide her life between the greys and the yellows, between the blacks and the reds, between what was and what might be. At night, looking at the remains on her dresser, she cried to think that she might be reaching out in another direction. She had felt dead for so long that coming back to life was painful and frightening. But no matter how difficult it was, she couldn't deny what was happening inside; she couldn't deny that she was returning to life.

"It is wonderful. It is terrifying. And sometimes I feel that if I take one more brand-new step, I will fly apart into a million pieces. I'm sorry if this sounds, I don't know." She took Clancy's hands. "You are so special to me. But, for now, this is all I can do."

All Clancy had said in return was, "Okay."

A few days later, she came to Clancy while he was washing the dishes and told him she wanted to move out, not because she didn't love it there, but because something told her that she wouldn't be able to make any other decisions unless she made this one. Clancy said, "Okay."

He and Bobby helped her move. They visited her regularly, and she came back to Clancy's several times a week, sometimes staying overnight, sometimes not. They didn't talk about what had happened the night Clancy had knocked on the bedroom door.

Weeks passed, and then one day she stopped by the house and told Bobby and Clancy that she knew what she wanted to do with the remains. She asked if they would help her. They both had said, "Okay."

They reached the green warning sign, a stick figure of a hiker with a white line drawn through it, and kept going. To their right and to their left, cathedral spires of sculpted silt reached for the heavens. Swallows busied themselves in and out of holes dug deep in the cement-colored walls. Hawks glided by, effortless and indifferent. Clancy smiled and thought, *My God, it never changes.*

They stepped out together onto the finger, where the wind never stopped and the paper-thin horizon seemed endless. Bobby put the canisters on the ground at Kate's feet. He looked at her, not knowing what to say. He put his arm around her shoulders and then stepped back. Kate looked at Clancy, who stepped forward and knelt down beside the canisters. He pried open both lids so that they lay loose atop the cans. Clancy stood up and faced Kate.

"Are you okay?" he said.

"Yes," said Kate.

She knelt down beside the canister of Mitch's remains. She

removed the top and looked at the ashes, the color of Chimney Bluffs. She began to cry as she stood. Kate turned her back to the wind and tipped the can over. The ashes caught the wind and took off in every direction.

"I love you," was all Kate said.

Then she took Danny's ashes in her hands. She looked at them, unable to imagine how everything could be reduced to this, and yet knowing it was true. She stood up and tipped the can over. The ashes caught the breeze and swirled into a tiny cloud, for a moment coming together and then just as quickly dispersing to the walls of the bluffs and the water down below.

"I love you, my sweet, sweet boy," she said through tears.

They stood silent for many moments. The shadow of one bluff slowly crossed the face of another. A freighter emerged from the horizon like a sea creature surfacing off the ocean. A sailboat glided, its sail a bushel full of wind. A tree, roots and all, lay on the shore, fingers of surf caressing it. The pebbled beach stretched north along the vaulted shore, catching the water in its arms time and time again. Tiny white daisies, no broader than a fingertip, leaned out from the cathedral wall, braving the wind and the height. And together, in their way, each welcomed the dust of life newly sprinkled on their world.

Kate turned to Clancy, saying, "I don't know what I'm doing."

And Clancy answered, "That's okay, neither do I."

Bobby looked again at the peaks, amazed at what seemed to him a mystery. He turned in time to see Kate and Clancy walking away, disappearing down the path, on their way to whatever was to come.

David B. Seaburn

If you enjoyed *Chimney Bluffs*, consider this other fine work by the author:

When eleven-year-old Jackie goes to live with a distant relative and meets disfigured hermit and infamous local legend Charlie No Face, Jackie's life changes forever. Jackie and Charlie develop an unlikely friendship that explores the surprising truth about Jackie's mother, who died, as well as what it means to look at others with one's heart.

About the Author

David B. Seaburn is the author of the *Charley No Face* (Savant 2011) and two other novels, *Darkness is Light* (2005), *Pumpkin Hill* (2007). He is also a retired psychologist, marriage and family therapist and ordained minister. Seaburn and his wife live in Spencerport, New York.

See more at http://www.davidbseaburn.com

273

If you enjoyed *Chimney Bluffs,* consider these other fine works from Savant Books and Publications:

Essay, Essay, Essay by Yasuo Kobachi
Aloha from Coffee Island by Walter Miyanari
Footprints, Smiles and Little White Lies by Daniel S. Janik
The Illustrated Middle Earth by Daniel S. Janik
Last and Final Harvest by Daniel S. Janik
A Whale's Tale by Daniel S. Janik
Tropic of California by R. Page Kaufman
Tropic of California (the companion music CD) by R. Page Kaufman
The Village Curtain by Tony Tame
Dare to Love in Oz by William Maltese
The Interzone by Tatsuyuki Kobayashi
Today I Am a Man by Larry Rodness
The Bahrain Conspiracy by Bentley Gates
Called Home by Gloria Schumann
Kanaka Blues by Mike Farris
First Breath edited by Z. M. Oliver
Poor Rich by Jean Blasiar
The Jumper Chronicles - Quest for Merlin's Map by W. C. Peever
William Maltese's Flicker by William Maltese
My Unborn Child by Orest Stocco
Last Song of the Whales by Four Arrows
Perilous Panacea by Ronald Klueh
Falling but Fulfilled by Zachary M. Oliver
Mythical Voyage by Robin Ymer
Hello, Norma Jean by Sue Dolleris
Richer by Jean Blasiar
Manifest Intent by Mike Farris
Charlie No Face by David B. Seaburn
Number One Bestseller by Brian Morley
My Two Wives and Three Husbands by S. Stanley Gordon
In Dire Straits by Jim Currie
Wretched Land by Mila Komarnisky
Chan Kim by Ilan Herman

Who's Killing All the Lawyers? by A. G. Hayes
Ammon's Horn by G. Amati
Wavelengths edited by Zachary M. Oliver
Almost Paradise by Laurie Hanan
Communion by Jean Blasiar and Jonathan Marcantoni
The Oil Man by Leon Puissegur
Random Views of Asia from the Mid-Pacific by William E. Sharp
The Isla Vista Crucible by Reilly Ridgell
Blood Money by Scott Mastro
In the Himalayan Nights by Anoop Chandola
Rules of Privilege by Mike Farris
On My Behalf by Helen Doan
Fifty-Eight Stones edited by Daniel S. Janik
Traveler's Rest by Jonathan Marcantoni
Keys in the River by Tendai Mwanaka

Soon to be Released:

Light Surfer by David Allan Williams
Path of the Templar - Book Two of The Jumper Chronicles by W. C. Peever
The Loons by Sue Dolleris
The Judas List by A. G. Hayes
Shutterbug by Buz Sawyers

http://www.savantbooksandpublications.com

www.ingramcontent.com/pod-product-compliance
Lightning Source LLC
Chambersburg PA
CBHW051249260626
47162CB00002B/685